Praise for Erin Nicholas's
Hitched

"*Hitched* is an excellent ending to what has been an entertaining, fun, and intriguing series."
~ *Guilty Pleasures Book Reviews*

"Erin Nicholas' typical chuckle-out-loud humor shone through. [...] The chemistry between Allie and Gavin was undeniable."
~ *BookLovers Inc.*

"One of the things I love about an Erin Nicholas story is that I can be guaranteed to have fun reading it and to fall in love with not just the hero and heroine but also the secondary characters as well."
~ *Book Reading Gals*

D1366489

Look for these titles by *Erin Nicholas*

Now Available:

No Matter What
Hotblooded

The Bradfords
Just Right
Just Like That
Just My Type
Just the Way I Like It
Just For Fun
Just a Kiss
Just What I Need

Anything & Everything
Anything You Want
Everything You've Got

Counting on Love
She's the One
It Takes Two
Best of Three
Going for Four
Up by Five

Hitched

Erin Nicholas

SAMHAIN
PUBLISHING

Samhain Publishing, Ltd.
11821 Mason Montgomery Road, 4B
Cincinnati, OH 45249
www.samhainpublishing.com

Hitched
Copyright © 2014 by Erin Nicholas
Print ISBN: 978-1-61921-709-6
Digital ISBN: 978-1-61921-431-6

Editing by Lindsey Faber
Cover by Angela Waters

First Samhain Publishing, Ltd. electronic publication: April 2013
First Samhain Publishing, Ltd. print publication: April 2014

Dedication

To my coauthors and friends, Kelly, Meg and Syd—how much fun was this?! To Kim, beta reader and cheerleader extraordinaire. To Kinsey Holley and PG Forte, without whom we would have called these books Book One, Book Two, Book Three and Book Four.

And to my family, who claim they really like having frozen pizza for dinner once a week, whether they mean it or not.

I also want to give a huge thank-you to Dana L. Petersen, DVM, for inspiring Gavin's interest in polar bears and work with the US Geological Survey and making sure I didn't screw up any of the details. ☺ (Well, if I did, it's all my fault—she answered endless stupid questions and gave me all kinds of great inside stuff!)

And a big thank-you, also, to Jennifer Bernard, who made sure that I got my Alaska facts straight as well! If she ever wants to write a book set in Iowa, I'm there for her! ☺

Prologue

"Dearly beloved, we are gathered here today to unite this man and this woman in holy matrimony."

"Oh, hell no."

Every head swiveled toward him as Gavin Montgomery strode purposefully down the center aisle of St. Mark's Methodist Church.

"*Gavin?*" Allie's shocked question was the first thing he heard over all the other noises—gasps, whispers, creaking pews.

The second thing he heard was the groom's question. "This is *Gavin?*"

The groom was Josh Brewster. Of course it was. The Brewsters had been close friends with Allie's family for years. Who else but Mr. Perfect would be standing next to Allie at the altar?

Nobody was more dearly beloved that Josh Frickin' Brewster.

"What do you think you're doing?" Josh demanded.

"I'm here to talk to Allie."

Josh moved to stand between Gavin and Allie. "We're kind of in the middle of something."

"Yeah, this can't wait." Gavin looked past Josh to Allie. "I need to talk to you. Now."

Her eyes were wide and she looked pale. Like she-might-faint-any-minute pale. But he wasn't so sure it was from the shock of seeing him. She'd looked terrible in the wedding announcement in the *Promise Harbor Times*, too. She was way too thin. She was too pale. She looked...sick and tired.

He suspected, based on the two a.m. phone call he'd

received, that she was also hungover.

He knew he looked like shit himself. He *felt* like shit. He'd been out in the field for the past two weeks and hadn't known Allie was getting married until last night. He needed a haircut, his beard had been growing, he hadn't slept or showered or eaten in...he wasn't sure. A long time. Once he'd heard the phone message from Hayley, his best friend in Promise Harbor, nothing had mattered but getting to Allie. Before she married another man.

Even with owning one-twelfth of a small private jet and living forty miles from the pilot, it took awhile to get from Alaska to Massachusetts. He'd landed in time to rent a car and drive like a bat out of hell to get here. Just as she'd been about to say *I do.*

In spite of the thinness of her cheeks and the dark circles under her eyes, she looked gorgeous to him. Seeing her for the first time in over a year shook him. He wanted to grab her. He wanted to carry her out of here. He wanted to hold her and take care of her.

He wanted to feed her.

Good lord, she'd always been thin, but now she was downright skinny. Her long, blonde hair was piled on top of her head in a mass of curls and baby's breath. Her dress was white and lacy and left her shoulders and arms bare, showing off smooth skin that was as white as the dress. She wore three-inch heels, putting her at five-ten, and her big green eyes were watching every move he made.

She looked dazed.

He could work with that.

He started toward her but Josh moved to block him. "I don't think so, Gavin."

Gavin sighed. He'd known this was going to be a spectacle, of course. Barging into a church during a wedding and stealing the bride created a spectacle by anyone's definition.

The church was completely silent, and he saw camera flashes going off from every direction. He was pretty sure this particular spectacle was going to end up on the Internet.

"Listen. I can do this here in front of the whole town. I don't mind. I'm leaving here with Allie one way or another. But I think keeping some of this private might be appropriate." He leaned around Josh to look at Allie. "I have some things I need to say before you say I do to another man, Al."

Josh sighed, stepped closer and lowered his voice. "Don't do this, Gavin. Haven't you messed with her enough? Just let her be happy."

"That's exactly what I want to do," Gavin insisted, not backing down an inch. "Is that what *you* want?"

"I'm standing next to her in a tux in front of a minister. What do you think?"

"I think that if you don't let her talk to me, you know that she'll always wonder. You don't want that, do you? To have your wife wondering about another man?"

Josh blew out a long breath and shoved his hand through his hair. Then he half turned to his bride. "Allie?"

"What would I wonder?" Her voice was weak, and again Gavin wasn't sure it was completely because of shock. She sounded and looked exhausted.

"You'd wonder what I had to say to you so badly that I would fly over four thousand miles so I could rush in here to stop your wedding."

She just stared at him for a long moment. There wasn't a sound in the church. Gavin couldn't breathe. She looked at Josh. Then she looked into the pews. Gavin knew without following her gaze that she was looking at her father. Then her gaze settled on the groomsmen. Gavin glanced over to see her two brothers, Charlie and Danny, standing in tuxes at the end of the line of groomsmen. Finally she pressed her lips together and shook her head.

But he saw the glint of tears in her eyes.

She was worried about them. As always. Her family and Josh's were close. Their mothers had been best friends. They wanted this. Gavin knew it. He knew in his gut that this was all more about everyone else in the church than it was about Allie. And maybe even Josh. Allie had never, ever, even once put herself first.

That wasn't true, he thought a second later. She'd put what she wanted ahead of her family one Christmas. The Christmas she'd spent with him instead. The Christmas before her mom got sick.

"Allie," he said, stepping forward.

"You're too late," she whispered. A tear slipped down her cheek.

"Bullshit," he said. She hadn't said *I do* yet.

He strode forward, bent and scooped her into his arms, then headed for the side door.

"Gavin!" She kicked and he tightened his hold.

"Just a damn minute—" Josh started.

Gavin turned. Several people were on their feet, including Allie's dad. All of the groomsmen had stepped forward. He picked Hayley out, also on her feet, in one of the front pews on Josh's side of the church. She looked concerned, but she didn't move to stop him. No one came any closer. At the moment.

"Give me a chance," Gavin said. "Let me talk to her. Let me tell her what I came here to say. Then if she wants to come back, I'll walk her down the aisle myself."

It was crazy to ask Josh to do that. But he didn't wait to hear the other man's response. He started toward the door again.

He knew it was over the top. He knew Promise Harbor was going to be talking about this for years. He knew that he was acting on pure emotion and adrenaline and might regret embarrassing Allie and Josh and their families like this. But dammit, he needed time. He couldn't just let her walk down the aisle and give her life to another man without at least trying.

Gavin had no actual plan at this point. His strategy had been to get to the church in time. Period. But he had Allie back in his arms. He wasn't going to stop now. "If you really love him, he has nothing to worry about," Gavin said low for Allie's ears only. "And if he loves you, he'll wait."

She looked up at him, then to Josh, then back to Gavin. "Am I dreaming?"

His mouth curled at one corner. "I'm real, darlin'. I'm here."

She sighed and Gavin felt it tremble through her whole body. He became aware of how light she was, how slight she felt. A surge of protectiveness and anger went through him. What the hell? Didn't they see that she wasn't okay?

They weren't taking care of her. He couldn't ignore that either. Allie's sense of responsibility and her need to take care of her family were deep and strong. Stronger than anything else. Even her feelings for him. So why he thought he could talk her out of this wedding, he wasn't sure. But the fact that she was obviously taking care of everyone but herself made him feel like snarling.

Someone had to take care of her. And he was the best one.

He reached the side door and the pianist rushed to open it for him.

The door banged shut behind them, and he'd taken three strides when he heard the inevitable sound of the door swinging open again.

"Wait!" Josh yelled.

Gavin stopped.

"What the fuck, Allie?" Josh demanded. "Are you leaving with him?"

Gavin knew she'd be pissed, but he had to get her away from the church. He could, and would, take Josh on if needed, but if all the groomsmen decided to stop him, he wasn't sure how he'd do. He sighed, then turned to face Josh. "Allie called me last night."

Josh's eyes went to Allie again and he frowned. "You did?"

Allie made a squeaky little noise. Her mouth was wide open, but she said nothing.

"She called and told me that she'd always love me." That wasn't entirely true. She'd sung it in a terrible rendition of Whitney Houston's "I Will Always Love You". But the message had been clear. On the night before her wedding to another man, she was thinking of Gavin.

If he hadn't already been on his way, that would have gotten him on a plane. As it was, that was what drove him up the steps of the church to crash a wedding.

He wasn't truly the caveman type. But when the woman he loved told him she felt the same way, he felt inclined to keep her out of another man's bed by whatever means necessary.

"Allie?" Josh asked, eyebrows drawn tightly over his eyes. "Is this true?"

She swallowed hard. Gavin could feel her rib cage moving rapidly as she breathed. Finally she said softly, "Well..."

Josh shook his head. "Jesus Christ." He fixed a glare on her. "Were you drunk?"

"Maybe a little."

"You called Gavin the night before our wedding and told him you'd always love him?" Josh asked, his voice rising.

"Not *exactly*," Allie hedged. "I didn't tell him to come or anything. I didn't *say* that I loved him."

"Allie. We're getting married. You don't just change your mind at the last second about something like this."

"I'm sorry," she whispered.

And that was good enough for Gavin. "That's all I needed to hear." He turned and headed for the car.

He might feel bad about Josh later, but right now Allie was his only concern.

Chapter One

Fourteen hours before the wedding

Promise Harbor, Massachusetts

She really liked tequila.

Allison Ralston signaled the bartender, who obediently put another shot glass and lime wedge in front of her. Normally, Matt might try to cut her off at this point, but she was getting married tomorrow, so everyone was doing what she wanted.

Allie tipped the shot glass back, swallowing quickly and shuddering as she put the lime between her teeth and bit down.

This was only her third shot. Or fifth. Something like that.

She just needed to keep going until after she managed I do. Just two little words.

Maybe the minister would let her say I should. That was much more accurate. Ministers and churches were big on truth. She should pledge to love and honor Josh Brewster. Josh was the best. Everyone thought so. He was handsome, funny, smart, and always did the right thing.

Like marrying his mom's best friend's daughter to make everyone—especially his mom—happy, regardless of his own feelings.

Allie signaled for another shot.

"Come on, Allie, dance with us." Bernice, her annoying cousin and one of her bridesmaids, tugged on her arm. "We're making requests. You have to dance with us to this one."

It was Beyoncé's "Single Ladies". Great. The perfect prewedding song, Allie thought sarcastically. If you like it...

Josh definitely liked her. He had since he was ten and she was seven. Liking wasn't the problem. Common goals, plans for the future, family dynamics, sharing a general life philosophy—

none of those were problems either.

Allie looked longingly at the empty shot glass on the bar. Matt hadn't refilled it yet, but that bar stool was a lot closer to the bottle than the dance floor was.

She made herself turn away from Matt and face the women who would be standing next to her tomorrow. Bernice, Crystal, Joanna and even Greta were already dancing. Actually, Greta was standing in the middle of the dance floor looking like she wanted to be anywhere else. But that made sense. Not only were the other girls being obnoxiously happy and annoyingly fun, but Greta was Josh's younger sister and didn't really know the other women well. Allie was pretty sure Greta was there only because Bernice had insisted. Bernice was good at that.

The other three squealed with delight as Allie moved onto the floor, bouncing up and down and singing the lyrics at the top of their lungs.

Oh, lord. Squealing bridesmaids, Beyoncé and tequila were not a good combination. Allie pressed her hand against her stomach as it pitched in response to the hip swivel she attempted. She took the boogying down a notch and just mouthed the words.

Thankfully, the song eventually switched to something slower.

The other girls had had a bit to drink as well, and they linked their arms and started swaying, again singing along to Shania Twain's "You're Still The One". Allie let them link her into the circle and she swayed with them, closing her eyes and thinking about the words.

You're still the one...

Stupidly, she felt her eyes stinging. Maybe she'd had enough tequila after all. She shouldn't be feeling lonely and sad. It was the night before her wedding. These girls were here with her, celebrating the biggest day of her life. Her house was filled with family and friends, getting ready for the next day. Somewhere a man was sitting with his friends, preparing to stand up in front of everyone they knew and loved and say that he'd spend the rest of his life with her. A good man. A wonderful man. A man any woman would be privileged to share her life with.

You're still the one...

Josh deserved better. He deserved better than a woman who was sitting in a bar, listening to a love song and thinking about someone else.

She should not be thinking about Gavin.

Allie took a deep breath, opened her eyes and smiled at her bridesmaids. Bridesmaids. She was going to be a bride. She was getting married.

Okay, she could do this. It was a good thing. A great thing. She was a very lucky woman.

"Josh is a great dancer," she said to Bernie. "Did you know that?"

"I'll bet." Bernie waggled her eyebrows.

He was. He was tall and when they slow danced, she could rest her head on his chest. His big hands easily spanned her low back, making her feel feminine and cared for. He had great rhythm, and his powerful thighs pressed firmly against hers because he always held her really close. That was just the kind of thing that should make a woman want to get even closer.

Dammit.

There was that word again—should.

"Greta, is there anything Josh isn't good at?" Allie asked, looping her arm around Josh's sister.

She was Allie's maid of honor, even though the girls didn't know one another well. Well, they knew each other of course— their families had been friends forever and spent lots of weekends and most holidays together—but Greta was younger and Allie had always had Josh as a confidante. It wasn't like the girls had shared any deep dark secrets.

Greta was the best choice for maid of honor, though. Their mothers had been best friends, and Josh and Greta's mom, Sophie, had taken Lily's death as hard as anyone. Truthfully, she'd been a mess. Her longtime battle with depression didn't help, and Allie and Josh had talked extensively about ways to get her through the hard time. Allie had always considered

15

Sophie a second mom and seeing her so distraught tore at Allie's already aching heart. Just like she was doing for her dad and brothers, Allie was intent on helping Sophie smile again. So far, planning a wedding where Sophie's son was the groom and her daughter was maid of honor was working very nicely.

Greta lifted her shoulder at Allie's question about her brother. "Josh has always been good at everything."

Yep, that was exactly right. Josh was nearly perfect. The guy didn't even snore.

Crystal approached with a small tray laden with shot glasses. "Let's toast!" she said with a grin.

That was a fantastic idea. At the moment, Crystal was her favorite bridesmaid. Hands down.

Allie wasn't sure of the wisdom of mixing tequila with the pink stuff Crystal had brought, but hey, it was liquor. It wasn't like she was going to be feeling great in the morning anyway.

She tipped the sweet concoction back and swallowed. Oh, yeah, that was good.

Her head spinning nicely, she looped her arm around Bernie's neck. "Thanks for picking out the dresses."

Bernie laughed. "When you still hadn't picked anything out and we were only a month away, someone had to do something." Bernie patted Allie on the head. Like a puppy. "Sometimes it's just easier to let someone else do it. I don't mind."

The dresses were god-awful. Allie had overheard Greta, Josh's sister, refer to them as Gone With The Wind dresses, and she couldn't disagree. Scarlett would have swooned at the sight of them, for sure. But Allie had been simply unable to look at another one after the fortieth. None were right. None felt good.

The song switched to another sappy love song, and Allie felt her eyes welling again. She really loved this song. She couldn't remember what it was called, but she loved it.

Humming and swaying with her eyes closed again, Allie thought about the man she loved. She was going to walk down the aisle tomorrow and the man at the end of the aisle was strong and charming, intelligent, wonderful. He had dark hair, brown eyes. He also had a smile that made her heart melt and when he ran his hands down her back and grabbed her ass she...

Her eyes flew open. Dammit. She really had been thinking about Josh. Or trying. But her thoughts slipped so easily to Gavin.

Crap.

She looked around, spotted Crystal and stumbled toward her friend. "I need another drink."

Crystal grinned. "Okay, let's do a blow job."

Allie started to clarify, but Crystal grabbed her hand and towed her to the bar. A moment later, a shot glass filled with a creamy brown mixture and topped with whipped cream appeared magically before her.

Whipped cream was a good sign.

Allie shot the drink back, sighing happily as the sweet liquid went down.

"You like a good blow job once in a while?" Matt asked with a wink.

"Of course," she said, winking back. Or at least she thought she winked. She might have blinked at him instead. She giggled and Matt laughed.

"Josh is a lucky guy," he said.

Yeah, Allie thought. Josh was a lucky guy. She was quite a catch.

She stumbled as she turned and started back for the dance floor.

"Whoa, babe." Crystal caught her by both elbows. "You okay?"

"I'm great!" Allie announced. She was sure her words sounded slurred only because it was so loud in here. "I'm getting married tomorrow!"

Crystal laughed. "I heard that somewhere."

"And he's the best," Allie insisted. She pivoted and grabbed a beer from the waitress as she passed.

"He is, definitely," Crystal agreed.

Allie drank, then shuddered, then spread her arms wide. "Gavin is the only man I'll ever want."

Crystal froze, her eyes widening. She was still holding on to to one of Allie's arms, which was fortunate because Allie felt a little off-balance.

"Al?" Crystal said, getting closer so she could lower her voice. "What did you just say?"

Allie frowned at her. "I said Josh is the best."

"And then you said Gavin is the only man you'll ever want."

Allie shook her head. "No. That's not funny."

Crystal squeezed her arm. "I know. It's really not funny. What are you talking about?"

Dammit. She should have never pulled that letter out last night. Allie closed her eyes and groaned. She'd been so pissed at him, so hurt. Her mom had died, it was absolutely the blackest time of her life and Gavin hadn't even called. He certainly hadn't showed up. He hadn't done a damned thing.

Then two weeks after the funeral she got a letter. Handwritten. Seeing his writing again had made her almost crack. She'd been holding everything together just fine. She hadn't cried, she hadn't broken down, she hadn't thrown anything, she hadn't told anyone to just leave her the fuck alone and quit asking if she was all right. She'd been composed and calm, she'd gotten everything taken care of, she'd gotten everyone taken care of.

She'd been fine. Until that letter came.

She'd almost lost it.

Instead, she'd read it once, folded it up and stuck it in her bedside table under some old CDs and a box of stationary. Then she'd forgotten about it.

Except that wasn't true. She'd pulled it out three times. She'd put it back without reading it twice. But last night she hadn't been able to resist. She'd read it. Four times.

And now he was so on her mind that she was screwing everything up. Of course.

"I didn't mean it," she told Crystal, shaking her head.

Allie immediately regretted that. Her head swam and she grabbed Crystal to keep from tipping over. She should have worn flats tonight instead of the high-heeled boots.

"Allie, you just...you can't be thinking about him," Crystal said. "What about Josh?"

"It's normal for people to think about their exes," Allie told her, hoping it was true. "We're getting married. That's a huge deal. It's natural to think about your past relationships. I'll bet Josh is thinking about Devon."

Devon Grant was Josh's most serious ex. He'd been completely in love with her. If she had been willing to move to Promise Harbor, he'd be married to her right now. For sure.

Devon and Allie had been as close as sisters at one time. In fact, Devon had met Josh through Allie. Allie had been thrilled that her two best friends had fallen in love.

And then real life and obligations and divergent paths had come between Josh and Devon too.

She didn't know every detail about their breakup. Josh hadn't wanted to talk about it, and Allie and Devon had drifted apart when things had gotten bad with her mom and things had gotten bad with Gavin...and things had just gotten bad.

In the end, it seemed to Allie that she and Josh just weren't destined for true love forever.

So they had each other. As always. It seemed fitting in many ways that they would end up together. She couldn't remember a Christmas dinner or a birthday celebration without him. So why wouldn't she agree to spend those events with him for the rest of her life?

They were...comfortable. They could completely be themselves. There were no secrets. They loved each other. Maybe not madly and passionately, but they had each other's backs. That was more than a lot of couples could say.

"Even if he is, he's probably not announcing it to the bar. You need to take it down a notch," Crystal said with a frown. "Let's go dance."

Allie went along, mostly because Crystal was still holding on to her and Allie wasn't sure she could stay upright on her own. She drank more of the beer and liked that it was more bitter than the blow job or the pink stuff. She was feeling a little bitter herself.

She drank again, swaying to yet another love song. This one was "Amazed", by Lonestar. Her bridesmaids were just going down the list of the sappiest love songs of all time. But she found herself singing along. And thinking of Gavin. They'd danced to this song.

They'd gone to high school together. They'd graduated in the same class and had known each other. The harbor wasn't big enough to not know everyone in your graduating class. They'd even flirted.

He and Jason Simpson had sat behind her and Devon in chemistry senior year. He'd cut in on her date at the homecoming dance and at prom. Every weekend from January until May he'd asked her to a party. She'd always said no.

But he'd never asked her out on a real date. Which was fine. She would have said no to that too. He was a bad boy, a rebel. She was a good girl who followed all the rules. He dated casually, if at all, and was just out for a good time. She dated nice boys, one at a time, and never did more than French kiss.

It was so cliché—the good girl fascinated by the bad boy—it was pathetic.

Then they'd gone away to college and hadn't seen each other again.

Until that party their senior year of college.

She'd been in love with him since then. She was now twenty-eight. That party had been just before she turned twenty-two.

Pathetic.

She tipped the beer bottle up, but found it was empty. How had that happened?

Suddenly the music died, there were shouts, then she could have sworn she heard, "Move. Police," followed by a loud crash.

"Oh my god!" Bernie gasped. "Jackson Knight just hit Hayley Stone."

Oh, that was just perfect. Allie felt her head throb. The best man in her wedding tomorrow had just hit a police officer. That was fantastic.

"What do you mean he hit her?" Crystal demanded.

"He was swinging at someone else but she stepped in. And she cuffed him," Bernice said with delight.

Crystal went up on tiptoe, trying to peer over the crowd. "Man, I'd love to have Jackson Knight in handcuffs and at my mercy for an hour."

"People are gonna be so pissed." Bernie's eyes were practically sparkling with the juicy news. "Jackson Knight is like a god."

"But he hit a cop," Crystal said. "She has to take him in."

Allie straightened. Hey, wait a minute...

"Take him in where?" she asked.

Crystal rolled her eyes. "Jail. Duh. You can't hit a cop."

"Jail?" Allie repeated. "The best man at my wedding tomorrow is going to jail?"

Hey. Maybe that was fantastic. They couldn't get married without a best man, could they?

"I'm sure he'll just have to pay a fine or something," Crystal reassured her. "It was an accident. And it's Jackson Knight."

Allie sighed. Yeah, yeah, Jackson Knight. The hot hometown hero. She was sure Crystal was right and Jackson would be out in plenty of time for the wedding.

The music came back up and the bridesmaids squealed and started shaking their stuff, the minidrama with Jackson and Hayley forgotten.

And Allie went right back to wishing for more liquor and thinking about Gavin. Not necessarily in that order.

"You know, maybe you should call him or something," Crystal said over the music.

Allie turned from looking for a waitress to face her friend. "What?"

"Maybe you should call him. Just, you know, check in. Get your mind focused."

"You think I should call Gavin?" Why did that sound like a great idea?

Crystal frowned. "Of course not. You should call Josh."

"Oh." She definitely shouldn't feel disappointed about that idea. Josh was the man she was going to be calling for the rest of her life.

Gavin hadn't even called her after her mom died.

She should not want to talk to him now.

And now that she was getting married? She definitely hadn't heard from him. Did he know? Did he care? Obviously not. Obviously he'd moved on.

But if he were getting married—she felt a sharp stab in her chest at that thought—she'd call him. She had no idea what she'd say, but she would call. Maybe say something like "Congratulations" or "I wish you the best" or "Is she anything like me?" or "Do you ever think of me?" or "Don't do it!"

Allie covered her face with her hands. She would not call and say any of that stuff if he were getting married. If he were getting married, it would mean that he was over her. Obviously.

But...what if it didn't? Her getting married didn't mean she was over him. It just meant that a really great guy wanted to make a life with her, a life that would be completely wonderful. She'd be an idiot to say no to Josh.

Josh would help her. Now that her mom was gone—another stabbing pain caught Allie in the chest, and she had to stop and breathe through it for a moment—her dad and brothers needed her more than ever. Almost too much. Someone had to help her with that, and Josh was the perfect one. He knew her family, knew their secrets, knew how to help. And he was here. Gavin sure as hell wasn't.

Yeah. That's why Josh was the best.

And everyone should know that.

Allie pulled her phone from her pocket and thumbed through her contacts. Gavin was the first G. She pressed his name and Call and waited for it to ring. She didn't even know if this was still his number.

It went to voice mail. But it was definitely his voice mail.

His deep, familiar voice swept over her and she felt like crying.

Then the beep sounded and she got mad again. It was the middle of the night and she was calling him. Shouldn't he at least be curious? If he'd called her she would most definitely be curious. She'd pick up for sure. If he was screening her calls, she was going to be pissed. Not that she would know. But still...

"Gavin," she said. "This is Allie. I want you to know that you should be here. That's what I need. You to be here. And I just thought you should know that. And you should know...all the other stuff too." She felt like she was trying to see through fog. Nothing was clear. She wanted him to know...something. Something about...someone. Who? Crystal? No, he didn't know Crystal. Maybe it was about her. Yeah, probably. "I want you to know that..." She frowned, wracking her alcohol-soaked brain. The next song started and Whitney Houston's voice floated over her. Oh, she loved this song. It was old, but it was a classic love song. She started to sway, the phone still against her ear. She pulled the phone away and stared at it. Gavin. She'd called Gavin.

The man she wished was here, the guy she wanted to be at the end of the aisle tomorrow.

Her eyes welled with tears. He wouldn't be, and she couldn't call him again after she married Josh. This was her last chance to tell him what she really felt.

She started to sing along. "And I...will always love you..."

It was amazing how much she sounded like Whitney, Allie marveled. Really amazing.

Ten minutes into the wedding

Allie blinked rapidly, trying to focus on the minister. She knew she was gripping Josh's arm too hard, just like she'd gripped her dad's too hard as they walked down the aisle. But she couldn't stop or she'd fall over.

It was okay, though. This was Josh. Josh would always be there to hold her up and help her out. She loved him for that.

She really, really did.

And had for a long time.

He'd punched Lane Neilson in the nose at recess when Lane had taken her swing in kindergarten. He'd taken her out for a fancy dinner on her seventeenth birthday after Travis Wilson dumped her. He'd driven sixty miles to pick her up when her car stopped running before she could get home from the concert her parents had forbidden her to see. He'd loaned her four hundred dollars in college when she'd fallen in love with a new online shoe company and had exceeded her ability to make the payments on her credit card.

Most of all, he'd been there in the hospital when her mom got sick, getting her water and coffee, talking to the doctors when she couldn't anymore, handling the never-ending phone calls from well-meaning friends and distant family. He'd also been there, in that very church, holding her hand through her mother's funeral. And he'd been firmly by her side, holding her up—literally at times—at the graveside.

By her side. Just like he was now. In front of the entire town. At their wedding.

Holy crap, it was hot in here.

She started to giggle—holy crap, in a church, that was funny—but pressed her lips together before the sound escaped.

It was Bernice's fault that it was hot and funny in here. She'd brought the mimosas and started the toasting.

Sure, Allie had given three of her own toasts, but Bernie had definitely started it.

"You okay?" Josh whispered, pressing her elbow against his side.

She must have swayed.

She nodded quickly. "Sure. Why not?" Ooh, had that been a whisper? She hoped so.

"You look...funny," Josh whispered again as the pianist continued to play in spite of Allie having reached the end of the aisle.

That made her want to giggle too. Except Josh thought she looked funny.

"I worked for two hours this morning to look like this," she whispered back.

"Are you drunk?" he asked with a frown as her breath wafted to him.

"It's Bernie's fault," Allie was quick to tell him.

Apparently that wasn't the right answer.

"You're drunk?" he repeated. "Jesus, Allie."

"You're not supposed to say 'Jesus' in church," she said. But she frowned. That didn't sound right. "You're not supposed to say 'Jesus' like that in church," she amended.

Josh was clenching his jaw when she looked up at him. At least he still had a hold of her. Her wedding shoes were white with three-inch heels and the biggest damned silk flowers Allie had ever seen on the tops.

They caught on the hem of her dress with every step she took—and she didn't need anything else making it hard to walk. The liquor still in her system from last night, the too-few hours of sleep between the bar and the hair salon, and the champagne just a little bit ago were more than enough to make it hazardous without over-the-top, gaudy, green flowers on her shoes.

Bernice had picked these frickin' shoes out too.

"Josh?" she asked as the song finally came to an end.

"It's okay, Allie. Let's...just do this."

Let's just do this. She stifled another giggle. She felt like they should stack their hands on top of one another and yell go team.

"Dearly beloved, we are gathered here today..." the minister began.

Allie felt like her brain was suddenly spinning. She had to stay upright. That's all she had to do. And say I do. Simple. No problem. They'd just get through this and everything would be...

"Oh, hell no."

She spun around, and immediately wished she hadn't. Josh no longer had a hold of her, and her shoes were threatening to dump her on her ass.

Still, her eyes found and froze on…a guy who sounded an awful lot like Gavin Montgomery.

"Gavin?"

This guy was the same size, had the build and the same hair color, but, speaking of hair, he had a lot of it. He had a full beard and his hair was shaggy and long enough to touch his collar.

Her Gavin—Allie caught herself and corrected the thought to just Gavin—shaved every day and wore his hair cropped short.

This guy looked like a mountain man.

"This is Gavin?" Josh asked her.

Josh was enough older than she and Gavin and Devon that he probably wouldn't have known Gavin. Gav hadn't been a star student or athlete, so he and Josh hadn't run in the same circles anyway. Even if he had known Gavin, he would have never recognized him now. She barely recognized him. Wow.

She nodded, unable to take her eyes off of the man who now stood only a few feet away, looking like a wild man. His eyes were bloodshot, he wore jeans and a T-shirt under a hooded sweatshirt that had seen better days—a long time ago. He wore lumberjack boots and the look in his eyes was…determined. That was the best word for how he was looking at her.

Allie became aware of the murmurings and rustlings of the crowd in the pews. The crowd of family and friends who had come to see her and Josh married.

Holy crap, indeed.

"What do you think you're doing?" Josh demanded of Gavin.

It felt like the moments were passing in slow motion, like they'd been standing there staring at one another for an hour, but it had only been a few seconds.

"I'm here to talk to Allie."

Oh, boy. Allie pressed a hand to her stomach. Now would so not be the time to throw up.

Josh moved to stand between Gavin and Allie. "We're kind of in the middle of something."

"Yeah, this can't wait." Gavin looked past Josh to her. "I need to talk to you. Now."

Her heart flipped over in her chest. God, she'd missed him. She wanted to touch him, smell him, taste him.

Quite inappropriate considering she was standing next to the man she was in the midst of marrying.

What she really wanted to do was throw herself into Gavin's arms and ask him to take her away.

No, she didn't. That was crazy.

God, her head hurt.

He started toward her, and she sucked in a quick breath as Josh moved to block him. "I don't think so, Gavin."

Gavin's eyes narrowed. "Listen. I can do this here in front of the whole town. I don't mind. I'm leaving here with Allie one way or another. But I think keeping some of this private might be appropriate." He leaned around Josh to look at Allie. "I have some things I need to say before you say I do to another man, Al."

Oh, her heart hurt too. This was...a dream. It had to be. That made the most sense. Her brain was floating in champagne and her blood alcohol level had to be...well, really high. Or low. Whatever it was when you were really drunk.

This whole thing was nuts. There was no way Gavin was here. The stress had finally gotten to her. She'd finally cracked up.

Josh sighed, stepped closer to Gavin and lowered his voice. But Allie could still hear him.

"Don't do this, Gavin. Haven't you messed with her enough? Just let her be happy."

Allie felt a twinge in her heart at Josh's words too. He was such a good guy. He was her friend. He really was trying to protect her.

"That's exactly what I want to do," Gavin insisted, not backing down an inch. "Is that what you want?"

"I'm standing next to her in a tux in front of a minister. What do you think?"

Crap. Crap, crap, crap. Josh was standing next to her in a tux in front of the minister because he was a really good guy who was trying to do a good thing. The right thing.

Of course he was. That was all he or Allie knew how to do.

He loved her. She knew that. She loved him. She was equally sure of that. They would have a great life together.

"I think that if you don't let her talk to me, you know that she'll always wonder," Gavin said. "You don't want that, do you? To have your wife wondering about another man?"

Allie felt her eyes widen. Damn, but that was kind of romantic. And sexy.

And no, she'd never love Josh the way she had loved Gavin.

Josh blew out a long breath and shoved his hand through his hair. Then he half turned to her. "Allie?"

Ah, crap. She was going to have to make a decision here? She hadn't even been able to pick out her bridesmaids' dresses or her own shoes.

"What would I wonder?" She meant specifically. She had about a billion questions and thoughts swimming through her liquor-saturated mind.

"You'd wonder what I had to say to you so badly that I would fly over four thousand miles so I could rush in here to stop your wedding."

Well...yeah. As would every other person sitting in that church.

There wasn't a sound in the church. Allie couldn't breathe. She looked at Josh. He looked angry and like he really wanted to hit somebody. That made sense.

Then she looked into the pews. She found her father sitting in the front pew. He seemed confused. That made sense too. Except that she knew he was more confused than most. This was bad. This would shake him up terribly. Things needed to happen with organization and routine for Owen Ralston. Everyone, especially her mom and Allie, had made sure that things in his life went according to plan.

This was not according to plan.

Could her brothers help her out here? This once. Could making sure her dad was okay fall on someone else's shoulders, just once?

She felt a surge of anger—or maybe it was resentment—flash through her.

She always did what was expected. She always kept it together for everyone else.

Her brothers, Charlie and Danny, were standing at the end of the line of groomsmen. They looked—curious, almost amused.

Amused?

Really?

Her life was being tipped upside down—and that was before Gavin even showed up—and they were feeling entertained?

Could she really trust them to step up and make sure things were okay for their dad?

Finally she pressed her lips together and shook her head.

Double holy crap with a cherry on top. She couldn't do this.

But oh, she wanted to. She wanted to pick up her skirts and run off with Gavin. Just seeing him again made her ache and want and need. If he touched her, she was a goner.

Allie felt the sting of tears in her eyes.

Nobody ever said life was fair.

"Allie." Gavin finally broke the silence as he took a step forward.

"You're too late," she whispered. She couldn't let him touch her. She felt a tear slip down her cheek.

"Bullshit," he said.

Bullshit? What did that mean? He couldn't just...

He strode forward, bent and scooped her into his arms, then headed for the side door.

"Gavin!"

Oh, no. He wouldn't really do this. He wouldn't really just march into her wedding and literally sweep her off her feet. No way. This was bad.

She kicked and he tightened his hold.

"Just a damn minute—" Josh started.

Gavin turned. Several people were on their feet, including her dad. He still looked confused—more so, really. She glanced at her brothers as all of the groomsmen stepped forward. Even Hayley Stone was on her feet.

But no one came any closer. This was Gavin Montgomery, after all. He wasn't a stranger. Most of the town probably didn't know she had a past with him, but he was hardly some bum off the street. In spite of how he was currently dressed.

"Give me a chance," Gavin said, addressing Josh. "Let me talk to her. Let me tell her what I came here to say. Then if she wants to come back, I'll walk her down the aisle myself."

Allie felt her heart do another double flip, then sink to her toes.

There was no way in hell Gavin was walking her down the aisle to marry another man.

Anyway, it was crazy to ask Josh to do that.

No way would Josh let Gavin just carry her off. Surely, he'd...

But Gavin didn't wait to hear the other man's response. He started toward the door again.

She thought maybe she should struggle, or cry for help, or something. Maybe she would. In a minute. Right after she enjoyed the feeling of strength and warmth that surrounded her. She felt like she melted a little when Gavin shifted her tighter against his chest.

He felt wonderful. He smelled wonderful. And she was pretty sure he'd taste just as good.

"If you really love him, he has nothing to worry about." Gavin's voice rumbled low enough that only she would hear him. She felt the vibration in his chest and sighed. "And if he loves you, he'll wait."

Yeah, he had a point there. If she was in love with Josh, then nothing Gavin could say or do would change that. And vice versa.

She looked up at him, then to Josh over his shoulder, then

back to Gavin. "Am I dreaming?"

His mouth curled at one corner. "I'm real, darlin'. I'm here."

She sighed. God, that sounded nice. It sounded so protective and reassuring. This felt good. Having Gavin swoop in after more than a year and carry her off from her wedding felt good.

There was something really wrong with her.

Allie buried her face into Gavin's neck as he turned and again headed for the door the pianist rushed to open for him.

They stepped out into the beautiful June day, and Allie didn't even flinch when the door banged shut behind them.

But the peace lasted only a few seconds.

"Wait!" Josh yelled from behind them.

Gavin stopped.

"What the fuck, Allie?" Josh demanded. "Are you leaving with him?"

Gavin turned with a sigh. "Allie called me last night."

Allie stiffened in his arms. What? He was ratting her out?

Josh's eyes went to her and his frown darkened. "You did?"

Oh...crap.

Allie made a squeaky little noise. Her mouth was wide open, no words coming out. Because her brain couldn't think of any. There was no way this could turn out good for her. A lie, in church, was surely a ticket straight to hell, and the truth would hurt one of the best men she knew.

"She called and told me that she'd always love me."

Allie groaned and closed her eyes, wishing Gavin had just kept walking. Or that he'd really done it right and ridden in on a white horse to whisk her off. They could be miles away by now.

What he said wasn't entirely true. She'd sung that she would always love him. Drunk off her ass.

But the message was the same—on the night before her wedding to another man, she was thinking of Gavin.

Crap. Damn. Hell.

"Allie?" Josh asked, eyebrows drawn tightly over his eyes.

"Is this true?"

She swallowed hard. She breathed hard. She prayed hard.

Finally she said softly, "Well..."

Josh shook his head. "Jesus Christ." Then he pulled himself to his full height, anger blazing in his eyes. "Were you drunk?"

God, yes. "Maybe a little."

"You called Gavin the night before our wedding and told him you'd always love him?" Josh's voice rose and she winced.

"Not exactly," she said. "I didn't tell him to come or anything. I didn't say that I loved him." Were white lies okay if you weren't technically in church?

Josh pinched the bridge of his nose. "Allie. We're getting married. You don't just change your mind at the last second about something like this."

She had no idea what to say. There was really no making this better at this point. What were they going to do—walk back in there and go through with the ceremony as if nothing had happened?

"I'm sorry," she finally whispered. And she was. Not sorry enough to go back inside, but sorry.

"That's all I needed to hear." Gavin turned and headed for the car that was parked at a crazy angle at the curb in front of the church.

Allie just hung on tight.

Chapter Two

Gavin headed for the rental car, mostly because he had no idea where else to go. It was right in front of the church, parked crookedly at the curb, the keys still in the ignition.

Just how he'd expect someone to park who was about to break up a wedding and steal the bride.

Break up a wedding. Steal the bride.

Hell. What had he just done?

Had he really just carried Allie out of her own wedding?

Gavin felt a trickle of sweat slip down his back—and it wasn't that hot out here.

Holy shit.

He'd really done it.

And looking down at the woman in his arms, he knew he would do it all over again.

It was moments like this that being a selfish bastard—as his father so eloquently put it—was a good thing. He wasn't going to lose any sleep over Josh Brewster and the wedding without a bride. Maybe Josh really loved Allie. Maybe his heart was in pieces right now. But Gavin didn't really care. This was about him and the fact that *he* was in love with her. Josh was on his own.

Yanking the passenger door open, he nudged Allie inside and slammed the door before jogging to the driver's side. He slid behind the wheel, shifted into drive and pulled away from the curb, aware of Josh's angry presence by the church's side door. Gavin kept his eyes on the street until they were a block away, then he glanced over at Allie. She was watching him with those big green eyes that had made him mush for years.

"You okay?" he asked, giving her a little smile. She would

be if she wasn't now. He'd make sure of it.

"Strangely enough, I think I might be," she said.

One corner of her mouth curled up at the corner, and Gavin knew he was right to interrupt the wedding. It wasn't like declaring that he still loved her and wanted her back could have really waited until *after* the wedding.

He smiled. "How do you feel?"

"Like the dream I had where you came home and swept me off my feet finally came true."

Those words were clear and they punched Gavin in the gut. "Yeah?" he asked gruffly.

"Yeah."

He couldn't believe he'd been within minutes of losing her for good. He took a deep breath. He'd come here to tell her how he felt, to beg her not to get married.

The not-getting-married thing seemed taken care of. For now anyway. Now for the I-was-stupid-to-let-you-go speech. "Allie, I—"

"I'm starving," she interrupted.

Ooookay. "What do you want?"

"A cheeseburger. With bacon."

He couldn't help his smile. Allie was one of those girls who could eat like crazy and never gain weight. Then he frowned. She'd never been *this* skinny though. She hadn't been eating any bacon cheeseburgers lately.

"You don't look good," he said simply.

Her eyes widened. "Well, thanks."

"Seriously. Did you sleep last night?"

"Four hours." She wrinkled her nose. "Maybe three."

"And you haven't eaten?"

She shook her head. "Couldn't."

"But you've been drinking." The way she'd slightly slurred her words in the church had made that clear.

"Definitely," she confirmed. "Lots."

"Today too?"

"Champagne." She spread her arms wide. "Happiest day of

my life."

Uh-huh.

That champagne was playing a huge part in her leaving the church with him.

Gavin shoved one hand through his hair, taking a corner too fast. He knew that her state of mind came, at least in part, from a bottle, and he knew that he should be torn about that. But he wasn't. He'd had to get her out of that church. At least long enough to tell her that he was still in love with her.

"How's your head?" he asked. Surely she was feeling the effects of the night before. On the phone it had been clear she was drunk. But he hadn't been able to help the thump of his heart when he'd heard her voice—and the words to the song.

"Swimmy," she answered, wrinkling her nose again. "Is that a word?"

He shook his head with a slight smile in spite of knowing he shouldn't find this funny. "I don't think so."

"Well, that's how it feels," she said. "Like my words are swimming around and around. Like they can't find the way."

"Okay, we need to sober you up. Then talk."

She frowned. "I'm really hungry."

A cheeseburger he could do. That was now the plan—focus on one thing at a time.

"Can we grab my bags out of my car?" she asked. "I've got crackers in there. And Twizzlers. And a Snickers. And lip gloss." She rubbed a finger over her bottom lip as if being without lip gloss and licorice was the biggest problem in her life. She grabbed the bottom edge of her bra through her dress and wiggled it. "I need a different bra, too. Bernice picked this one out."

Gavin wasn't sure what that had to do with anything. "Al, I can…"

She reached up and pulled her veil from her hair, then looked down at her dress, lifting the skirt with her hands. "I need a brush and some different clothes."

Finally, he just grinned. With that list, how could he doubt she needed her bags? And he was on board with her not needing to keep the dress on. That was a good sign she didn't intend to go back to her wedding any time soon. "You bet. Where is it?"

"It's right by the north door of the church. The blue Focus."

Right. Her car would be at the church. Great.

Praying for a little divine intervention—that he was pretty sure he didn't fully deserve—he took a left and headed back for St. Mark's. He pulled up by the door, hoping no one would be spilling out of the church just yet. Angry mobs weren't his thing. And they'd have a right to be angry. He got that. But this was big. This was bigger than what his hometown thought of him—not that his reputation was spotless anyway—and what everyone thought Allie should have done. He was sorry about the cake and flowers, but a guy didn't just stand by and let the love of his life marry someone else.

The Focus was unlocked, so he grabbed the two bags out of the backseat, slammed the door and headed back for Allie.

She was stretched lengthwise on the front seat, facedown.

"Allie?"

She didn't answer or move. Gavin shoved the bags into the backseat of the rental, then leaned in the driver's side door.

He shook her by the shoulder. "Allie? Come on, babe, wake up."

She mumbled something incoherent. Was alcohol poisoning a real possibility here? She'd just been talking to him, but suddenly he was concerned.

His hand on her bare shoulder reminded him how pale she was. "Honey, you have to—"

The side door of the church banged open and Gavin glanced up to see a little crowd frozen in the doorway.

Okay, change of plans. He used both hands to slide Allie over and got behind the wheel. She moved then—just enough to sit up, curl her legs under her and lean against him. Once the car was in gear, he wrapped his arm around her, tucking her more firmly along his side. He resisted squealing the tires, and instead, calmly and coolly, pulled out onto Ash Avenue and turned left.

Not for any particular reason, except that it got them out of sight of the church.

"Allie?" he tried again. "Honey, I need to be sure you're all right."

He used the rearview mirror to look at her. Her eyes were shut. He tightened his arm around her, still trying to convince himself this was real. It hit him again how tiny she felt, how bony even, and a renewed surge of anger went through him at all the people back there who were supposed to care about her. Didn't they see that she looked sick? Didn't they notice that something was wrong? And how about the drinking and drunk dialing? Clearly something was up when a woman got sauced to walk down the aisle.

Just as Gavin was contemplating turning around and beating Josh to a pulp after all, Allie shifted to turn into him more fully and sighed. She settled against him like she was seeking warmth or comfort. Her hand rested on his thigh, her cheek against his chest.

Damn. That felt familiar. And really, really good.

But she was out of it.

He shifted, trying to reach his phone. Allie shifted too...and slid down until her head was resting in his lap. Gavin cleared his throat and moved again, trying to get his fly out from under her cheek. This was no time to get a hard-on. But this was as close as his cock had been to Allie's mouth in over a year, and his body didn't appreciate the finer points of her being drunk, emotional and still in her wedding dress.

At least now he could reach his phone, and Gavin was sure that talking to his friend Carter would take away any amorous thoughts.

"It's me," he said when Carter picked up.

"Where the hell are you?" Carter demanded. "I've been—"

"What are the signs of alcohol poisoning?"

That stopped him. "How much have you had?"

"Not me," Gavin snapped. "Someone I'm with. She's clearly drunk but now she's sleeping and it's really hard to—"

"Just tell me where you are. I'll come to you," Carter said.

Gavin appreciated the offer, but even if it were a possibility, he wasn't quite ready for Carter to know what he'd done. "You can't. It's too far. Just tell me what to do here."

Carter sighed. "How much has she had?"

"Not sure."

He sighed again and Gavin gritted his teeth. "So sorry to inconvenience you, Doc," he said. "Just tell me the symptoms."

"Confusion?"

"Uh, a little. Maybe."

"Vomiting?"

"No." Not that he knew of anyway.

"Slow breathing, low temp, pale skin?"

"Maybe. Kind of." She was pale and her skin felt cool to him, but she seemed to be breathing all right.

"Are you close to an urgent care or ER?"

He was. There was one in Waterford, which was only twenty miles and would afford them some anonymity that would not be possible at the medical clinic in Promise Harbor. "Twenty minutes give or take."

"Get her some Gatorade to rehydrate, then take her to the urgent care. Then call me immediately after." Carter disconnected.

Gavin did appreciate that his friend could just concentrate on the issue and not push. For the moment, anyway.

Urgent care. Okay. Allie sighed in her sleep and he glanced down, brushing a stray strand of hair away from her cheek. His finger caught on a sprig of baby's breath and loosened another tendril from the circle of pearls that held her hair up and back.

The pearls matched the ones on the neckline of her wedding dress.

She was still wearing her wedding dress.

Fuck.

As he turned left to get on the street leading out of town, Gavin blew out a breath. He couldn't show up at urgent care with Allie in her wedding dress. It also occurred to him that this whole urgent care thing could be very complicated. He didn't have her purse. Did she have her ID and insurance cards in her bags in back? If not, how was he going to pull that off? He could just pay for the urgent care visit out of pocket, but they would want to see her ID, wouldn't they? And there would be paperwork. He was a veterinarian and they had a ton of paperwork.

He couldn't even fill in her full medical history. What if they needed to know something he wasn't sure of? He could claim to be her boyfriend, but her drunken state and lack of ID might make them suspicious.

If they were back home in Bend, the tiny town Gavin had landed in when he'd moved to Alaska, Carter could take care of her.

Gavin quickly thought that through. The plane was waiting for them at the airport, so they could leave right away. If they got in the air immediately, they could be back in Alaska in about ten hours. Would she be okay until then? He'd deal with the police questions if necessary, if it was truly a medical emergency, but if she was just drunk and exhausted, getting her home would be better.

Gavin grabbed his phone again and redialed Carter.

"I can't take her to urgent care. She doesn't have any ID or—"

"You don't even know who she is?" Carter asked in disbelief. "Seriously, man, this is—"

"Carter, stop talking!" Gavin demanded. "Of course I know who she is. Don't be a dumb ass. We just left without her purse or anything."

"You can't go back?"

Gavin glanced in the rearview mirror. Going back was not an appealing option. "Not easily."

"If she's got alcohol poisoning, it could be really serious, Gav. That's not something to screw with."

"How do I tell? What can I do?"

"She's unconscious?"

Allie sighed and wiggled, her cheek pressing into his thigh and making Gavin swear silently. "She's sleeping."

"Does she respond to stimuli?"

"Stimuli like what?"

"Pain?"

Gavin scowled at the road in front of the car. "Pain? What the hell?"

"Pinch her," Carter said.

"I'm not going to pinch her."

"You have to. I have to know how out of it she is."

Gavin swore again. "Fine." He reached down. "Sorry, babe," he muttered before he pinched her arm.

She pulled away and frowned.

"She responds to pain," he told Carter.

"Try to wake her up."

"Fine. Fuck." Gavin looked for traffic and then pulled over to the side of the road. He put the car into park, put the phone up on the dash and turned in his seat. "Allie. Honey, you gotta wake up for me." He pushed her up into a sitting position and cupped her face. "Al? Open your eyes."

She sighed heavily.

"Allie?"

Dammit.

He grabbed his phone, keeping her propped up with one hand. "Nothing."

"You have to do more than that," Carter said, sounding disgusted. "Slap her."

"Dammit, Carter, I'm not slapping her."

"Pinch her again. Something."

Gavin threw the phone back on the dash, harder than he should have. Fine. He'd wake her up. He leaned in, cupped the back of her head with his hand and kissed her.

For six seconds, nothing happened. Then she sighed, wrapped her arms around his neck and kissed him back.

It was as if the past year evaporated.

The heat built quickly and steadily from "yum" to "*damn*". Gavin tipped her head, slid his hand down her throat, stroked his tongue deep. Allie arched closer, her hands gripped the front of his shirt and she groaned.

Gavin sat back in his seat, bringing her with him. Allie tugged on her dress and moved to straddle his lap. When she settled her weight onto him, his quick, hard erection pressed up against her and they both moaned. He dug his fingers into her hair, pulling the pearls and bobby pins free, tossing them one by one onto the floor, until her hair fell free and loose. She ran her hands up the back of his neck into his hair too. His hair was several inches longer than he usually wore it, and he thought of his beard rubbing against her skin. He'd never worn a beard with Allie before. Did it feel weird?

He pulled back, breathing hard. She didn't let go of him, keeping their faces close, and they stared into each other's eyes for several seconds. She didn't look like anything felt *weird*, exactly.

"Whoa," she said softly.

"So, you're awake," he said unnecessarily. His voice was husky.

"Yeah."

"Good."

Still looking at her as she pressed her lips together, he reached for his phone. "She's awake."

"Is she responding appropriately?" Carter asked.

"Um, yeah, very appropriately."

"Then she's probably okay. Get her hydrated, make her eat, sober her up as much as you can. Then get her over here. I'll check her over."

"It's, um..." Gavin couldn't remember the last time he'd said "um" so many times in a conversation. "It's going to be a while."

"Where are you?"

"Massachusetts."

There was a long pause on Carter's end of the phone.

"You're *where*?"

"It's a long story."

"You're coming home now?"

"In a few hours." Several hours would have been more accurate.

"I'll see you then."

Oh, Gavin was sure that Carter would be in his face within moments of touchdown. And he wouldn't be alone. Not much exciting happened in Bend, Alaska, and Gavin's love life was the most boring thing of all.

He disconnected the phone call and looked at Allie.

No one was going to think he was boring now, that was for sure.

"You still want a cheeseburger?" he asked.

"I kind of want to stay right here and go back to what we were just doing," she said.

"You're drunk," he pointed out.

She started to shake her head, but lifted her hand to her forehead and said, "Yeah, maybe a little."

"Or a lot. Let's find food and coffee."

Allie slid back into the passenger seat as Gavin pulled the car back onto the street. Wow, no one could say their chemistry wasn't still strong. He moved in his seat, trying to relieve some of the pressure in his jeans. Maybe they should get a hotel room.

But when he glanced over at her, she had her head resting against the window and she was staring out as their hometown passed by.

"I don't want to sober up," she said quietly.

"What?" He looked from her to the road and back.

"I don't want coffee. I don't want to be sober. Can't I just go to sleep and you take me somewhere wonderful where I don't have to make any decisions or worry about anything or anyone?"

Wow. That was...wow. "Yeah, Al, I can do that," he said gruffly. "Is that really what you want?"

God, he'd known it. He'd known that she was collapsing under everything. If only he could have been there. But they had gone their separate directions, knowingly, willingly. She'd known what he wanted. She'd chosen Promise Harbor over him.

"It's really what I want," she said, closing her eyes. "Really, really, really."

Glancing at her, he felt his heart clench. He could definitely do that.

He'd been doing it for years. When they were together, whenever she went to Promise Harbor to spend time with her family, he planned a way to help her decompress when she got back to him. Sometimes they'd go out, sometimes they'd stay in. But his focus was on making her smile, making her forget the pressures and frustrations, taking care of her.

She never asked him for any of it. She never had to. He just knew what she needed, and the drive to make her happy was impossible to ignore. He might have hated that she'd go home to her family nearly every weekend and always come home tense and tired, but he did like being her refuge.

He knew that now she was still under the influence. Her words were still slurred and he figured her thoughts were still "swimmy", but what she wanted made sense. She wanted a break, she wanted to get away, she wanted to have someone else take charge. Maybe she wouldn't have let those thoughts and words out if she were completely sober. Maybe this was a good thing—without her inhibitions, her rock-solid sense of responsibility, her constant worry about her family, she could be honest about what she wanted and needed.

Whatever the case, he was taking her at her word. She wanted him to take her somewhere? He knew just the place.

"Okay, Allie, I've got you. I'll take care of everything."

She sighed and turned to curl against him again. "A dream came true," she mumbled, just before she fell asleep again.

They landed at nine p.m. local time. Not that local time mattered. Gavin's system was so screwed up with changing three time zones out and back in the space of twenty-four hours that he knew he'd be feeling the effects for days. On top of that, it was right before the summer solstice, so it never got completely dark. Nine o'clock at night looked like two in the afternoon.

Allie was still asleep. He'd also slept, as well as could be expected on the plane, for several of the ten hours of the flight.

As he deplaned, he shook hands with Major, the pilot who had traded the spontaneous flight to the East Coast for a year of free veterinary care for his ten mushing dogs, six cats, four horses and seven goats. In addition to his regular fees. "I'll be out to check on Eddie soon," Gavin said.

Major chuckled and lit up a cigarette. "It was the most interesting trip I've had in a long time," the older man said. His eyes flicked to where Allie lay curled in her seat. "Good luck, boy. Looks like you have your hands full."

Gavin turned to look at Allie. He couldn't believe she was here. Hands full? Maybe. Okay, probably. But he knew what it was like to have his hands empty of her...he wasn't doing that again.

He carried her to his truck, loaded her bags in back and headed for home. They pulled in just before eleven thirty.

Gavin tried to rouse Allie to walk into the house, but she was having none of that. Instead, she seemed to melt into him when he picked her up off the truck seat. Not that he minded. She weighed next to nothing and he liked the feeling that he was taking care of her. He knew Allie. She was a do-er. She took care of people. She always had a plan, went nonstop and gave one hundred and ten percent to everything. For her to fall into this deep of an unconscious state with him meant she was either completely exhausted or completely trusted him. Or both. Whichever it was, she needed him and needed to be here.

He deposited her on the king-size bed in his bedroom. He had a guest room on the main level, but Allie wasn't sleeping under his roof in any bed other than his. And he was going to be right beside her.

He was damned tired of seeing her in that wedding dress though.

With a deep breath, he realized he needed to change her clothes. For one, she'd be more comfortable, and for another, he couldn't very well burn the dress with her still in it.

"Allie? Babe, let's get you out of this thing," he said, pulling her up to sitting.

She pulled back, trying to lie down.

"No, no, come on," he said, tugging her upright.

He reached behind her and lowered the zipper on the dress. The bodice gaped and slipped forward on her arms. Gavin stoically kept his eyes from dropping lower than her face. This wasn't sexual. That wasn't what was happening here. He was going to undress her, put her in one of his T-shirts and tuck her in. Period.

The dress hadn't dropped away from her breasts completely, so he also unhooked her bra and then rose to grab a T-shirt from his dresser. She'd flopped back onto the pillows, the bodice loose, but still covering her when he returned to the bed. He slipped the T-shirt over her head and then pulled it down as he pulled the dress and bra down. He didn't see any bare body parts—but he knew they were there. And his body reacted.

Gavin stubbornly ignored the tightness behind his zipper and slipped the dress and bra out from under the shirt, pulling the dress the rest of the way off her hips and down her legs. He left her panties on and tossed the dress to one side. He was going to roast marshmallows over the fire he made with that dress tomorrow.

Then he stripped off his own clothes except his boxers and managed to get the comforter and sheets pulled down from under Allie. She sighed contentedly, burrowing down into the pillow, and he slid in next to her, flipping the covers over them both.

The big windows were covered with blackout shades, making it feel like it was nighttime in the bedroom at least. But there was enough light from the light in the hallway that he could lie and watch Allie's profile. She was here. He finally let his body and mind relax enough to absorb that fact. He and Allie were in his bed together in Alaska.

This was where she belonged. With him. And finally it was

going to happen.

His actions and reactions had been fueled by emotion—panic, fear, love, determination—for the past twenty-six hours. Now everything just drained out of him. It was over. He'd gone to her. He'd done the right thing. He'd rescued her.

Everything was good now.

Gavin felt his body start to sink into the mattress, and he reached to pull Allie against him. She wiggled close, her butt right in his groin, her legs against his, her back to his chest.

His body hardened as his heart softened.

Everything was very good now.

"Walking pneumonia."

There was a beat of silence then, "What the *fuck?* She's actually *sick?*"

"It's a mild pneumonia. Treated with antibiotics. She'll be fine."

"It's not just stress and liquor?"

Allie heard Gavin mutter something else and the other male voice say, "Extreme stress, fatigue, lack of sleep, not eating well—all of that can contribute to physical and mental exhaustion and, yes, getting sick."

Extreme stress—check.

Lack of sleep—check.

Not eating well—check.

That all sounded about right to her.

Allie buried further under the covers of the most comfortable bed she'd ever been in and closed her eyes again. The guys were just outside the bedroom, the door open, and she didn't want them to know she was awake.

"What the *fuck* were they all doing? Just sitting around, picking out his and hers towels and thinking that it didn't matter that she was obviously not doing well?"

Allie felt her chest get warm at Gavin's words. Obviously he was frustrated. He'd never been very good at hiding his feelings.

She'd always loved that about him. If he was happy, you knew it. If he was angry, you knew it. If he wanted you, you knew it.

But this frustration was over her. He was concerned, protective, willing to fight battles for her.

A shiver of desire went through her but, as always when it concerned Gavin, it was twisted up with a bunch of other emotions—love, of course, and the ever-present sense that she needed to hold on tight and absorb every minute because it might not last. She squeezed her eyes shut and breathed. She was not going to think about how it hadn't lasted before, how she had to keep saying good-bye to him, how no matter what she did or how it felt, it wasn't enough to keep him.

She wasn't going to think at all, in fact. This just curling up and sleeping for hours and hours seemed to be working just fine.

"Gavin, what she needs is rest. Sleep. Her body knows that. We'll get her some antibiotics. When you wake her up to feed her, have her take them. In a few days she'll be fine. No one can sleep forever."

Well, she was going to give it her best shot.

"And look at it this way. Obviously she totally trusts you and feels safe with you. That's what she needed. A safe haven. Looks like you're it, buddy."

That was exactly what she needed and exactly what Gavin was. What he'd always been.

Even after they'd broken up and decided they shouldn't see each other anymore—all three times—all she had to do was call and he'd stay up all night talking, or she'd tell him she needed to see him and he'd immediately book a flight to a city halfway between them so they could be together. Even if was just for a weekend.

The only time he hadn't been there was at her mom's funeral...

Allie stubbornly closed her eyes, shut down her mind and drifted off to sleep again. She was here now, with Gavin. He'd take care of her. That was all she needed.

"Detective Stone."

Damn. He'd been hoping for voice mail.

"Hayley, it's me."

"Have you lost your *mind*?" she hissed in a sudden whisper.

"No. And don't tell me you're surprised by this."

"That you showed up? No. That you kidnapped her? A little."

Hayley was probably the only person in Promise Harbor who knew all about him and Allie. And that he'd never really gotten over her.

"I didn't kidnap her," he said, knowing it was unnecessary. Hayley wouldn't have believed that of him. If she had, she'd have been all over his ass. She knew his address and she carried a gun. He wouldn't mess with that. "She wanted to come with me. She asked me to take her away."

"This is crazy, Gav," Hayley said, her voice still hushed. He'd called her at the station on purpose. She wouldn't be able to yell at him in the middle of the Promise Harbor Police Department.

"Maybe. Or maybe it makes complete sense." He hoped the latter was true. He was still having trouble believing it had all happened too. "Maybe I'm a frickin' hero. Because if I'd ever set foot in Promise Harbor again, she would have been cheating on Josh with me."

"Oh, you're such a big talker," Hayley said, finally laughing lightly. "You would have never done that."

She was right. Cheating was one thing Gavin absolutely didn't tolerate. Even before he'd learned his dad's dirty not-so-little secret, Gavin had thought cheaters were assholes. After finding out that his dad didn't just cheat, but that he actually thought he had good reasons for it that should make it forgivable, Gavin couldn't even be in a room alone with him.

"Gav," Hayley said, suddenly hesitant. "Um, speaking of scumbags, your dad was at the wedding."

Hayley knew that when he was sixteen Gavin had walked in on his dad in his office, screwing his best friend's wife on the desk. Hayley didn't know about the argument they'd had when

Gavin confronted him or his father's reasons for doing what he'd done, but she still hated him. The whole truth would have probably caused her to find a reason to Taser him.

Gavin closed his eyes. His dad at the wedding meant his mom and probably his brothers had been there too. Well, of course they were. It was Promise Harbor and his family was a part of the community. Nothing big happened without their attendance, and nothing was bigger than the Brewster-Ralston wedding.

He didn't give a shit what his dad thought. In fact, embarrassing and frustrating his father had been a hobby of his from age sixteen to eighteen, when he left home, and he'd gotten damn good at it. But he hated that it also affected his mother. He hated hurting her.

"This is all your fault, you know," Gavin told Hayley.

"My fault?" she asked. "If you'd asked my opinion about this plan of yours I would have locked you a cell until the whole thing was over."

"If you'd told me they were getting married before the other day I could have come home and talked to Allie long before it got to this point," Gavin said.

"I called you about it two weeks ago," she argued. "It's not my fault you don't check your messages when you're out playing with your bears."

Gavin rolled his eyes. The work he did with the endangered wildlife program was hardly "playing", and his involvement with the polar bear capture and release program was something he was very proud of. Which Hayley knew well. "You knew about the engagement for more than two weeks," he said.

There was a long silence on her end before she said, "You told me to stop telling you about Allie."

He took a deep breath. He had said that. And meant it. It tore him up every time Hayley called him. The first time had been when Allie's mom, Lily, had been diagnosed with cancer. It had been hell knowing what Allie was going through and not being there. The idea that she was hurting, sad, stressed out had eaten at him. His role had always been protector, savior.

But she hadn't called him. She hadn't reached out or needed him.

Because she had Josh.

Gavin felt the acid churn in his stomach. Other than the fact that she'd been standing next to Josh at the end of the aisle in a church, Gavin hadn't really let himself think about it. But Allie had been standing next to *Josh.* Josh Brewster. Mr. Fucking Perfect.

Of course she had been. Who else would have been there?

Gavin blew out a breath.

Every time he'd talked to Hayley after Lily's diagnosis it seemed that she had bad news. Lily wasn't doing well, the disease was progressing, Allie was holding it all together. And he'd known that meant that Allie was taking care of everyone and not thinking about herself for even a second.

The old bitterness had reared its head, and he'd had to remind himself that even when they were a couple, talking about a future together, she had thought of her family first, put their needs ahead of what she wanted and needed. He hadn't been able to convince her she was worth consideration even when she was madly in love with him. After he'd broken her heart, he knew she wouldn't listen to him tell her that it was okay not to do it all herself.

Even now it was painful to think about it. He knew he'd failed Allie when her mom was sick and then passed away, but he hadn't known what to do then and didn't know how it could have been different now.

The solution had always been for her to be with him in Alaska. That seemed simple enough. She was a teacher. They needed teachers in Alaska.

But her family was in Promise Harbor.

"I know," he finally said to Hayley. He paced to the window and looked out over his property. He owned twenty acres and his veterinary practice. He loved Alaska, the people he'd met, the outdoors, the animals, the space, the freedom. He sighed. "I didn't want to hear about Allie. It hurt too much."

"Ugh," Hayley groaned. "I knew about it for five months,

Gav. It was killing me not to tell you, but I knew you'd freak. And then I finally couldn't take it anymore. But you weren't calling me back and I didn't know if you'd gotten the message or what. I *knew* you were going to freak," she said again.

"Well, I think it's safe to say you were right on that one," Gavin said.

"So, she's in Bend with you?"

"Yep."

"Does she like it? Is she staying? Is this for good? Are you going to get married?"

He chuckled, even as he wanted to sigh heavily. He didn't know the answer to any of those questions. They hadn't had a conversation beyond him waking her up, making her eat and drink and then asking *Are you ready to get up?* and her saying *Not yet.*

"She's been in bed since we got here."

"Good for you," Hayley said.

He laughed out loud at that. "Thanks for the vote of confidence, but not like that." Then he did sigh. "She's exhausted. And sick." He felt pretty exhausted himself.

"But she wants to be there. I think that's a good thing," Hayley said, sounding more like the friend who was always on his side.

Even when he acted like an idiot, Hayley had his back. Not that she wouldn't arrest him if he deserved it. Plenty of times she'd told him to pull his head out of his ass when he needed it.

But even she hadn't been able to advise him on the impasse he and Allie had reached sixteen months ago. Allie was determined to stay in Promise Harbor and he was just as determined to be anywhere else.

"I think she needs to be here," he told Hayley. "She needs someone to take care of her for a change. She needs to be far away so that they can't need her."

"I hope it works out this time, Gav," Hayley said sincerely.

"Thanks. I need you to be sure everyone knows she's okay. She's here with me and she's staying. Just make sure no one's freaking out. Like Owen," Gavin said of Allie's dad. "Or Sophie."

Sophie Brewster was Josh's mom, but the families had always been so close that Gavin knew Sophie thought of Allie as another daughter. Allie's mom had been Sophie's best friend, and Gavin was sure Lily's death had hit Sophie as hard as anyone.

"Or Josh?" Hayley asked dryly.

"Yeah, you can tell Josh that he's lucky I don't come back there and kick his ass for letting Allie get this stressed and sick."

Hayley chuckled. "Couldn't tell him even if I wanted to. He took off."

Gavin scowled. "What do you mean?"

"He left."

Gavin could tell that Hayley was grinning widely.

"Left?"

"Went to Greenbush Island."

There was something in Hayley's tone that caught Gavin's interest. What wasn't she saying? "Why there?"

"All I know is that he'd booked the honeymoon suite at the Oceanside Inn there."

Yeah, that was all she knew. Sure it was. Hayley was a great cop and loved knowing stuff other people didn't. She had contacts all over. If Josh Brewster left town and she wanted to know where he went and why, she'd know.

"So he went on the honeymoon?" Gavin asked. Hey, the guy had paid for the tickets. Maybe he wanted to get drunk on a beach instead of drinking in Promise Harbor, where everyone knew he'd been left at the altar. Gavin couldn't say he blamed him.

"Technically he went to look for Allie."

"Allie's not on Greenbush Island."

"I know."

"You lied to him?" Gavin knew Hayley was a good friend.

"Didn't have to. He didn't ask me."

"Convenient."

"Everyone knows we're close, but maybe Allie didn't tell him we still keep in touch. Whatever he didn't know before the wedding, I'm sure his mother filled him in on."

Gavin grinned. He and Hayley had definitely had some fun. It had been minor things—parties at the river, underage drinking, sneaking into the swimming pool after midnight, taking the principal's car for a joyride—stuff that hadn't hurt anyone but had made them a bit notorious.

"Well, maybe looking for her is just his excuse to go off by himself and lick his wounds," Gavin said. He paused for a moment, wondering if he'd feel a stab of guilt over Josh Brewster's wounds. Hmm. Not a one.

"Oh, he didn't go alone," Hayley said brightly. "He took Devon Grant."

"He took another woman?" Gavin asked, amazed. Sure, Allie had left him at the altar for another guy. Sure, Gavin had broken up the wedding—in front of the entire town, including his own family. But Gavin was possibly even more amazed that perfect Josh Brewster, everyone's favorite golden boy, had done something so spontaneous and gossip-worthy.

"You remember Devon?" Hayley asked.

"Sure. She and Allie were tight in high school."

"Right."

The realization dawned slowly. "Josh took off on his honeymoon with Allie's best friend?"

"Ex-best friend," Hayley said, clearly enjoying sharing the news. "Josh and Devon were really serious for a while after college."

"No way." Gavin thought about the information. Then slowly he felt his grin spread. "That's awesome. Good for him."

"You don't care about Josh," Hayley said with a laugh. "You're just glad that this means he and Allie won't be getting back together."

Gavin's scowl returned. "He and Allie *won't* be getting back together."

Hayley said, "I'm not the one you have to convince."

"Yeah, I know."

"Keep me informed, okay?"

"Definitely."

"And Gav?"

"Yeah?"

There was a long pause, and for some reason Gavin braced himself. He knew Hayley. Well. There was something in that pause that made him frown.

But in the end she just said, "Take care of yourself. And maybe stick around long enough to at least have a drink with me next time, okay?"

He wanted to push, to ask her if everything was all right. But this was Hayley. She was tough as nails and she knew he'd be there for her. If she needed something, she knew all she had to do was ask. He finally said simply, "Promise."

As he hung up, Gavin looked at the ceiling. Allie was still up there, *still* sleeping.

When he'd wished to have her in his bed, this wasn't exactly what he'd had in mind.

Chapter Three

"It's been *two days*."

"I know. How long can a person sleep?"

"She's fine. When her system is ready, she'll wake up."

"This is ridiculous."

"You don't even know her *name*?"

"Allie."

"No last name?"

"Nope."

"He's not saying a word to me either."

"I found a *wedding dress* on the floor. He hasn't told you *anything*?"

"Look, he said something about his and hers towels. I don't know what that means."

"It means he eloped with her!"

"He would have told us that. Wouldn't he?"

Allie groaned and pulled a pillow over her head. Couldn't these people have their gossip session somewhere else? They had to be outside her bedroom door—well, Gavin's bedroom door—to talk about her?

She recognized the male voice as that of Gavin's friend, Carter, who was apparently the local physician. He'd been the one here checking her vitals and taking blood out of her arm anyway. The other voices were female and she had no idea who they were. She also figured it was Gavin's problem what they thought was going on with the wedding dress and everything.

"I know she's from Massachusetts. Or at least that's where he was when they got together. He's not giving up any other information."

"Isn't he from the East Coast somewhere?"

"I thought he was from Kansas."

"That's where he went to vet school."

"Well, thank god he finally got called out. He's been driving me crazy."

"Me, too."

"Me, too."

"He's stomping around here, irritable, biting my head off. I'm about to tell him to fuck off."

Allie threw back the covers with a little growl. The pillow wasn't shutting out enough noise. She stomped across the room to the half-open bedroom door and yanked it the rest of the way open.

"Could you go tell him to fuck off now? It would get you away from this door."

They all jumped and turned as one to stare at her.

"We, um...didn't mean..." Carter stammered.

Carter stood between the two women. He was short, with dark hair and glasses and looked embarrassed at having been caught gossiping about her.

The woman closest to the bedroom door was thin and tall, nearly six feet, and had straight, blonde hair and intelligent blue eyes. She looked to be about the same age as Carter, Gavin and Allie. Her mouth was actually open as she stared.

Allie knew she looked like a mess. She was wearing another of Gavin's T-shirts that hit her midthigh, panties and nothing else. She was sure her hair was wild because she'd gone back to bed with it wet after her shower yesterday, and she had no makeup on. And she didn't care.

It was actually a freeing feeling. Typically she took great care with her appearance, making sure that her hair and makeup were done even to go to the grocery store in the harbor.

The other woman was only about five one, had streaks of red in her chin-length dark hair, wore a nose ring and was clearly much younger than the other two. She was the only one who let her gaze obviously travel over Allie from her hair to her toes and back again.

"Okay, let me help you out here," Allie said, putting a hand on her hip, her other hand still on the doorknob. "Her name is Allie Ralston. Gavin knows her from high school and from *dating* her after college. In fact, they just broke up a little over a year ago. Yes, she's from Massachusetts, as is Gavin. She's feeling a lot better, thank you. And she had a wedding dress on because she was getting married when Gavin showed up and stopped it." Allie tipped her head. "Anything else?"

"No, no...that's fine... We'll just—" Carter started.

"You were getting *married*?" the shorter girl demanded. "And Gavin showed up to *stop* it?"

Allie lifted a shoulder. She didn't have much to add to that. "Yep."

"*Why*?"

Allie frowned. Why? What kind of question was that? And what was with the disbelieving tone of voice?

"Because he didn't want me to marry someone else."

The younger girl's eyes widened and she looked Allie up and down again.

Hey.

"I'm so glad you're feeling better, Allie," Carter said, taking each of the women by an elbow and trying to turn them toward the stairs. "I'll be back to check on you later. Be sure to take all of the antibiotics."

"You just left your wedding?" The girl shrugged Carter's hand off. "And came here from *Massachusetts*? In the middle of the night?"

Allie put both hands on her hips and pulled herself up tall, aware that it drew the hem of the T-shirt higher on her legs. But she didn't care. Her legs were one of her best features. "Yeah."

"And now you plan to spend all your time in bed?"

There was something about this woman that rubbed Allie the wrong way. Possibly the way she pointed out the things about this situation that sounded really stupid out loud. "Now that I'm feeling better," Allie said, chin up. "I'm planning to talk Gavin into exactly that."

The girl's eyes narrowed and Allie resisted sticking her tongue out.

She wasn't saying it to mark her territory. Okay, she wasn't saying it *just* to mark her territory. She'd been sleeping next to Gavin for two nights now, right up against him. She hadn't let herself turn in to him, run her hands all over him, put her mouth in all the places she'd been fantasizing about, because if she was feeling good enough for that he might make her get out of bed during the day. She wasn't ready for that. So she'd feigned sleep.

Now, though, looking at the three people in front of her, she was pretty sure her cover was blown. Gavin was going to know that she was out of bed, sounding quite coherent and sassy. Bitchy even.

She might as well plan to make the most of being awake and well.

"Now we're going," Carter said, finally successful in moving the women several steps toward the stairs. "Gavin's out on a call. He should be back in a couple of hours. If you need anything, Lydia would be happy to help you."

Ah, Lydia was the younger girl. She glared at Carter for his comment and Allie decided she wasn't going to need anything from any of them.

She was quite used to taking care of herself and everyone else.

"No problem. I'm just going to jump in the shower so I'm ready when Gavin gets back." She let the issue of what exactly she would be ready for just hang in the air between them.

"Great, great," Carter said, nudging the two women down the stairs in front of him. "I'll let him know."

She was sure he would. Now Allie was going to have to face Gavin fully sober and awake.

Allie finished her shower, singing loudly as she quickly washed and shampooed so as not to think about how she was in Gavin's shower, using Gavin's shampoo and Gavin's soap. She grabbed a towel, not thinking about how it was Gavin's towel, and was in the midst of wrapping her hair up when she finally made a mistake in her avoidance routine.

She looked out the window.

It was an understatement to say that the landscape outside Gavin's bathroom window was a lot different from the view she was used to. Even from inside the bathroom, the sheer awesomeness of the land outside hit her. It was so raw, so rugged. Everything was huge and rough and it seemed to go on forever.

Allie clutched her towel tightly and swallowed hard as reality—which she'd successfully kept out of her consciousness for the past two days—crashed into her.

Usually she was an expert at keeping reality under control. She let measured amounts in and only to a certain level of awareness. The deep, emotional part of her brain she'd kept nicely numb ever since her mother's cancer diagnosis. She wasn't about to start using it now.

But a little truth slipped past and landed square in the middle of her mind.

She was in Alaska. *She* was in Alaska. She was in *Alaska*.

Being unconscious was really preferable to the way her head started spinning.

Allie grabbed for the countertop and plopped onto the toilet, sparing only a millisecond to be grateful the lid was down.

Oh god. She'd walked out of her wedding, she was here with Gavin, she was in *Alaska*.

What the hell had she done?

She'd left home. Left her dad and brothers. Left Josh.

Oh god.

She leaned forward, resting her forehead on her knees and rocking back and forth. Oh god. She was here with Gavin.

Just like he'd always wanted. Just like he'd insisted she needed to be.

She tried to work up some anger toward Gavin. He'd brought her here. He'd taken advantage of her pathetic, drunk, sick state to get her here.

But it didn't stick. Not even for a second. Gavin hadn't done this. She had. This was all her fault.

She wanted to go back to bed.

Instead though, and incredibly proud of herself for it, she forced herself up. She didn't need to go to bed. She just needed to keep busy. Move. Work. Plan. Do. Anything to keep from *thinking.* She knew for a fact that it worked. It's what she'd been doing for the past nineteen months.

Drying off quickly, Allie headed into the bedroom for her bag. She'd showered yesterday while Gavin was gone, but she hadn't been too concerned about anything in her luggage. She'd used his soap, shampoo, deodorant and brush. Then she'd pulled on another T-shirt from his dresser and had gone back to bed.

Grabbing her bags, she threw them onto the bed and unzipped the first, looking for lotion, a ponytail holder and body spray. Digging didn't help her find any of those, so she finally upended it, dumping the contents onto the bedspread.

Her phone was the first thing to catch her eye.

Ugh.

She'd tucked her wallet and phone into this bag so she was sure to have them when they threw everything into Josh's car after the reception. The *wedding* reception. The wedding reception that they would have been leaving as husband and wife.

She stared at all the travel bottles. She'd truly been prepared for the honeymoon trip. When she packed, she'd had every intention of being Josh's wife when she next needed those bottles.

God, Josh must hate her.

And his mother must hate her. Allie closed her eyes and turned to slump onto the edge of the bed.

Sophie.

She had to be beside herself. Her dream wedding—the only thing that had really made her smile in the past year—had turned into a fiasco because of Allie.

Was Josh watching her more carefully now? Greta was

there, so that would help. But if Sophie slid into one of her depressions because of this, Allie would never forgive herself.

Allie felt a tear slip down her cheek. *They* were never going to forgive her. She'd ruined everything.

She swiped angrily at the tear. No. She was not going to cry. Not now. Not because of *this*. She didn't get to cry about this. She could have controlled this, she could have prevented it, she could have gone through with the wedding and kept everyone happy. This was all her fault.

She thought about Gavin storming up the aisle at the church and scooping her up to carry her out the side door.

Okay, this was eighty-five percent her fault.

But if she didn't cry about the things that were out of her control, then she certainly didn't get to cry about the stuff she messed up.

She got off the bed and made herself get dressed, stoically ignoring her phone as she pulled on white cotton capri pants and a green sleeveless blouse. She had no idea if she was dressing appropriately for Alaska, but she didn't have much choice. The clothes in her bag had been intended for the honeymoon.

Stubbornly, she shut down the thoughts of Josh and their wasted trip. She stuffed her phone back in her bag, tossed the bag back on the floor and took five steps toward the door—then stopped.

Dammit.

She hadn't been more than a foot away from that phone since the morning her mother called her with the news that the biopsy was positive.

Since then, Allie had officially taken over her mom's position on four different committees—two for school, where they'd taught together, and two for the city. She'd stepped in to push her youngest brother, Danny, toward a college major and to push her middle brother, Charlie, toward a job. All the while doing their laundry and cooking for them just like Lily had. Allie also had a list of things she needed to take care of for her dad and a ton of expectations from Josh and his family. They all needed her to be strong and decisive and *there*. They all needed her to replace Lily.

And, dammit, she had.

Not a wrinkle or a blip was noticed by anyone. Not a single ball Lily had been juggling got dropped. Not one of the many hats she wore fell off.

Because Allie was there.

Could she step away from the phone now?

Allie eyed the pillow where she'd spent the last two days. Maybe she could just crawl back in there and close her eyes again and this would all go away. Sleep was the only place where she could really escape.

She knew they needed her. What were they going to do without her? Was Charlie going to think to check on the bills and make sure the payments were going in on time? Was Danny going to get up for class without her there? Was her dad going to think to do laundry before he completely ran out of shirts? And would he remember to turn the iron off after he ironed the shirts? If he thought to iron at all?

Allie took a deep breath.

She had to stop. She was here, in Alaska, with Gavin. She couldn't do a damned thing about Danny's classes or her father's shirts.

To deal with that she was either going to climb back into bed or find something else to keep her busy.

Being busy was all that kept her going. She felt like if she stopped for too long everything would pile up on top of her and she'd never be able to climb out, so she just kept working and doing, planning and organizing. Her to-do list was like a security blanket. As long as she had something more to do, then she never had time to really think. Or feel.

So she needed a to-do list here.

First thing, make herself presentable.

In the bathroom, she dried her hair and pulled the sides up on top of her head with a gold clip while thinking about talking Gavin into a tour of his place and the town. She'd never been to Alaska but she knew it was gorgeous. She wanted to see some glaciers. And whales.

As she applied light makeup, she thought about all of Gavin's favorite foods and made a mental list of ingredients. She'd go through the kitchen before he got back to see what she had to work with and figure out if she could surprise him with dinner.

Feeling better now that she had a plan, Allie ventured out of the bedroom for the first time since arriving in Alaska. She ignored the butterflies in her stomach. That was stupid. Nothing bad was going to happen just because her phone was on a different floor, she had no email access and she was thousands of miles from home.

Or if it did, it wouldn't be *because* she was away from her phone and email and was thousands of miles from home.

She groaned. That wasn't really helping.

Then she stepped through the doorway into the rest of the house.

That helped.

The house was amazing.

The bedroom was actually a loft above the main room of the house. She stepped out onto a landing that overlooked the living room. The room had twenty-foot ceilings and the wall facing Allie was made up of windows overlooking what had to be acres of wilderness with mountains in the distance. It was breathtaking, and for a moment she just stood and stared.

No wonder Gavin loved it here. Waking up to that every morning was not a bad way to start the day.

As she moved down the staircase, she took note of the furniture Gavin had picked: the packed bookshelves, the stone fireplace, the huge entertainment center. The browns and tans were warm and masculine, everything was big and solid, and it made her feel comfortable and safe. All just like Gavin.

She wished he was here. The thought hit her as she stepped off the bottom step and looked around. She was lost. Not just in this house but in general. She didn't know her way to or around town—she couldn't even remember the name of the town at the moment. She certainly couldn't find it on a map.

She was standing in the middle of a place she couldn't even find on a map.

Allie made herself breathe and grabbed the banister.

She really wished Gavin was here.

When he was with her, this made sense somehow. She wanted this, wanted him, and when he was in front of her, walking away from everything else she knew and loved didn't seem crazy.

But at the moment, things definitely seemed crazy. And scary. And like going back to bed was a really good idea.

Allie turned back toward the stairs and even lifted her foot, but she glanced out the window again before she could step up.

In bed she couldn't see *that*.

It was gorgeous and vast and wild and...different. It seemed surreal, like something in a movie, retouched to make the colors brighter and everything bigger. The land was covered in trees, and it seemed to stretch forever. The mountains in the distance could have been in a painting. It was almost impossible for her to grasp that it was all real. It was so different from what she was used to. And it was beautiful. Though that didn't seem like an adequate word.

Okay. She could do this.

She turned to the room and looked around again. The kitchen couldn't be too far away.

Across the room, a large, arched doorway led to a room with ceramic tile visible from Allie's vantage point. A moment later she stepped into a gigantic modern kitchen. Everything shone in the morning sun that swept in through windows almost as large as the living room's, and there wasn't a crumb to be found.

She didn't remember Gavin being so neat. She appreciated that trait immensely. She'd cleaned up after enough men to last her a lifetime. She wondered if her brothers would think to buy Dad's favorite cereal when they finally had to go to the store because the peanut butter jar didn't magically refill itself. Then she stubbornly pushed those thoughts away. She couldn't do a thing about that from here, and her dad certainly knew his way to the grocery store if he needed something. What he'd get once he was there was anyone's guess, but she couldn't do anything about that from here either. Frozen pizza wouldn't kill him. Thank god he was working for Sophie at the Brewsters' landscaping business. He'd gone to work for the Brewsters after his accident, and having Sophie and Josh look out for him during work hours gave Allie a lot of relief. But there were twenty-four hours in a day.

Allie glanced toward the living room and the staircase to the bedroom. She could quickly text one of her brothers. Or call her dad. Or see if Mrs. Paulsen could take a casserole over.

Dammit.

She gripped the counter, closed her eyes and counted to ten. For god's sake. She didn't need to do any of those things.

She needed to do something *here.* For a change she was going to cook for a man who didn't *need* her to, for a man who could fend for himself very nicely. Doing something for someone because she wanted to do it instead of because she had to do it would be a welcome relief.

Newly determined, Allie started opening cupboards, inventorying the pots and pans and utensils as well as the food.

As she went, she decided to pull things out and rearrange to put things in a more logical place for use. Gavin probably didn't think about this stuff—and she was willing to bet he'd never used his crepe pan—but if she was going to be staying for a while, it made sense to make the kitchen as user-friendly as possible.

She was just fitting the beater into the mixer for the snickerdoodles she'd decided to make when she heard, "What in the hell do you think you're doing?"

She swung around to find Lydia staring at her from the doorway that led down another hallway she hadn't investigated yet.

"I'm making Gavin cookies." Allie pushed the beaters into place and plugged the mixer in.

"No you're not."

Allie looked at the flour, sugar, eggs and butter sitting on the countertop. "Uh, yes I am."

Lydia came into the room, her cheeks pink, her eyes glittering. "*I* make Gavin cookies on Fridays. He still has chocolate chip left from a few days ago."

"Well, these are snickerdoodles and he likes them better than chocolate chip," Allie said, cracking the eggs into the bowl.

Lydia's eyes widened as she watched. "He does not. He loves my chocolate chip."

Allie cut the stick of butter into squares and dumped it in the bowl.

Lydia gritted her teeth.

"Chocolate chip are his second favorite," Allie agreed. "But snickerdoodles are number one."

"You're *not* making cookies. This is my kitchen. *I* cook for Gavin." Lydia folded her arms.

"This is *your* kitchen?" Allie asked. She measured and added the sugar and Lydia gasped.

"*Yes.* I take care of Gavin. I clean the house, answer the clinic phone, shop for groceries, cook *and* bake."

Allie looked at the girl, realization dawning. Lydia had a crush on Gavin.

That could be...complicated.

She set her spoon down. "I'm just trying to stay busy. I'm going a little nuts."

Lydia cocked an eyebrow that said she was pretty sure Allie was already there.

Allie gave her a frown. "Anyway, I just need something to do until Gavin gets back. I'm just going to finish these and—"

"No, you're not."

Allie blinked at her, surprised. "Yeah, I am."

"No."

Allie picked up the mixer. "Yes."

"This week is Rice Krispies bars," Lydia said stubbornly.

"Fine. Make Rice Krispies bars. I'm going to make these." She put the beaters into the bowl and pushed the on switch.

The mixer whirled for five seconds before stopping. "What the..." She looked up to find Lydia holding the end of the cord where she'd pulled it from the outlet.

"You're not making those. Give me the bowl."

Allie frowned. "No way."

"Yes. I make the cookies. Snickerdoodles aren't for two more weeks."

Wow, and *she'd* been accused of being a type A personality. "Then I'll eat these. Or give them to Carter or something. Whatever. I just want something to do." She pulled the cord from Lydia's hand and turned to plug it in to a different outlet.

When she turned back, Lydia was holding the bowl. "You can go make Carter cookies at his place."

"I don't know where Carter lives." Allie grabbed the other side of the bowl and pulled.

Lydia pulled back. "I'll give you directions."

Allie pulled harder. "I'm not here with Carter. I'm here with Gavin."

Lydia's eyes narrowed. "I've been here with Gavin for a year." She yanked hard enough to cause a drop of the sticky precookie dough to splash onto her shirt. She didn't seem to care.

Allie knew that there was nothing going on with Lydia and Gavin. Lydia was twenty, maybe, and if Gavin was *with* her—or anyone—he wouldn't have been at Allie's wedding. That was something she knew for certain.

She had no reason to fight with this girl over Gavin.

But she really wanted to make the cookies.

She. Needed. Something. To. Do.

Cripes, if Lydia had any idea how crazy Allie might get if she was just sitting around here thinking, the girl would be gathering recipes and offering to run to the store just to keep her sane.

"Lydia," Allie said, pulling on the bowl again. "I have no desire to take over your jobs. I'm not honing in on anything here." Not that there was anything to hone in on except the kitchen duties. "I just need to keep busy. Please."

Even the "please" didn't sway the other woman. "Go get busy somewhere else."

Right. Somewhere else. What was she going to do? Watch TV? She hadn't sat in front of a television in months. Head into town? She didn't have a vehicle and she'd be lost within five minutes of putting it into drive anyway. She could play solitaire, but that was a sure recipe for crazy. She could read but...well, okay, she could read. But she wanted to make cookies.

"I'm already doing this." She yanked on the bowl again.

"Stop it. You..."

"What is going on?"

They both let go of the bowl at the sound of Gavin's voice. The pink plastic hit the wood floor, and both women jumped back as the gooey mixture of sugar, eggs and butter splattered on both of their shoes, the bottom cupboard and the floor.

"Ladies?" Gavin had his arms folded.

"I was trying to make some cookies," Allie said.

"In *my* kitchen," Lydia said, stomping toward the sink. "Without asking."

"If I'd asked you would have been okay with it?" Allie asked.

"No. But it's the polite thing to do." Lydia returned with a wet rag and knelt to begin the cleanup.

Allie started to reach for the bowl to help but Lydia grabbed it first, pulling it out of Allie's hand. "Hey."

"Don't worry about it. I'll take care of it."

Allie frowned. "I'll help." She headed for the roll of paper towels.

"Don't bother."

"It's fine. I know how to scrub a floor."

"No one's asking for your help."

Allie wet several towels and knelt next to Lydia. "You don't have to ask."

When was the last time someone actually asked Allie to do something? Everyone just expected it would get done.

"I'd rather do this myself," Lydia said, not looking up as she wiped the cupboard clean.

"Well, I'd rather—"

"You have something else you need to be doing." Gavin's strong arm came around Allie and he picked her up.

"Hey!"

"You're coming with me." Holding her against him with just one arm clamped around her waist, he tossed the bag he'd been carrying toward the hallway where Lydia had appeared. "Take that to the clinic, okay?" he asked.

"You got it," Lydia said.

Allie rolled her eyes. Was there anything Lydia said no to where Gavin was concerned?

She let Gavin carry her as far as the living room, out of Lydia's hearing. Then she wiggled. "Let me down."

He did, but he crossed his arms again and stood practically on top of her. "Why are you harassing my housekeeper?"

"I wasn't harassing her." Allie frowned at him. "I was making cookies, for god's sake. I didn't know there was a background check and secret handshake required to be in the kitchen."

Gavin smiled at that. "Lydia doesn't even let me in there, if it's any consolation."

Allie sighed. "I was just trying to keep busy."

"She's a little...territorial," Gavin said.

"Yeah. Of you."

"No." He shook his head. "I know it seems that way, but she's just loyal to me. I gave her a job when no one else would, and she feels like she owes me. She works hard and is proud of what she does."

"Why wouldn't anyone else give her a job?" Allie asked.

"She killed a man."

Allie stared at him. She swallowed. Then she asked, "She what?"

Gavin held the serious look for only a moment before his grin broke free. "No. She ran away from home and ended up here. Somehow. Anyway, hiring a stranger without references wasn't a risk anyone else wanted to take."

Running away from home. It seemed Lydia and Allie might have something in common after all.

"Why'd she leave home?"

Gavin shrugged. "I don't know. She doesn't want to talk about it."

"And you're okay with that." She knew he was. He didn't like to talk about his family and Promise Harbor either. That had always been a sore spot in their relationship. Their feelings toward their families and home were so different, and it had eventually pulled them apart.

"I'm okay with it," he said with a nod. He was looking into her eyes, as if he was searching for something. "But I'm not okay with it from you. So don't even think about it."

"I have to talk?"

"Yep."

"To you?"

"Yes. Deep, dark secrets, how you feel, dreams and wishes, the whole bit."

She stared at him. This wasn't Gavin. They didn't do deep, serious stuff. They'd talked about dreams and plans. Until they'd realized that their plans would take them in two different directions. They'd then ignored those conversations just like they ignored anything stressful or frustrating or downright screwed-up that ever happened.

Their time together was about fun and romance and living in the moment and enjoying. They had their own little bubble and they both protected it.

"Since when do you want to know about deep, dark, serious stuff?" she asked with a frown. That was *not* what she wanted or needed. Her life had been deep, dark and serious for a long time now. She needed Gavin to be...Gavin. Fun and sweet and spontaneous.

The kind of guy who would storm into a wedding and steal the bride.

He frowned back at her. "I've grown up."

She couldn't help that her eyebrows went up.

"I have." He looked offended by her obvious disbelief.

"That's just...a weird thing to say," she told him. "You've always been a grownup." It wasn't that Gavin was juvenile or immature or anything. He loved to try new things—new bands, new foods, new museums. He was well educated, well read, loved to travel, followed world events and politics.

"Well, then I've gotten serious," he said.

Hmm. If that was true, it might be a problem. "Why?"

"Why did I get serious?" he repeated.

That didn't seem right either. It wasn't that he hadn't been serious. He'd been dedicated in vet school and then very focused when starting his career. Even when they were together having fun, he'd been...determined. That didn't sound like it should go with "fun", but it was true. Gavin pursued fun like he'd pursued her, and school and work—the things that mattered to him. "I mean, why with me? We've always avoided serious, haven't we?"

His frown deepened. "Yeah, well, you were about to say I do to another guy. That's very serious to me, Allie."

Ah. He was twisted up about her almost-marriage. That was good. She'd hoped he'd have some emotions about the situation. It looked like it had gone so far as to knock good-time Gavin serious.

"But I didn't. So it's a moot point. No need to get all *serious* about it." She really didn't want to talk about Josh or her Wedding That Wasn't or all the people who were disappointed and upset and even angry now.

She really, *really* didn't.

She wanted to have fun. She wanted to go roller-skating or rafting, or play paintball or strip Old Maid or dirty-word hangman.

"If you need someone's deep, dark secrets, ask Lydia," Allie said, not making eye contact.

"No."

"Why not? She might really need someone to talk to."

"If she does, she knows where I am."

"But you're not going to insist with her?"

"No."

"Why?"

"Because I'm not in love with her."

Allie's gaze came immediately back to his and she stared at him. God, hearing those words sent emotions spiraling through her, rocking her.

"But I am in love with *you*," he said. "I want it all from you. You're going to have to spill everything."

Damn. She hadn't been expecting this at all. When he'd shown up like a superhero at the very last moment to save her, she'd been sure this would be more of what Gavin did best—making her feel good, taking care of her.

He was her haven. When she was with him, they laughed and made love and tried things like rock climbing and hot-air ballooning. They were spontaneous and didn't worry about schedules. Of course, school was important and they'd both worked to help with the bills, but when they had time off, they made the most of it. Together.

He'd had a sixth sense for what she needed. She'd go home to the harbor, without him, and spend the weekend with her family. When she got back to Boston she'd be tired or frustrated or worried, but Gavin always made it good again. Sometimes they'd head out to a sexy couples yoga class, sometimes a trip to their favorite dessert shop, sometimes to a late-night showing of an Audrey Hepburn movie. Sometimes they'd just drink great wine and dance on the balcony. Whatever it was, it erased the stress of the weekend and effectively focused her back on him and their life together, where things were just how she wanted them.

She wanted that.

To feel good. To have Gavin make her feel good.

She wanted massages and dessert and sex. Lots of hot, sweaty, forget-everything-else sex.

But no. Now he wanted to *talk*. About her *feelings*. Ugh.

She couldn't do it. It was too much of a risk. It was too

dangerous. He didn't know what he was asking.

If she let even one little thing out—like how she was afraid to open any of the drawers in her dad's kitchen because she might find a pack of gum with a stick missing and know her mother had chewed that one piece, or worse, an old grocery list in her mother's handwriting—she'd curl up into a little ball, start crying and never stop.

Allie pressed her lips together and shook her head.

"Oh, yes," Gavin said, lifting his thumb to free her lower lip. "I want everything, Al."

She wanted to push him away as badly as she wanted to hug him.

Hugging was also something she hadn't let many people do. It was dangerous too. The dam she'd put up to hold all the emotions back was at risk of crumbling. Josh was the only one she'd talked to about problems and feelings, and they'd had an understanding—they talked about their families' problems and feelings, not their own.

But with Gavin it was different. She needed this—to feel him, to know he was real and *here*. She leaned forward and he immediately took her into his arms. Her body molded to his as his arms went around her. She pulled in a deep breath of his scent, absorbing how warm and solid and strong he felt into her bones.

This was where she belonged.

It all made sense when he was here.

All the yucky, sad stuff went away and instead she got to feel cared for and like nothing bad could ever happen.

As long as Gavin held her and touched her and kissed her and smiled at her, reality was a distant and dim memory.

"I'm so sorry I wasn't there for you when your mom died."

Unless he talked about the yucky, sad stuff.

She stiffened and tried to pull back but he held on. "I don't want to talk about that."

"I know. I know we don't talk about this stuff. But I have to tell you this."

She steeled herself. Gavin was her shelter and he knew it. Deep down, she'd suspected that had something to do with why he hadn't come for the funeral—for *her*. Because that wasn't what they did.

Gavin was a pro at making her forget. And now he was making her think.

"I didn't know that she'd passed away until two weeks after the funeral. By then I knew it was too little, too late to call and say I was sorry. A plant or flowers would have been dumb at that point and..." He trailed off and took a deep breath.

Allie felt his chest rise and fall under her cheek, but she didn't dare look up at him. She felt tears begin to sting, and she tightened her arms around his waist and held on.

"I was a selfish bastard, but I chose to stay away instead of come home, because I knew if I came back to see you, I'd never leave," he said quietly.

She tried to focus on the selfish bastard part, to work up some anger or hurt. It was true. He was more comfortable being the good-time guy, the hero who saved her from all the hurt. In Promise Harbor after her mom's death, the hurt was everywhere, in everything. He couldn't have saved her, and she was sure that was part of why he hadn't come.

But, she'd wanted to be saved. She'd wanted—dreamed of—him coming for her just like he had at the wedding. Sweeping her off her feet. Carrying her away from it all.

"I ached to see you. I lay awake every night, thinking about what you were going through. I was a complete asshole to everyone around here for weeks. You can ask them. I'm sure they'd confirm it."

She smiled against his shirt but still said nothing. What could she say? That it was all right? It wasn't. She'd needed him and he hadn't been there. But they could go forward from here.

She tipped her head back to look up at him. "You want to make me feel better?"

She needed him to stop talking. She needed to stop thinking.

"Of course." He ran his hands up and down her back.

"That's why you're here. To get better. To feel good again. To let someone else take care of you for a change."

"Then kiss me."

Heat flared in his eyes as her request registered. He swallowed. "I'm not sure that's a good idea."

"I think it's a great idea," she countered.

"I'm not sure you're ready for that." But he didn't move back or try to let her go.

"How could I not be ready for it?"

"It's just...fast. With everything else that's going on. I just want you to be here, to relax, to rejuvenate..."

"You don't want to have sex with me?"

He swallowed again and his gaze dropped to her lips. "I didn't say that."

"This isn't exactly new territory for us, you know," she said. "I know what to expect. And I *know* it will make me feel better."

He drew in a long breath. "It's kind of new. It's been awhile. A lot's changed."

She thought she knew what was going on. She was a mess. Gavin had never seen her like this. No one had. She didn't just handle things, she handled them well.

She was strong, and that made Gavin's job of helping her forget about her worries and frustrations easy and guilt-free. She didn't need to be coddled and cuddled. She needed to be distracted.

Sex with Gavin definitely distracted her. It made her forget her own name most of the time.

"I'm not delicate, Gavin. I'm not going to break."

"Yeah, well, you don't know what I have planned for you," he muttered.

She grinned at that. And it felt really good. "Is that right?"

"I have some big-time pent-up emotions going here," he said.

Allie couldn't help the warmth that spread through her. It was the weird combination of desire and comfort she always felt with Gavin. How could she not be addicted to him? No guy had ever made her feel the way he did. He made her smile even when he was turning her on.

"Kiss me," she said again, pulling back and going onto tiptoe. He wouldn't say no. Gavin always wanted her. The sex was amazing. Way amazing. Not-fair-to-the-other-guys-in-the-world amazing.

Gavin sighed and pulled her hips closer. "Having you in my bed again has been wonderful and horrible," he said, his gaze traveling over her face. "Having you in my arms makes me sure that you'll be okay, that I can take care of you, but sleeping next to you and not touching you has been torture."

"We've never spent the night in the same bed without sex," she said, realizing it herself for the first time. That he'd held her, and only held her, meant a lot.

"I know. I'm a strong advocate for that habit," he said with a grin. "But this was nice too."

Allie felt tears threatening. God, she hated that. Why was she *constantly* on the verge of crying? This was no time to cry. Gavin had been sweet and protective and wonderful. That wasn't anything new or surprising.

But it felt so good.

Sex. Hard, fast, awesome, sweaty sex. That's what she needed. All these mushy feelings would go away if they could just get naked.

She ran her hands up under the edge of his shirt. "I've never had sex in Alaska."

His grin fell away and want was immediately clear in his eyes, as if it had been just under the surface and he'd been trying to cover it up. "Me either."

She stared at him. Did he mean... Had he seriously... "What?" she asked.

"I've never had sex in Alaska either."

She believed him. But she was amazed. Not that she'd expected him to have a different girl every night or anything, but he certainly hadn't been a virgin when they'd gotten together, and he was seemingly insatiable with her.

Gavin was gorgeous and masculine with a voracious sexual

appetite that was also varied—they'd done it all from various positions to toys to role-playing.

How was it possible that he hadn't had sex for a year?

"You go into Canada for sex?" she asked.

He shook his head. "I haven't been with anyone since you and I met in Denver."

That was the last time they'd been together. It had been three months after her mom got sick. Allie hadn't intended to call him, certainly not to see him, after they'd broken up the last time. But she had to get away. She had to lose herself for just a few days in the midst of all the sadness and pain. And he'd been the first one—the only one really—that she'd wanted to see.

He hadn't even asked why. He'd just said, "I'll be in Denver tonight."

That had been a wild weekend too. They'd been naked in the hotel suite for a solid forty-eight hours. He'd made her scream and laugh, and she'd loved him in that weekend more than she ever had. He'd met her, without question, and given her exactly what she needed, somehow knowing without her saying a word. She hadn't wanted to talk about things at home. She hadn't wanted to think about home. She'd just wanted to feel good.

Like now.

He was doing it again. Saving her without question.

She didn't know what to say to him. He hadn't been with anyone since her. He hadn't been with anyone else while they were together—not that he would have had time or energy for anyone else anyway—and she'd only been with Josh...

No way was she thinking about her ex-fiancé right now.

She turned and pulled Gavin with her up the stairs to the bedroom. He followed without a word. The minute they were through the doorway, she turned, put her hand at the back of his head, pulled him forward and kissed him.

That was all it took.

His fingers curled into her hips and he lifted her up against him. His lips opened, his tongue stroking boldly, possessively.

Then he ran his hand down to her thigh, lifting it and turning her at the same time. He backed her up against the door, his erection pressing against her, and Allie gasped. All she could think about or feel was Gavin. His body, his heart rate, his heat, his scent. She wanted it all to wrap around her and fill her up.

Every sense was overwhelmed by him. Exactly what she needed.

Chapter Four

Gavin couldn't remember a time with Allie where he'd felt completely satisfied. That wasn't to say the sex wasn't amazing and fulfilling and exhausting. It was all of that and more. But it was a general feeling of always wanting more. Even if he'd just had her—and had her well—he could still want her.

How he'd managed a year without her, he wasn't sure. It was like a part of him had just been numb. But now that she was here, now that he was touching her, now that he was *tasting* her, anything that had been numb was most definitely awake, fully functional and ready to go.

"Allie," he groaned as she pulled her mouth away to run her lips down his neck, then licked at the base of his throat.

"Please, Gavin, I need you. I need this."

He couldn't say no to her. Never had been able to and had given up trying a long time ago.

"Anything, Allie," he promised.

She took him at his word and started to pull his shirt up over his head. He tossed it away, groaning again as she ran her hands over his chest and shoulders.

"I've missed you," she whispered, watching her hands touch him.

Missing her didn't even begin to cover it.

There were times when constant daylight was a pain in the ass. But there were times when lots of brilliant light was just what he needed. Like now. He hit the button to raise the blackout shades. Sunlight poured in and over them through the huge windows.

He tugged her shirt up and off as well, drinking in the sight of her breasts cupped in green satin and lace. Her skin was pale, much more so than he remembered, and with her weight loss her breasts were smaller. But his mouth still watered at the sight. He reached to unhook the bra and pulled it off as well.

Her nipples puckered in the air and under his gaze, and he drew the pad of his thumb over one, loving her quick intake of air. They'd been together enough that he knew exactly how to make her hot and ready, and he plucked at one nipple while dipping his knees so he could take the other in his mouth. Sucking, he felt Allie tangle her hand in his hair and grip him tight, holding him there as she arched her hips against him.

Needing to see and touch more, Gavin cupped her ass, lifted her and started for the bed. Her breasts pressing against his chest made him want to throw her down, push her pants just far enough out of the way and thrust home. Who needed foreplay? In fact, he'd done exactly that to her more than once.

But he hesitated. Even as his body strained for hers and he wanted to bury himself deep, he held back. She was...different. Her mom's death had hurt her and he hadn't been with her through or after that. He didn't know anything really except that she seemed more delicate. Not just in appearance, though her thinness was certainly part of it. Allie had always been thin, but she was toned. She worked out, ate well. Her hair and skin were gorgeous, her eyes bright, and she was full of energy and smiles. This Allie seemed so sad. He knew she was, of course, and he knew she'd been sick. But the dark circles and pale skin were only part of it. The sadness and frailty—no matter what she said—went deeper. She wasn't as bright and energetic and... *happy*.

Of course, she'd been asleep most of the time they'd been together so far.

It was more of a gut feeling he had. That things weren't quite right, that she wasn't the same girl he'd known and loved.

He laid her gently on the bed, his gaze moving over her face and breasts and shoulders and stomach. It was all so familiar. How could he feel like he didn't know her?

He knew her. Better than any man. He knew how to please her, how to touch and kiss her, how she liked to be loved.

Dammit, he could prove it.

He unzipped his jeans, loving how she propped up on her elbows to watch. Allie loved his body and he loved giving her free rein over it. He pushed the denim to the floor, not quite ready to get rid of his underwear. He needed a barrier there for some control because he was about to get her completely naked.

Allie dutifully lifted her hips as he reached for the button and zipper of her pants and pulled them down her legs and off. Her panties were also white, and he traced his finger up and down the front of them, not rushing to strip them off like he wanted to.

"Right there," she breathed as his finger slid over her clit.

He did it again, then pulled the white silk to one side. Running his finger over her without the silk in between made them both groan.

Allie moved her knees apart. "Gavin," she said breathlessly. "More."

"I love making you sound like that," he said, watching as he moved his finger again, stroking over that sweet spot.

She arched toward him. "You love making me sound even better than that too."

He grinned. "Yes, I do. And I'm damn good at it."

She laughed, then gasped as he leaned in and kissed her inner thigh. "You are," she breathed.

He licked the spot he'd kissed, then moved higher and kissed and licked again.

"Let's get you loud," he said huskily just before licking over her clit.

"*Ah.*" Her fingers tightened in his hair and she lifted her hips closer.

He licked, swirling his tongue as her "ahs" got louder.

Finally he sucked.

"Ah!"

He slid a finger into her tight heat, loving how she writhed and cried out. Stroking deep, he added a second finger, curling just right to hit the spot that would send her quickly over the edge.

"Gavin!"

There it was. She came around his finger, crying his name.

"I don't think I can properly express how much I love doing that," he said, crawling up her body.

She grabbed him around the neck and pulled him close, hugging him tightly.

For a moment he held her and just breathed in and out. When he tried to move, though, she held tighter, not letting him shift away even an inch.

"Al?"

She didn't respond, and he became aware that her breathing was ragged and there was something warm and wet on his shoulder.

"Allie, are you crying?"

She sniffed, but still said nothing.

"Honey, I can't breathe." It was more from the tightness he felt in his chest at the idea of her crying, but he needed to move so he could see her.

With a big sigh, she finally loosened her hold on him.

He lifted himself up off of her and she tried to roll away. He pinned her hips to the mattress. "No way. Allie, what's going on?"

She had her eyes closed and she shook her head.

The sex had always been amazing. Even overwhelming at times. He'd felt a multitude of emotions after being with her as well. But there had never been tears.

Even when they'd broken up—any of the times—there hadn't been tears. At least, not that he'd seen.

Gavin shifted so he was to one side, but he wouldn't let her turn. "Allison, talk to me."

"I just..." She covered her face with one hand and breathed in and out, deep. "I don't know."

"You're crying."

"I know." She sniffed.

"In bed."

"I know."

"With me."

"I know."

"After an orgasm."

"I *know*," she wailed.

"You can understand where I might be feeling confused...and offended." He'd meant to make her smile. Instead she grabbed a pillow and covered her face, her whole body shaking.

Dammit.

"Al?"

He started to pull her toward him but she resisted, and when he let go she rolled and headed for the bathroom.

The next thing he knew the bathroom door shut—and locked—behind her.

Fuck.

Gavin scrubbed a hand over his face. Now what? He had almost no experience in comforting crying women. But Allie didn't cry. She was always in control, poised, in charge.

This was...not good.

Gavin pushed himself up off the bed and strode to the bathroom door. "Allie?"

"Just give me a minute. Or an hour. Go back to work," she said, her voice muffled by the door.

"No way. Come out here."

"No."

Gavin rolled his neck. He liked things upfront. When they were breaking up, they'd been straightforward and completely honest. They loved each other but they wanted completely different lives. It made sense to end it. When he wanted her back, even though she was getting married, he walked into the church and told her how he felt.

He wasn't going to tolerate a door between them when she was crying.

"I'm going downstairs to get my tools. When I come back up, either the door gets opened by you or the hinges are coming off." He started to turn away, but the door swung open behind him.

"Are you kidding me?" Allie demanded from the doorway. "I can't have a ten-minute breakdown by myself?"

Her eyes were red and puffy, but the tears had stopped. She was wrapped up in one of his big bath towels and she looked—dammit—fragile.

He crossed his arms. "No."

"I just want to be alone."

"Too bad."

"That's not very sympathetic."

"No. But I have a feeling that you've had plenty of sympathy. Everyone's been tiptoeing around, *not* talking to you about how you're feeling for a long time now, right?"

She opened her mouth to reply, then snapped it shut, frowned, and finally said, "I don't want to talk about it."

"You got away with that for a year. I guess if you wanted to have everyone leave you alone—even when you were getting sick and exhausted—then you should have stayed in Promise Harbor."

Her chin came up. "Maybe I should have."

"But you know as well as I do that you didn't want to be in Promise Harbor. You wanted to get out. You wanted to escape." He took four steps closer, his toes just on the other side of the threshold into the bathroom. "You wanted me."

"Maybe I just came for some hot sex."

"Maybe," he said with a nonchalant shrug. "But I'm not the one who just had an orgasm and bolted out of bed crying. Seems that if that's all you wanted, you would have stayed put and gotten more."

She looked surprised that he brought it up like that. Then her cheeks got pink. "I didn't...it wasn't *because* of the orgasm."

"What was it?"

She swallowed hard. "I don't know. It just all came out. I couldn't stop it."

He reached out, rubbing his hand up and down her upper

arm. "Honey, it's okay. In fact, I think it's great. I'm not mad. My pride's not wounded. If you want, I'll take you back over to the bed right now and show you how *not* wounded I am. But," he went on when her mouth curled, ever so slightly, "I know that I'm dealing with a lot of emotions right now being with you again. I can only imagine all the feelings that are messing with you."

She shook her head. "I'm fine. It's not—"

"Allie, your mom died."

She flinched. "I'm aware."

"That's big. Huge. And I know you. I know that you haven't told one single person how devastated you are."

She pressed her lips together, not meeting his eyes. "They know how devastated I am."

"But them knowing isn't the same thing as you admitting it. You've been too worried about your dad and brothers and Sophie to probably even admit it to yourself. And I know none of them asked."

He felt a familiar churning in his gut when he thought about Allie's family. Or rather her blind devotion to them. They weren't bad people, by any means. He'd liked her mom and dad—what he'd known of them. But when he and Allie were dating, they hadn't involved their families. They'd been off at college and spent all their time together outside of Promise Harbor. He didn't go home to visit, and when she did, he stayed behind. It worked.

But Gavin had seen her when she was getting ready to go home for a visit. She'd been tense and distracted. Then when she came back to him she'd been tired and stressed. Nothing like how she'd looked in the church at her own wedding, but the strain around her eyes had always pulled at him, made him feel protective and possessive. He'd wanted nothing more than to erase that look and make her smile. Not talking about her family and her weekend at home had seemed the best way to do those things. And so their Sundays of fun had started.

Eventually, though, the inevitable happened. When it finally came down to choosing between him and them, she chose them. She had this idea that they couldn't survive without her, and now that Lily was gone, he was sure that had multiplied a thousand times.

Gavin made himself relax. She was here now. He could take care of her. Her family was too far away to lean on her.

"Can we go back to bed?" she asked, dropping the towel.

As far as diversionary tactics went, that was a good one.

But Gavin was strong. He shook his head. "If you think you're going to get out of talking by distracting me with sex...you're almost right."

She smiled.

"But I can play that game too—until you talk to me and tell me about the serious stuff, no sex for you."

She stared at him. "You don't mean that."

"I do." At least, he was going to try hard to mean that. There were more important things here than sex.

When she was standing in front of him naked, it was nearly impossible for him to remember what they were without fierce concentration, but he knew there were some things.

"I need you, Gav," she said quietly, moving closer and putting her hand on his chest over his heart.

He covered her hand with his. "I know you do. But you need me for more than a daring rescue from the church and hot sex that makes you forget everything else."

She frowned at him and he raised his eyebrows at her.

"You're surprised that I know that you're trying to *not* think and talk and feel? Babe, we've been doing that routine for years."

"Let's keep doing it. That's what I need."

He cupped her face. "No."

"No?"

She was right to be surprised. The only time he'd said no to her was when she'd asked him to come to Promise Harbor with her.

"I'm the best playmate you ever had, right?" They'd played hard in the bedroom for sure, but they'd played hard in the world too. They'd skied, snorkeled, had food fights, sung karaoke.

She knew what he meant. "Yes. Definitely."

"Now I want to be the best everything else too."

He'd almost lost her. He would never forget the feeling of panic that had coursed through him when he'd heard Hayley's message that Allie was getting married. It was like his world shook and broke apart, looking completely different in the next moment. He needed her and was going to keep her this time.

She swallowed hard, clearly not sure what to say to that.

He turned her by the shoulders and nudged her into the bedroom. "Get dressed. I want to get started on the everything else."

"Maybe I'll go back to bed," she said moving toward the king-size mattress. "Even if I'm alone. I can do quite a bit alone." Her tone and smile made it very clear what she was referring to.

"Nope. Nice try." Though his body didn't care that she was only teasing him. Without even trying, he conjured some very specific and graphic images of her alone in bed, doing "quite a bit". "If you're not downstairs in five minutes, I'll come back up and get you. And it will be even longer before you get lucky."

Allie groaned, obviously believing him.

"See you in five." He was grinning as he shut the bedroom door behind him. He was sexually frustrated, but he was feeling optimistic about everything else.

In fact, he was going to be the king of everything else.

Allie took her time getting dressed. She didn't remember Gavin being so bossy. She would have remembered because it was kind of a turn-on. Not that she wanted to talk—at least, not the way he intended—but she couldn't help the little shiver of desire that went through her every time he declared he was going to take care of her.

Maybe she didn't remember the bossy side of him because she hadn't needed it before.

She knew that Gavin hadn't liked the way she put her family before everything else. She knew he thought they were ridiculously dependent on her. The boys, including her father, anyway. Her mom hadn't been dependent, but she'd made no secret of wanting her daughter to follow in her footsteps, taking care of others and serving the community.

Her mom had helped raise her three younger cousins after her aunt died. Of cervical cancer. So it came naturally to Lily, and she'd indirectly and directly passed it on to Allie. In return, Lily had been beloved, appreciated and respected. Allie would never forget how packed the church had been—standing room only—for her funeral.

Allie shuddered and shut the thoughts down again. She was getting good at that. Just like she shut down the urge to run to the doctor and have a PAP test every other month. She knew the risk factors for the cancer, and she was doing what she could to prevent it. She knew eating right and exercise and regular PAPs and safe sex were the main things in her control. And she was doing them. She had to be okay with that.

Well, she was trying to do them. She'd had her PAP and she'd only had sex with two men in the past six years, but she needed to eat more fruits and vegetables and, well, everything. Sighing, she admitted that Gavin was right about that.

The mirror confirmed what she already knew—she looked like crap. She could blame it on being sick and in bed for the last few days, but the truth was that she'd looked and felt like this for months. She wanted to exercise, but she was so tired all the time. Then because she wasn't exercising she felt even more tired. It was a vicious cycle she was aware of on some level, but she had yet to truly do something to change it.

Turning away from the mirror, she pulled her blouse on and walked to the window. Gavin's property was gorgeous. This was hardly the frigid white world that came to mind when she thought about Alaska. Getting outside for a walk was not a bad idea.

It was approaching the five-minute mark and she didn't have the energy to fight with Gavin anymore right now, so she started for the staircase.

That was why he'd never been bossy before. She hadn't needed it. They agreed on most things, like restaurants and movies and how to spend the weekend. The only thing they'd ever disagreed about was family and Promise Harbor, and they'd simply avoided talking about them rather than fight. She went home to visit and he stayed in Boston. It was that simple. Even when it meant the end to their relationship, he didn't fight. He got upset. He asked her to stay with him. But when she'd said no, he'd accepted it.

Now, though, he clearly felt the need to step in. And it made her feel good. She couldn't deny it.

Besides, this more demanding side of him was hot.

Maybe she'd let him get away with it for a while.

She descended the steps, expecting Gavin to be waiting at the bottom for her. Instead, she was surprised to find Lydia standing there. With a glass of something orange, a plate with a muffin, and a surly expression.

"What's this?" Allie asked when she got to the bottom step.

"Your breakfast. I guess."

"You made it?"

"Yep."

"Why?"

"Gavin asked me to."

"Ah." Allie reached for the glass and sniffed it. "Orange?" It was too thick to be juice.

"Orange, mango and peach smoothie."

Allie lifted an eyebrow. That sounded good. "You take a drink of it first."

Lydia didn't seem surprised or offended by the request. She took a big drink out of it, complete with a satisfied "ah" after she swallowed.

Fine. She'd drink it. "Blueberry?" Allie asked of the muffin.

Lydia did look offended at that. "Cranberry orange."

Allie decided not to ask if there was a muffin schedule like there was for the cookies.

"Well, thanks," she said, taking the plate.

"Whatever." Lydia headed back for the kitchen.

Allie made a note not to get hungry if Gavin wasn't around. Lydia wasn't going to cook for Allie out of the goodness of her heart.

She took a sip of what was quite likely the best smoothie ever made. Then she tasted the muffin and decided that she should probably start being nice to Lydia. The girl could cook.

Chewing, she glanced around. Where was Gavin? Surely he'd be coming back soon to check on her with the five-minute timeline he'd given her.

She wandered toward the kitchen. "Lydia, have you seen Gavin?"

"Yes." The girl was standing at the sink rinsing dishes.

Okay. "Can you tell me where he is?"

"In the clinic. He just took a walk-in."

Yeah, that wasn't a lot of help. Did she wait here? Lydia banged a spoon hard against the pot she was washing and Allie decided that no, she wasn't waiting *here*.

In fact, she wasn't going to wait at all.

She stepped out onto the deck through the sliding glass door.

Breathing deeply, she walked to the far end of the deck. The mountains in the distance looked like a postcard and the sun warmed her skin. Eyes closed, Allie tipped her head back, just feeling the clean air. The soft breeze stirred her hair and she felt some tension melt out of her muscles.

This was nice. Quiet too. Really quiet. And it wasn't just the lack of sounds around her, it was the lack of even *potential* sounds. No one knew she was here. There was no phone ringing, no doorbell ringing, no brothers asking for favors, no father digging through a drawer trying to find something that he hadn't seen in two years and couldn't describe to her when she tried to help.

The tension was back, so Allie forced herself to take a big drink of smoothie, then a big breath of Alaska air, and empty her mind.

She was here now. She should take advantage of the clean, fresh air, the gorgeous scenery, the good food and the gorgeous man who'd given her all of this.

But in order to take advantage of him, she'd have to talk.

Even if she wanted to talk, where would she start?

"You take this view from beautiful to gorgeous."

She didn't open her eyes or move. She'd been expecting him at some point. "That's a cheesy line."

Gavin chuckled. "It's still true."

She felt him move in next to her. He didn't touch her, but the wooden railing around the deck moved slightly when he leaned against it, and the air got warmer on that side of her.

Allie breathed again, keeping her eyes shut. She needed to steer the conversation or he would try. He couldn't make her talk about any topic she didn't want to, but even his questions brought surges of emotions. Emotions she didn't want.

"Do you remember the time you made up naughty versions of fairy tales for me?"

Somehow she could tell he was smiling when he said, "Of course."

"I especially liked the Cinderella story where she and Prince Charming got it on in the broom closet before midnight."

She felt him turn toward her. "And, of course, how Hansel propositioned the witch to get him and Gretel out of trouble," she said.

Gavin lifted his hand to her head, stroking her hair.

Allie kept her eyes shut, breathing deep of his scent, which was even more energizing than the fresh, natural air. "And who could forget what the frog really needed from the princess to turn human?"

"I know what you're doing."

His voice was husky but she could tell he was watching her. "Reminiscing?"

"Tempting."

Finally she opened her eyes. "Am I?"

"Yes." His eyes were hot as they stared into hers. "But it

won't work."

It was clear that the memory of that night, when he'd told her his versions of the favorite stories, was as strong in his mind as it was hers.

"What if I tell you that I've come up with a few stories of my own?" she asked.

"It won't matter."

"You don't think I can distract you with a story about Snow White and the seven dwarfs?"

"You're going to turn a beloved childhood story into a gang bang?"

She smiled. "Well, I hardly think any dwarfs would be grumpy or sleepy if that was going on. You have a dirty mind."

"Yes, I do. More so when you're around."

"One of your most endearing traits, in my opinion."

His eyes narrowed slightly. "I know."

"Let's go upstairs," she said, moving in close. "Where I can really take advantage of that."

"Love to. Just tell me how your dad and brothers are doing."

Dammit. She felt her smile waver. "I don't want to talk."

"I want to know how you are, what's going on in your life, Allie."

"I'm fine," she said, making herself meet his gaze.

"Liar."

"How could I not be? Especially now. I'm on vacation in this beautiful place, with the sexiest man I've ever met, nothing to do or worry about."

Gavin frowned. "This isn't a vacation."

"Well, it's not my real life, that's for sure. But," she said when he started to reply, "isn't that the point? You're the one who stole me away from my real life. You don't want me living my real life, right?"

He sighed. "That's not exactly it."

"My real life includes my father and my brothers—a lot of them, all the time. And committee meetings and my phone always ringing and someone always needing me. And..." she took a deep breath, "...Josh."

Gavin's jaw tightened. "Then no, I don't want you living your real life."

"So, help me forget about it. Give me something else to feel and think about and care about."

The tightness left his face and he lifted his hand to her cheek again. "You already feel for me and think about me and care about me."

He was right. There was no way she could convincingly deny it. "No, none of that was ever the problem," she said quietly. "Caring about you was easy."

"Easy, huh?"

"Definitely."

Something flickered in his eyes. "That's what finally cost me, isn't it?" he asked softly.

Allie took a breath. "What do you mean?"

"I was easy. Easy to be with. Easy to care about. And I made your choice easy."

She tried to breathe again, but the air already stuck in her lungs wouldn't let her.

"If I'd been more high maintenance, like they are, if I'd needed you more than they did, we would have stayed together. You went home because you thought they couldn't be without you. But that I could."

His words hit her directly in the heart. He was right. But she was stunned he'd figured it out.

Clearly he'd been paying attention. And thinking about this a lot.

Part of his appeal in the beginning had been that he was someone she could love who didn't *need* her. That had been so attractive.

But yes, that had also made it easy to leave him.

He'd survive without her. She'd known that. She'd known that he'd go off and make an amazing life and be happy even without her, so it had been easier to say good-bye to him than to the family that did need her.

Allie felt her throat tighten and had to blink to keep him in focus. "You still don't need me." He'd left her and done just fine. She grabbed his arm as he leaned back. "But it's a relief, Gavin. That's what *I* need. I've got nothing left to give right now."

"I need to have you here with me," he said, his voice quietly intense. "I need to know you're okay, that you're healthy and happy, Allie. I need that a lot."

She swallowed hard. He looked determined. She was starting to like that look on him.

"I'm feeling a lot more of all of that when I'm here with you."

He looked into her eyes for what seemed like an eternity. Then he leaned in and kissed her softly.

The gentleness of it almost knocked her over. More than all of the passion and heat and intensity she'd experienced lip to lip with Gavin, this was the one that nearly undid her.

Stupidly, tears filled her eyes, and in spite of her best effort, one escaped. Gavin just watched it slide down her cheek. Then he lifted his finger and wiped the wetness from her skin. He didn't panic and he didn't insist she talk about it. He just took her hand.

"Let me show you around," he finally said. "I want you to see my clinic, the rest of the house, the property, the town—everything I've got here."

He'd kissed her, he'd carried her in his arms, he'd made her come with his mouth and tongue, and yet his hand holding hers was what made her chest warm and her mind quiet. As long as Gavin had a hold of her, she'd be okay. He seemed determined not to let go.

Allie followed him back into the kitchen. Lydia's back was still to them and she just gave a noncommittal "uh-huh" when Gavin told her he was giving Allie a tour and to page him if anyone needed anything.

Gavin gave Allie a wink as they stepped into the short hallway off the kitchen. "She's suspicious of you."

Allie shrugged as they walked along the bright hallway with

windows everywhere. "She should be. I show up here in the middle of the night in a wedding dress, unconscious, with no explanation? Seems weird, you have to admit."

"I think it's more about her not thinking any woman is good enough for me."

She looked up at him. "Thought you said nothing was going on there."

"She actually feels more...motherly toward me, I think."

"Sure."

He laughed. "Seriously. She's always picking up after me, feeding me, criticizing me. And she tells me which women in town want to date me and why I should steer clear."

"Because she wants you all to herself," Allie said. Men were really dumb.

He shook his head. "She and I have talked about this. Her reasons are things like the girl being slutty, or having a bad temper, or drinking too much."

"You and Lydia have talked about this?" Allie rolled her eyes. Of course they had. Gavin was in-your-face honest. There was little that was subtle about him. If he had an opinion, a question or advice, he let you know it. He did it nicely. But if you asked Gavin if your hair looked good, you'd better be prepared for the truth.

"Yeah." He pushed the door at the end of the hall open and they stepped into what was clearly his office. "I was wondering why she was so critical of all the women too, but when I asked if she was in love with me, she crossed her arms, looked me up and down, shook her head and said, 'Sorry, but no'."

Allie felt her mouth curve. "She apologized?"

He nodded. "She was very gentle on my ego. She said she liked me, felt loyal to me, like I said, and just didn't want me to get with a girl who wasn't good enough, but that she had no interest in me beyond that."

"And you believed her?" How could any woman not want Gavin? He had it all. She sighed.

"Yep. She told me, very politely, that she thinks I'm a great guy but she's not attracted to me, there's no spark."

Allie laughed. "Clearly she's not normal."

He tugged her toward him. "I love when you laugh."

She looked up at him and couldn't reply right away in the face of the warmth in his eyes. "I don't avoid it on purpose or anything."

He gave her a little smile that seemed almost sad. "I know. But we're going to make it more regular."

She was all for it. "Nice office," she commented, even though she'd barely glanced at it.

He looked around. Two walls held floor-to-ceiling bookshelves, one wall had a huge window—of course—and the other held the door that obviously led to the rest of the clinic. His desk was huge and cluttered. There were distinct piles but there were a lot of them, and he had at least four coffee cups, a bowl and spoon, and three textbooks along with the usual desk stuff—penholder, phone, lamp, clock.

He smiled. "This is the one room in my life Lydia doesn't touch."

"It shows."

"I know." He pulled her toward the door to the clinic. "But a guy needs some space to just be himself."

"Even if himself is messy and unorganized?" she asked, following.

"Even then," he agreed with a grin.

His office opened into a break room with a fridge, microwave, small table and coffee pot, which then led into the front lobby. It seemed to be a typical vet office with chairs in the waiting area, a tall desk where patients—or their owners anyway—signed in. What was a little unusual, though, were the huge color photographs that covered the walls.

Polar bears.

Everywhere.

But not just nice wildlife photographs of random polar bears. Gavin was in every photo.

He was bundled in cold weather gear from head to toe, his eyes covered with dark goggles, but she knew it was him. It was the grin.

She'd know that smile anywhere.

She moved toward the big photo in the middle of the far wall. It was Gavin holding two polar bear cubs and looking like he'd never been happier. Her heart ached at the sight of that smile. God, he was gorgeous, and warm, and amazing.

"These are beautiful," she said, lifting her hand to touch the face of one of the bears.

"Thanks. Those were taken last summer. Those are twin girls."

Something in his voice made her turn to look at him. He was looking at the photo with pride in his expression.

"Where is this?" she asked. Did they have polar bears wandering through their neighborhoods in Alaska?

"Up on the Northern Slope," he said. "It's one of only seven polar bear populations in the world. One of two in North America."

"What were you doing?"

"It's a capture and release program through the US Geological Survey that's been around about thirty years. Three times a year—spring, summer and fall—we go out with the goal of capturing and monitoring about one hundred bears. We gather samples—like skin, hair, fat—and take lots of measurements. We also tattoo ID numbers on them so we can track them long-term. Most of the bears are monitored for years."

His face lit up as he spoke about this obvious passion, and Allie found herself fascinated.

"Where's the Northern Slope?" she asked.

He moved to a huge map of Alaska he had mounted on another wall. "North," he said with a grin.

"Ha-ha."

He pointed. "I've worked near both Deadhorse, which is a town of oil-field workers, and Barrow, which is a native community of Inupiat people."

"Tell me about it," she said.

"Really?"

Something that made him look that happy? She definitely wanted to hear more. "Yes, really."

He didn't need any further nudging. "The season is usually four to six weeks, and the work depends on the amount of daylight and how lucky we get finding the bears. They're tracked with GPS coordinates from their collars, but the satellites only upload coordinates every forty-eight hours and a bear can cover a lot of ground in that amount of time, so sometimes we go a couple days without seeing anything. Other days we find ten bears at once. So we stay up there while we're working. The days can be long and the weather can be nasty, but...I love it."

That was clear.

"What's this?"

The photo she was looking at showed a helicopter lifting a huge bear in a slinglike contraption.

Gavin moved to stand behind her and she leaned back into him. She loved feeling the rumble of his voice through his chest as he talked. She also loved the warm weight of his hands on her shoulders.

He chuckled looking at the photo. "That guy weighed just a bit over one thousand pounds. Can you imagine four or five of us trying to get him into that sling when he was completely knocked out? It was a great workout."

Her eyes widened. "A thousand pounds?"

"Yep. The helicopter is the only way to move a big boy like that. That's Wilson, one of our best pilots. I love going out with him. The most dangerous part of the work is when the helicopter is following a bear before it's sedated. We tranquilize the bear by shooting it with a Telazol dart from a shotgun. It takes an amazing helo pilot to not crash while staying close enough that we can get a shot while the bear is trying frantically to get away. Once we get the dart in, we go up higher and follow until the bear falls asleep—and to make sure they don't try to go into the water, then drown when the drug starts to work."

"And you're in the helicopter while they're chasing the bears?" she asked with a little shiver.

"Yeah. That's how we get up there. There are no roads in that part of Alaska, babe."

Ugh. No roads and one-thousand-pound polar bears. She wasn't in Massachusetts anymore.

"The next danger is working on a bear when there are other bears nearby. The work on one bear can take up to two hours, so sometimes we move the bear to a safer location. And we're all armed and there's always someone standing guard."

Allie looked back at the photo. Wow. Stuff like that didn't happen in the harbor for sure.

"I didn't know you were doing that," she said, trying to keep the emotion out of her voice.

It was strange to think that there were things about Gavin she didn't know. If she'd really stopped and thought about it, of course she knew there were things about his life she didn't know—like how beautiful the land in his new home was, or that he had a housekeeper named Lydia, or that he worked with polar bears—but this was the first time she'd really let that sink in.

It also seemed unfair with everything he clearly knew about her. His insight into who she was, how she liked to fix people, how she coped with stress and tried to make everything better, was scary.

"I got started when I got to know a PhD student in Kansas. He was working with the Geological Survey and got me hooked up. I fell for it right away."

Not just pride, she decided, but true love—that was what she was seeing in his face as he looked at the bears.

Yeah, one more reason Gavin was probably happier in Alaska.

She shook that off. "This clinic is great."

"Thanks. I'm proud of it. The practice was already here, but over the past year it's grown nicely. It's good I have Nancy to help out."

As if on cue, the tall blonde from earlier that morning

stepped from one of the rooms off the lobby. She pulled up short. "Oh, hi."

Gavin gestured between the women. "Nancy, this is Allison Ralston. Allie, Nancy Steirs, my assistant."

And one of his watchdogs, Allie thought. But she didn't say anything. "Hi, Nancy."

Nancy didn't quite smile but she said, "Hi, Allison."

"You can call me Allie."

"Okay."

"How's Max?" Gavin asked, seeming unaware of the awkward silence between the women.

"Gave him the shot, cleaned that ear out and gave her instructions," Nancy said, handing Gavin a folder.

"Great. I'll poke my head in for a minute. Be right back," he told Allie.

She watched him knock once and enter the room, shutting the door behind him.

Then she and Nancy were alone.

"Carter thinks I should tell you that I'm not interested in Gavin," Nancy said.

Allie wondered if it was the fresh air up here that made people so frickin' honest all the time. "That's handy, since he's taken," she said.

"Is he?" Nancy asked smoothly.

"Why else would he have not slept with anyone for the year that he's been here?" Allie asked, finding that the blunt thing was kind of fun. "I'm sure there have been lots of willing women."

Nancy met her gaze. "You always believe everything men tell you?"

Allie shook her head. Lord knew that she rarely believed the things her brothers told her. Her father told her he was "fine" when he definitely was not. She had believed most of what Josh said to her, but not everything. Not that he actually wanted to marry her. She knew he *would have* married her. But that was different.

"No, just Gavin." She had always trusted Gavin. Besides, she'd not only slept with someone else, she'd accepted that man's proposal. Gavin didn't have to lie about his love life—she had no room to judge.

Nancy watched her for a moment, then asked, "You know him really well, huh?"

Allie nodded. "Better than I know anyone."

"What's his favorite breakfast food?"

It stood to reason that they worked early morning shifts together and Nancy might know Gavin's favorite. Especially since he ate it five days a week. "Oatmeal," Allie said. "And not the flavored instant kind. The real stuff."

Nancy gave her a nod of acknowledgement. "Favorite music act of all time?"

Ah, a trick question. But Allie definitely knew this one. She'd been dragged to three concerts. Each. "It's a tie between Tim McGraw and Brad Paisley."

Nancy seemed mildly impressed. "What does he find funny that absolutely is not?"

Allie grinned. "Talking animals in movies."

Nancy actually smiled at that. "Favorite sexual position?"

Allie raised an eyebrow. "Do *you* know the answer to that question?"

Nancy shrugged. "That was a bonus. For the rest of us. It's been a frequent topic of conversation at The Hub."

Allie didn't doubt it. Gavin was definitely the type of guy to draw attention—especially of the female type. But she was thrilled no one knew the answer. "The Hub?"

"The bar downtown."

Of course. "Well, I'm feeling generous. His favorite is the cowgirl."

Nancy grinned. "Okay, you passed the test."

"The test of how well I know Gavin?"

"That. And the test of how cool you are. I'll tell Lydia to lighten up."

"You were teaming up to test me?"

"No. I was testing you. Lydia just doesn't like you."

Allie sighed. "Got it."

Chapter Five

"It's actually nothing personal," Nancy continued. "Gavin's made Lydia feel important and she doesn't want to lose her spot."

"Well, tell her there's no fear there. I'm a good cook, but I don't like to do it and I have no trouble letting someone else scrub toilets."

Nancy wrinkled her nose. "That's not exactly the attitude that will work. Lyd does a lot more than that. Those things are on the side because she realized Gavin needed someone to make sure he eats vegetables once in awhile. She does all the clinic scheduling and billing, she troubleshoots any and all computer issues and she organizes Gavin's life."

"Oh." Allie realized how her comment sounded. "Sorry." And what was with Gavin harping on her about not being healthy and eating right? He needed his assistant to make him eat veggies?

"Just don't...*do* anything and you'll be okay with Lydia," Nancy said.

Allie stared at her. Don't *do* anything? Allison Ralston not do anything? Nancy had to be crazy. Or Allie was going to be. Either way, this didn't bode well.

"So how did Gavin end up...here?" Allie asked Nancy as the other woman headed for the front desk.

Nancy gave her with a funny look. "A friend of a friend of a friend from vet school."

Allie looked around. "He's the only vet in...town?" Dammit, what was the name of this place? She looked at the brochure on the front desk about canine flea treatments. Denali Veterinary Clinic was stamped on the front. Was Denali the name of the town?

"He is the only vet in...town," Nancy confirmed, mimicking Allie's hesitation.

Allie decided to ignore that. "Did he build the clinic?"

"No, Dr. Happerly was the vet for years before Gavin. He built the clinic and the house."

"He retired?" Allie asked.

"Passed away," Nancy said.

"Oh." Great conversation.

"When he found out he was sick, Doc met with Gavin. Gavin impressed him right away. Happerly didn't have a wife or any children, so he left everything—the house, the practice, the equipment—to Gavin so that Gav could afford to move up here and take over right away."

That made sense as to how Gavin could afford all that he had only two years out of school.

"So, he's been successful...here?" Allie asked. *Wherever here is.*

Nancy chuckled lightly. "Yes. Of course it helps that he's a veterinarian and everyone here is very dependent on their animals. They would need Gavin even if they didn't like him."

Allie wandered to the bulletin board. Maybe there'd be a hint there about the name of the town. Or at least a reason to change the subject. There was an ad for flight tours to Mount McKinley.

Okay. So that was a great clue. She was in a town near Mount McKinley. A mountain. A really big mountain. And if she were any good at geography, that might matter.

"This sounds great," she said, even though she didn't know where she was. "Have you ever done one of these tours?"

Nancy glanced over. "Oh, sure. Those are fantastic. Rob Ingalls flies one of those tours."

"Is he good?"

Nancy gave her a wink. "He's *very* good. And he's a great pilot."

Allie grinned. "Got it."

Another flyer caught her eye. The photo showed a man in

cold weather gear in the midst of a pack of Alaskan huskies. He had his arms around two of the dogs and was grinning widely. "Dogsled tours," Allie read out loud. "These dogs are gorgeous."

"They're gorgeous," Nancy agreed. "And our bread and butter."

"The clinic takes care of these dogs?"

"Those dogs and all the dogs of all the other mushers around here," Nancy confirmed, sliding the file drawer shut.

"You can support a whole clinic just on sled dogs?" Allie asked.

"We do other animals too," Nancy said. "But around here? Yeah, we can support the whole clinic just on the mushing dogs."

"There are a lot of them?" Definitely not something seen in Massachusetts.

"It's the official sport of Alaska," Nancy said.

"It's a year-round thing?" Allie asked. The flyer advertised summer hours.

"Definitely. Besides competing, there are tours year round and there are several people around here who prefer dogsled for local transportation. It's cheaper than cars and trucks, cleaner than gas and keeps their dogs in shape."

"Gavin's been dogsledding, I bet," Allie said. Gavin had always liked the outdoors, and there was very little not to like about Alaska from what Allie had seen so far.

"All the time. And he loves it. Obviously."

Allie turned. "Obviously?"

Nancy pointed to the picture on the flyer. "Doesn't he look happy?"

Allie swung back to look at the bulletin board. Now that she looked closer, she realized the smiling man on the front of the flyer was Gavin. "Yeah, he does look happy."

Which made her heart feel heavier. Stupid. It wasn't like she thought he was going to pack his stuff and hop on the next plane to Massachusetts with her. But it did emphasize that he'd successfully established a life here in Alaska and hadn't spent too many nights pining for her. When would he have had the time?

"Tell me about the town," Allie said, pulling her eyes from the huge grin on Gavin's face.

"Which town?" Nancy crossed to the coffeepot and poured a cup.

"This town."

Nancy leaned back against the counter. "Denali or Bend?"

It had to be Denali, right? That's what the brochure said. But then why did Nancy ask it that way? "The one we're in right now," Allie said stubbornly.

"Technically we're not in a town right now. We're about four miles north of Bend, on Gavin's twenty acres."

Allie huffed out a breath. "Okay, you got me. I don't know which town we're in or near or whatever. What's Gavin's official address?"

Nancy chuckled. "Bend. Denali is the national park."

Allie rolled her eyes. "Okay, tell me about Bend." She'd Google Denali later.

"What's to tell? It's named because the very creative people who settled it noticed we sit at the bend of the river. It's a tiny town in Alaska that caters primarily to climbers and outdoorsy tourists. We have lots of hiking, fishing and, of course, the mushing. We're laid back, can guzzle beer with the best of 'em, and we all really like Gavin."

"So we have one thing in common."

Nancy grinned. "You can guzzle beer?"

"Nope." Tequila was a different story, of course. She most definitely wasn't laid back either. "But I'm crazy about Gavin."

"Huh." Nancy rifled through the folder in front of her.

"Huh?" Allie repeated. "What's that mean?"

Nancy looked up at her and just paused for a moment. She evidently decided to go ahead with what she was thinking. "You haven't been around. I've never heard of you. You didn't even know the name of the town Gavin lives in."

Yeah, okay, that didn't seem like someone who was crazy

about him. At least Nancy hadn't mentioned the almost-marrying-someone-else thing.

"And you showed up in a wedding dress that I assume wasn't for Gavin."

Damn.

"Things with Gavin and I are complicated," Allie said, hoping that would be enough. She didn't owe Nancy an explanation, of course, but her comment sent Allie's mind spinning back to the last time she and Gavin had been together.

They'd agreed that a complete break—no phone calls, emails or texts—was the easiest, safest way to go. If they weren't going to make a life together, they needed to work on making two lives apart. As painful as it was to say good-bye, repeatedly saying good-bye after occasional phone calls or visits was worse.

"Well," Nancy said, moving to the file cabinet. "Gavin's life here is pretty simple."

And the implication was clear: he liked it that way.

Allie could understand the temptation for simple, that was for sure. "Complicated" had been the main word to describe her life for a long time now.

"He's only been here for a year," Nancy went on. "So he's still an outsider, but if he sticks he'll be okay."

"If he sticks?" Allie asked. "What do you mean?"

"If he stays."

Allie's heart tripped. Maybe he wasn't as settled as he let on. "Why wouldn't he stay?"

Nancy chuckled. "This is Alaska. It's not an easy place to live. Not many people make it through their first winter."

"But he did." Gavin had already been in Alaska for a full year.

"Yep. Once."

Not sure what to say about any of that—she was probably the type to whine through a long, hard winter—Allie turned back to the bulletin board, pretending to study the flyers and announcements. But she quickly found herself actually reading them and getting excited.

This could be a lot of fun.

There were flight-seeing tours—planes and helicopter rides up to see the mountains, complete with glacier landings. *Glacier* landings.

There were dogsledding tours of the area—even in summer. There were mountain climbing and wildlife sightings and fishing and hiking.

There was plenty to keep her busy and to keep her mind off of home. That and some hot, sweaty sex with Gavin and she'd be good to go. The winter was a long way off.

The door to the exam room opened just as she took a brochure off the board. Gavin looked up as she spun to face him. He came up short at the wide smile on her face. He smiled in return, handing the folder he held to Nancy. "What's up?" he asked, striding forward.

"Mountain climbing."

Allie knew she put more enthusiasm into her voice than was really warranted, but it was such a good idea. Just what she needed.

"What do you mean?" He looked at the flyer she was clutching to her heart.

"Mountain climbing *school*," Nancy corrected, also glancing at the flyer.

"I don't know, Al," he said.

She felt her eyes widen. Was he serious? "Why not?"

"It's pretty challenging around here. Climbing here is for pros."

"I assumed that was why there's a need for a *school*," she said.

"But you've never climbed."

"Again, I'm pretty sure that's where the school thing comes in." Oh, brother. Gavin never hesitated to jump into things like this. "And we've done some rock climbing."

"Yes, *rock* climbing," Gavin said. "Not *mountain* climbing."

She rolled her eyes. "What's with you?"

"I just don't know if you're up to it."

Her eyes widened again. "I'll take it easy."

"You just had pneumonia."

"I feel a lot better."

"Maybe in a few days."

This was completely out of character and it was freaking her out a little. She took a huge step forward and grabbed the front of his shirt as he said, "I thought we'd just—"

"What is going on?" she demanded. "I want to *do* something. I want to have some fun."

"I thought we'd just..."

He trailed off as her eyes narrowed.

"What?" she asked. "You thought we'd what?"

"Curl up on the couch and watch a movie together. Just us. Nice and quiet."

"Curl up on the couch," she repeated. Her eyes narrowed further. "Will we be naked on this couch?"

Gavin cleared his throat. Nancy also coughed, but Allie thought maybe she was covering a laugh. She didn't look away from Gavin to check.

"No. Not naked," he said.

"Then I want to mountain climb."

She was *not* going to lie on the couch and watch a movie. She'd go insane. There wasn't a movie ever made that could keep her mind off of home and the disaster she'd left behind. She needed way more activity than that. Way more.

"Mountain climbing naked could be dangerous," Nancy commented.

Gavin glared at her and Nancy covered her smile with a folder as she headed into the back room.

"I don't think mountain climbing is a good idea." Gavin spread his feet wide, making him look even bigger, and Allie knew it meant he wasn't messing around.

She let go of his shirt. She wasn't asking permission, but she also didn't see the point in fighting with him. The mountain wasn't going anywhere.

"How about the flights up to the glacier?" She grabbed another flyer from the board. "I'll bet that's pretty amazing."

"I'm sure it is," Gavin said.

His tone was a touch condescending, but she chose to ignore it.

"You haven't done it?" she asked.

"No."

"You've been living here, in Alaska, at the base of Mount McKinley, and you haven't gone up and landed on a glacier even once?" She couldn't believe it. "You're the spontaneous guy, the one who's always up for something new and amazing."

"I know."

"So...why? Why haven't you gone up and done this?" She was honestly stunned. This was right up Gavin's alley. She couldn't believe *he* hadn't suggested it to *her*. "This seems exactly like something you would—"

"I'm settling down. That's what I want to show you. I want you to see that I can be serious. Husband material even."

Husband material? What the—

Allie dropped the flyer and quickly backed up three big steps. "Wh...what?"

Gavin looked calm and cool as he watched her. "Husband material," he said again. Clearly. Firmly. "I want to show you that I do regular things, can just be a typical guy. No one's fun and crazy all the time."

Ah, crap.

"I don't want serious, Gavin." She pinched the bridge of her nose. "God, I've had serious up to my eyeballs for the past year. Longer, even. I want fun. I want to be...happy. *Not* serious."

He still looked unruffled. "I can be serious *and* make you happy."

"No." She shook her head adamantly. "No serious stuff. I want to see glaciers and mountain climb and dogsled. Not watch movies on the couch. Hell, I can do that anywhere, with anyone."

"This is part of settling down," he said stubbornly. "Normal couple stuff."

"Oh, for god's sake," she muttered. This wasn't what she wanted. She wanted to get lost in Gavin, with Gavin, like it had always been.

Normal couple stuff was exactly what she'd left behind in Promise Harbor.

"What's going on?" she asked, looking at him evenly. "We've had a really good thing going for a long time."

"Yes. And now I want a really *great* thing *forever.*"

Forever. That was right up there with *husband material* for giving her the heebie-jeebies. Not that she didn't love Gavin. Not that she didn't think she would still love him in fifty years. But loving him and wanting him in her bed were different things than wanting to live with him.

They'd never done the day-to-day, have-a-mortgage-and-combine-everything-in-their-lives thing. They'd dated. They'd had fun. They'd seen each other several times a week, and sure, they'd done a few loads of laundry and cooked dinner together from time to time. But overall, Gavin was her *escape* from reality. When the normal, everyday stuff got to be too stressful or too complicated or too boring, she turned to Gavin.

She didn't want him to be part of the stressful, complicated, boring things.

Marriage was a great idea. For some people. But she'd seen what *for better or worse* and *in sickness and in health* and *for richer or poorer* really meant. Her dad's accident, rehab and the residual effects had taxed her mom emotionally, physically and financially. Accidents and bills happened in life. Things like that would happen in *her* life.

She just would really love to have Gavin living in Alaska when they did.

She would really love to know that she could call him up, hop on a plane, and be wrapped up in the fun-and-hot-sex Gavin-cocoon for a few days whenever she needed it.

Not that she intended to be married to someone else and use Gavin just when she needed a break. Walking away from that altar and Josh—talk about perfect husband material—had felt so good, so freeing. She didn't want to get married at all.

But a long-term, hot-weekend-only, get-away affair? Definitely.

"Gavin—"

"I've changed."

Yeah. And there was the problem.

She closed her eyes. "I can't handle any more change." She needed something to be the same, something she could lean on. "I need something to be steady."

"My feelings are the same, Al. But how I love you has to be different. I want it to be all day, every day. Not just the nights, not just the weekends. All the time, in every way."

Even when they'd lived in the same city, their relationship had been "after hours"—after studying, after work, after her family was taken care of.

Now he was settled.

That sounded strange even in her head. Gavin had always been restless, looking for more, working his ass off. He hated when things came too easy. He believed in hard work and sacrifice. He even played hard. He did everything with an unflinching determination.

She sighed. Why did she think he'd approach her and their relationship any differently?

"You want to watch TV and eat pot roast and play Scrabble?" she asked. That would never work. It sounded so...boring. She would have never expected to be at risk of being bored with Gavin.

"Maybe dirty-word Scrabble," he said, moving closer.

"I still want to mountain climb."

He glanced at the board behind her. "How about we compromise?" He leaned to take a flyer off the board. As his arm reached past her, she took a deep breath of his scent. She wanted that. All over her.

"We'll go to Anchorage next week," he said, leaning back.

"Anchorage?" She read the flyer he held up. "The Solstice Festival?"

"Longest day of the year. Great excuse for a party."

Hmm. Well, it wasn't TV and pot roast. "Drinking and dancing?" she asked, reaching for the brochure that clearly depicted people drinking and dancing.

He held it up out of her reach. "No drinking for you."

She grimaced. "Not a bad rule. Unfortunately. But dancing?"

"If you're good."

Before she could come up with a sexy quip about how good she could be, Lydia said, "No fun for you until you go see Eddie. I've made excuses for you for two days."

Allie leaned around Gavin to look at Lydia. Geez, the chick could be soundless when she wanted to be. She could easily sneak up and scare the crap out of someone—or set up a booby trap. Allie made a mental note to carefully survey her environment.

"Okay," Gavin agreed. "You're right."

"Eddie?" Allie asked.

"He wouldn't go while you were sleeping," Lydia said with an exaggerated eye roll.

"Eddie lives about forty miles out. I didn't want to be that far away while you were sick," Gavin explained, "but I do need to check on her." He paused and tipped his head to look at Allie. "Want to come?"

"Yes," she answered without hesitation. She didn't care who Eddie was or where she lived or what was wrong with her. She wanted to get out of the house, period.

"Okay, let's go. We'll talk about Anchorage on the way."

Things were looking up. This was way better than Scrabble.

But as soon as Gavin helped her up into the high passenger seat of his F350 and shut the door, she realized she'd made a tactical error. She was now a captive audience. It was a forty-mile drive. That would take a while. There were no distractions, nowhere to go. That meant the potential for a lot of talking.

She groaned.

Things were looking up. Gavin resisted humming as he got behind the wheel and started the truck, but just barely.

Taking Allie with him to check up on Eddie and her pups was perfect. They could be together; she wouldn't be fighting with Lydia, drinking tequila or mountain climbing; and, best of all, she'd be a captive audience for a talk.

And Allie was going to see some of his real life—his grown-up, responsible, serious life.

He grinned and pulled the truck out onto the road before she could realize the same thing and jump out.

Besides, he'd be forgiven as soon as she met the dogs. Allie was as much an animal lover as he was. He couldn't wait to tell her more about the polar bears, too. In fact, that was the main reason Anchorage had appeal for him. The Solstice Festival was a typical celebration—food, drink, music, staying up all night—literally. They had nineteen hours of daylight this time of year. Not that it actually got *dark* at all. And it was the first official day of summer. But it was a great reason to take Allie to the zoo and introduce her to his girls.

Neither of them said a word for the first few miles. Allie kept her head turned, watching out the window. Finally she gasped and turned to look at him. "I'm in *Alaska*."

He looked at her with a combination of amusement and concern. "Yes, you are."

She covered her face with her hands and rested her head back against the seat. "Omigod."

He reached over and put his hand on her knee. "You okay?"

"No." Her answer was muffled by her hands.

"No?"

Her hands came down. "I might be on the verge of hyperventilating."

"You've been in Alaska for almost three days now."

"But I've been ignoring it. Every time I start to think about it, I make myself stop. And if I'm with you it doesn't seem to matter. But now..." she swept her hand toward the windshield, "I'm right out in the middle of it. I can't ignore it now. It's everywhere."

He squeezed her knee. "You're okay. I'm here. This is all good."

She started shaking her head. "No. It's not good. What about my family, what about my *dad*? And all those people. What about Josh?"

Dammit.

Gavin swerved to the side of the road, throwing the truck into park. He turned to her and pulled her across the seat and into his lap. "Breathe," he commanded, rubbing his hand up and down her back.

She covered her face again and he tugged her hands down to her lap.

"Breathe," he said again.

She did.

"Now look at me."

She did that too. There were no tears. Just something worse that tore at him—regret.

"Oh, no," he told her firmly. "You're not going to regret this."

"Just...what did I *do*?"

He cradled her face between his hands. "You came to Alaska with me. Have some perspective, Allie. You didn't steal anything, you didn't kill anybody. You didn't lie to anyone. You did the most honest thing you could. You did what your heart told you to." He would never forget how it felt for her to choose *him* in front of everyone.

She'd been pressing her lips together. Now they parted as she breathed in deeply.

"Kiss me."

That wasn't a good idea. He was weakening anyway, the longer they were together. Out here, far from interruptions, with that look of need in her eyes, it was almost certain he'd crumble. The old Gavin would have stripped her by now. To hell with proving he was ready for serious, ready to be everything she needed.

But the new Gavin knew how it felt to just stop, to enjoy a moment, to not rush and push and work all the time. Being with Allie, helping her through those times when she just needed to let go and feel free had been great. They'd had some amazing experiences. Fun, over-the-top experiences. But he wanted more now. He wanted to sit back, to know he could make her happy with less, without all the craziness, by just being him.

How could he keep up that exciting, spontaneous, take-her-breath-away pace forever? And forever was what he wanted.

"Allie—"

"When you kiss me, it all makes sense. I feel like I'm right where I'm supposed to be. I feel like I'm spinning out of control, but when you kiss me, the spinning stops." She put her hand against his cheek. "Please."

Well, fuck. Like he had any hope of resisting *that*.

He pulled her in and she met his lips hungrily. She held his head still, her lips moving against his as if she couldn't get enough. Her tongue slid along his and she turned to straddle him. Somehow his hands ended up under her shirt.

Just feeling the skin of her back wasn't a problem though, he reasoned. But the moan when he ran his palms up and down the length of her spine *was* going to be a problem. Because he wanted more of that. A lot more. He moved his hands to cup her breasts, his thumbs stroking over the tips, eliciting an even better, deeper moan. She pressed down against him and *he* moaned.

"Yes, like that," she panted against his mouth. "More."

Another truck drove by, the rumbling on the road pulling Gavin out of his lust-filled daze. "Al." He glanced into the rearview mirror as, predictably, the truck's brake lights lit up. No one drove past without stopping to be sure all was fine.

"Al." He squeezed her hips and shifted her back off of his erection.

"More," she whispered, staring at his mouth.

"Later."

She pushed her hair back from her face and said, "I couldn't even bring myself to pick out my bridesmaids' dresses."

"Wh—"

"Hey, Gavin. Everything okay?"

Jeff Pinkett, the local mechanic, grinned through the truck's open window. He leaned on the door, clearly enjoying what he'd stumbled upon.

"Well, Jeff, I have a gorgeous woman on my lap. Yeah, I'd say things are okay."

Jeff grinned at Allie. "So, everything's working the way it should here?"

She chuckled instead of blushing, and Gavin looked at her in surprise. She was usually all about not causing a scene or embarrassing herself—or anyone else.

"We haven't checked *everything* out yet but I have no concerns at this point."

Jeff hooted with laughter and Gavin found himself grinning at her.

"'Kay, I'll leave you to it then," Jeff said. He gave them a wink and sauntered off.

Gavin was sure The Hub—and therefore all of Bend—would hear all about it later. Truthfully everyone would love some gossip about him. He was straitlaced here. No one knew his family, his past. He had nothing to live down or prove. He could just be whoever and however he wanted to be.

As Jeff drove off, Allie started to laugh. At first it was just a giggle, but it quickly built and the next thing Gavin knew she was laughing so hard she had to wipe her eyes.

God, he loved seeing and hearing that. And with the way she wiggled in his lap, he *felt* it too.

She quieted after a moment and drew a deep breath. "*That* was awesome."

She slid off his lap and onto the passenger seat, still breathing in deeply and smiling. He told himself it was for the best and put the truck in gear. But he knew if she wanted to climb back up, he wouldn't fight her off.

"Welcome to Alaska." Gavin adjusted his fly for a more comfortable fit.

"He didn't seem a bit fazed," she said, tipping the mirror on the back of the visor down to check her makeup. "Has he seen you like that before?"

"Nah. But it's not uncommon to see moose and stuff getting frisky along the side of the road. He's an outdoorsman."

That sent her into another gale of giggles. "I've never been compared to a moose before."

He snorted, his smile refusing to fade.

They drove without speaking for another few miles. Then she said, "See, kissing you always makes me feel better."

"Kissing you makes me feel a lot of things," he muttered.

She laughed at that too. "See? Win-win. We should do it a lot more."

He had a feeling it was going to happen whether it *should* or not.

"You mentioned bridesmaids' dresses," he said, hoping to divert further talk about their physical relationship. His cock was still wondering what had happened to all the hot and happy feelings from just a few moments ago.

"Ah, damn, you heard that."

"It was a little out of context," he said. "It caught my attention."

"I only told you so you'd keep going," she said. "I thought you stopped because you'd remembered your rules about no sex until we talk about...things."

"Glad to know you've been listening."

"To your stipulations? Yes."

"I prefer the term *compromise*. We both get something we want out of it."

"You get two things you want," she pointed out. "Sex and me spilling my guts."

"You get two things you want too," he said reasonably. "Sex and proof that I'm good husband material."

There was a beat of silence, and out of the corner of his eye he saw her tuck her hair behind her ear.

"There's that term again," she finally said quietly.

He glanced at her. She was sitting facing him, with one foot tucked up under her.

"It's not going away," he told her. They were going to talk about what had been going on her life in the past year, but they were also going to have plenty of conversation about her life moving forward. With him.

"Where did it come from? We've never used that word before."

"Husband?" Gavin had to relax his grip on the steering wheel. "You've used it with Josh."

"Ah."

She was watching him when he glanced at her again.

"Ah what?" he asked.

"That bothers you."

"That you were about to marry another man? Yes. Does that surprise you?"

"No, not really. But I think it's more about rescuing me than it is about wanting to take Josh's place."

He breathed deeply, trying to keep his cool. "If I thought you were happy with him I..." Would he have let it happen? The question slammed into him. If it had been some other guy he didn't know? If it hadn't happened right after her mom's death? If he thought it was what Allie really wanted and needed? Was there a circumstance where he would have left her alone?

With her here now, he couldn't imagine it.

"My dad cheated on my mom," he said instead of answering any of those impossible questions. Hell, if he wanted her deepest secrets, maybe he should give up a few of his.

"What?"

"More than once. At first, I only knew about the one time I'd walked in on him in his office. I told him that if he didn't tell Mom, I would. He believed me. The next day he told her about that woman...and all the others." Even now, years later, his gut churned remembering the day he'd caught his dad with his pants down—literally—and the day he'd watched his dad break his mom's heart.

Allie said nothing but he could tell he'd stunned her.

"And he made me stand there and listen while he explained it all to her," he went on before Allie could interrupt him. "That was how he punished *me* for finding out about his cheating and forcing him to confess—he made me watch him devastate my mother,"

Gavin gripped the steering wheel and breathed, thankful Allie didn't say anything.

When he relaxed his jaw enough to speak again, he said, "Apparently he was very sexually...proficient. And he knew that women held a lot of power. He not only slept with powerful women—like the middle school principal and the chair of city council—but he slept with women who could influence powerful men. He had an affair with the mayor's daughter—thank god, she was twenty-one at the time. He slept with the superintendent's wife and several councilmen's wives, and even the mother of the high school football coach—he was a first-year coach and didn't have a wife to tell him what to do."

Gavin took a deep breath. It was amazing how good it felt to dump all of this out there. He had never talked about it to anyone. Hayley knew some of it, but not all the gritty details.

"None of the affairs were ever love affairs. It was all about sex. He was, apparently, that good. He was a simple, blue-collar guy who couldn't *buy* everything he wanted to give us, so he found another way to provide for us. The women just wanted some great sex with a guy who wouldn't expect them to wash his socks or cook him dinner. And in return, they pressured the men in their lives to do Dad favors—not that the men knew why. Women can be very manipulative that way, I guess."

He sighed. "So, everything important my brothers or I ever had—a starting place on the football team, a spot on the honor roll, recognition by the local paper, a scholarship from the Promise Harbor women's group—came to us because Dad was a boy toy for the powerful women in town."

"I, um...wow," Allie said.

He knew it was a shock. Allie had grown up in Promise Harbor and knew every single person he'd just mentioned.

"Yeah."

"And he *told* you all of this?"

He nodded. That had always amazed him too. "I was sixteen." He glanced over to find Allie's mouth hanging open. "That's why I didn't get along with my dad the whole time I was in high school and why I left home right after graduation."

"He didn't stop?"

"Oh, I don't think so," Gavin said with disgust. "He sure as hell was never apologetic about it—not to me and definitely not to my mom. When she started crying, he told her to think about the life he'd given her and whether she would really trade all of it in. And he reminded her that it wasn't like he never had sex with *her*. He said he loved her and the other women were just about taking care of his family."

Allie wrinkled her nose. "Yuck."

"Yeah."

They were quiet for several seconds.

"It was hard for me to know what to think and feel about my mom after that too," he confessed. "She didn't yell at him—at least not in front of me. She didn't kick him out, she didn't leave. After that night it seemed that everything just went back to how it had always been."

Then she said softly, "That's why you've always been so good about taking care of me."

"Yes." God, absolutely. That also bugged the shit out of him. There was no way his father could have truly loved his mother. If he felt for her how Gavin felt for Allie, he wouldn't have even been able to look at another woman.

"And that's why you work your ass off at everything."

He gave a jerky nod. "I had to prove that I could succeed without people doing me favors. Then I came here to Bend. No one knew me or my dad. No one owed my dad anything. I just came and did my work honestly and very well, and when they were happy to see me or appreciated me or trusted me, I knew it was because of *me.*"

Silence. Not a sound. Nothing.

But he was on a roll. "That's why it's finally time for me to be serious about you. I'm settled in every other aspect. I'm ready for this now too. For you."

"You've proven that you don't need your dad and that you can make a life without following in his footsteps. You're a better man than he is," she assured him.

"Yes." And it was such a relief. There had been moments over the years when he wondered if the whole world worked the way his dad's world did and Gavin had been naive to think any differently.

But his dad's way wasn't the only way to get ahead. And Gavin had proved it.

"And now you want to prove that you can be a better husband than he is too."

He finally looked over at her. "Yes," he said honestly. "That's not the only reason I want to be with you, but I'm determined to be a good husband. Nothing like my dad."

"It's why you've always been so determined to make me happy, to make me feel special."

"Yes." He had to look back to the road, and he wished he could look into her eyes as he said, "When you love someone, you take care of them. You protect them from getting hurt. And you definitely don't become the thing that hurts them most."

She didn't say anything, and when he glanced over she was crying. Again.

Argh. He hated that. "I've never seen you cry and now it's like it's a constant."

She sniffed and wiped her cheeks. "I know. Sorry."

"What are these tears for?"

"You just..." She sniffed again. "You couldn't really protect me, or fix the stuff that was making me crazy with my family when we were dating—it's not like any of that was going to go away—but you worked your butt off, as usual, to keep me from being sad or angry or frustrated. That was..." another sniff, "...really amazing. And it must have been hard on you not to be able to make it all better."

He felt his heart squeeze. It had been horrible to not be able to really fix things for her. And trying to hadn't been amazing. He'd *needed* to do it. He'd felt driven to find something, anything, to make her smile.

He had to change the subject. The topic of his father gave him a stomachache and made him want to hit things. "Now tell me about the dresses."

"I couldn't choose," she said without any further encouragement. "Every time I thought I'd picked one, I'd wake up the next day and hate it and change my mind. Everyone was ready to strangle me. Finally it was the last day to order to get them in time. I couldn't do it. I hated every single one of them. So my cousin Bernice said she'd pick and I said fine."

"What was that all about?" Gavin asked. Allie loved clothes. She always knew exactly what to wear. She lived to accessorize.

"Well, gee, Dr. Freud, you suppose maybe it meant that I didn't want to get married?"

He looked at her. "You knew you didn't want to get married even when you were picking out dresses?"

She shrugged. "Yeah. But I ignored it. I talked myself into wanting to."

"Did you have to talk yourself into saying yes to the proposal?"

She wet her lips. "I knew it was coming. Josh's mom kept talking about how great it was that Josh was there for me, and how having me around meant part of my mom was always around." Allie's gaze went to the road in front of the truck. "Sophie was so sad. My dad was so sad. *Everyone* was so sad. But when we were all together, especially me and Josh, they smiled and laughed. I knew it was working on Josh. Ever the obedient son, I knew it was making him think."

"You were thinking too." Gavin didn't mean for it to sound quite as surly as it did. But this was *not* his favorite subject. She had, after all, been the one to say yes.

"Yeah," she finally said, quietly, "I was thinking too."

He wasn't sure he was ready to hear all the details about

her thoughts. About how wonderful Josh was, how happy their families had been about their engagement, how she regretted hurting them by coming with him.

He had a twinge of guilt when he pushed harder on the accelerator, but was relieved to see the end of Major's driveway. They didn't speak as they drove the mile along the dirt road leading up to the house.

As they pulled in, Gavin looked over the house and yard through Allie's eyes. Major's place was like every other in Bend—or anywhere in Alaska, for the most part. There were three four-wheelers, one of the primary modes of transportation around here, parked along one side of the house. Further out by the trees were two beat-up, broken-down pickups. They weren't just parked there because Major was too lazy to haul them to town. Everyone kept a hold of anything that could be used for parts. They called them "resources". There were also stacks of tires in the yard. Some had studs for driving in the snow and ice that would hit in winter, and others that were kept on hand to replace any problems.

There were a number of buildings behind the house as well. A few were sheds that stored even more "resources", one was the wood shed as Major heated his house with a wood-burning stove, and one, Gavin knew, was Major's outhouse. He winced and hoped that Allie wouldn't need the bathroom while they were here. That might be too far out of her comfort zone.

They pulled up beside the dog yard and kennel area. Gavin opened his mouth, but anything he would have said, if he could have come up with anything anyway, was interrupted as Allie asked, "Are those doghouses?"

It seemed obvious—there were dogs lying on top and in front of several of the insulated houses. But what probably made her wonder was that the houses were huge and there were ten of them. The houses lined the fence and opened up to a large, clean central area with bowls of water and lots of room for the dogs to move.

He shifted into park. "Yeah, those are Major's mushing dogs."

"Like for dogsledding?" she asked.

Gavin was so grateful for the new topic—one he was quite confident in—that he launched into a description of how the dogs were kept and trained.

Major mushed year-round. The sleds were for snow, but he had rigs for the warmer times and the tourists enjoyed it no matter what. Major got around almost exclusively by dogs or by plane.

Just then Major banged out of the gate to the yard with Eddie right behind him.

"I thought Eddie was a girl," Allie said.

"She is. That's Major. He's the owner."

She opened her door and started to get out. "So who's Eddie?"

A *woof* and a giant set of front paws were planted on her stomach the moment her feet hit the ground.

"That is," Gavin said, watching Allie gasp, then smile at the Alaskan malamute who was introducing herself.

Allie set her hand on the dog's head. "Nice to meet you, Eddie."

The dog gave another soft *woof*, then dropped her paws back to the ground. Allie laughed and turned to Gavin. "Is there something wrong with her?"

"She's damned cranky," Major groused from near the fence to the dog yard.

Eddie had always been particular. "She's a new mom," Gavin said. "Give her a break."

"She's a new mo—" Allie's question was interrupted as five puppies came tumbling out of one of the houses.

Allie was through the gate and on her knees in the dirt with the puppies in under ten seconds. The five furry, wiggly bodies fought for space on her lap as she laughed and tried to gather them all to her at once.

No one seemed to care—or even notice—that her pants were white. Least of all Allie.

Gavin just stood watching. He wasn't sure what hit him

hardest—that she didn't care about getting her clothes dirty or how breathtaking she was when she smiled like that. She hadn't even reacted to the smell. The dogs were beautiful, but dog yards stank. Period.

At the moment, if she wanted to get back in his truck and take her clothes off, he'd be at her mercy.

Chapter Six

Eddie and the puppies were completely healthy and Gavin finally got Allie to the truck again.

She felt great. She knew she looked like a mess though. She tucked her hair behind her ear as she looked down at her clothes. "I have paw prints everywhere."

Gavin glanced over. "I noticed."

There was something in his tone and his eyes that made her eyes widen. His gaze flickered down and she followed it to see multiple mud prints on her breasts and the front of her pants. She'd definitely been felt up.

But just Gavin's eyes on her good parts made them tingle. She'd trade that hot look in his eyes for litters of cute puppies.

"You want to sit in my lap?" she asked. "It's all yours."

"I do," he said, putting the truck into drive. "Or have you on mine."

"I'm not the one who thinks that's a bad idea, remember?" she asked, tingling even harder.

"I'm having trouble recalling my argument, frankly," he said, staring—almost glaring—at the road. "If I can find you playing with puppies hot, I think I'm pretty far gone."

She grinned. "I'm covered with mud and smell like dog. How is that hot?" Though she loved that he was hot for her—whatever the reason.

"You being happy, carefree, uninhibited is hot."

Something was coursing through her. Getting out into the beautiful countryside, the fresh air, the puppies—she didn't know for sure but she was feeling *something*. Playful, daring, free. Things she hadn't felt in a long time. It was such a relief. She felt like she'd finally taken a deep breath.

"Can we go dancing before next week?" she asked.

"If we do, I'm really in trouble," he said.

"Why?"

"I want you right now so dammed bad I can hardly drive straight, and you have mud on your cheek. If you get dressed up and we go dancing, I'll have you up against the nearest wall before the first song is over."

Perfect. As soon as she caught her breath she said, "In that case, I'll make things easier and not wear panties."

Gavin swerved slightly and she gave a soft laugh. When she looked over at him, he seemed tense. It wasn't just sexual tension either.

"You're mad," she observed.

"At myself."

"Why?"

"Because I want to get you naked more than I want to talk to you."

He really did seem disappointed. Which was sweet. And he'd taken her to see puppies. He was trying to take care of her and she did feel better. Like maybe talking wouldn't turn into a maelstrom of emotion and tears. Maybe it would be okay even. Gavin deserved to know she was better.

She took a deep breath. She was willing to try this. "No one knew my mom's favorite flower. And it made me nuts. That one thing, more than anything, made me crazy. I threw a vase against the wall at the funeral home because I was so pissed."

Gavin swerved again because he was looking at her. But he corrected the wheel and slowed down.

Allie stared out the windshield, but she knew he was surprised. He'd never seen her cry and he'd definitely never seen her temper. Why would he? They got along great. They never fought. They disagreed but it was always the same stuff— their families and Promise Harbor. They'd just gone their own ways when it came to that. She'd never shown him just how angry or hurt or frustrated she was about her family. He recognized her tension, but she never cried or ranted and yelled about it. It had been obvious he didn't want to be involved with all of that, so she'd kept the specifics to herself.

"Of all the things, *that's* when I lost it," she went on.

There had been so many things during her mom's sickness and after her death that had made her crazy. Her brothers hadn't done one single load of laundry the entire time. Just for instance. But that day they'd gone to the funeral home to discuss the service had been the final straw.

"I held it together up until then," she said.

Breaking down wouldn't have done anyone any good. The laundry would have still been dirty, her dad would have still needed lunch for work the next day and her mom would have still been gone.

"But then we were sitting there and the funeral director wanted to know what kind of flowers we wanted to use and no one knew her favorite flower. Not my dad. Not *me*." That still bugged her. "I got up and stomped out of his office. On my way out the front door, I noticed this vase of daisies. It was beautiful. Then I realized that daisies are *my* favorites and I still didn't know what my mom liked best. So I picked the vase up and heaved it at the closest wall before storming out."

There was a beat of silence before Gavin said, "I would have liked to have seen that."

That pulled her attention from the road. "Really?"

He nodded. "It seems like the only emotions we've ever had together were happy or passionate, you know?"

"That's bad?"

"No. But it's...not real."

She blew out a breath. "Yeah, well, real life can really suck."

He reached over and took her hand, eyes on the road. "Yep. It really can."

She linked her fingers with his, tempted to let it go. That's what they did. They let things go. She didn't think about her worries or frustrations when she was with Gavin. He never asked either. They concentrated on the fun. But...come to think of it, he was maybe okay with the less than wonderful emotions.

"Do you ever have to put animals to sleep?" she asked.

He glanced over. "Yeah. Sometimes."

"What do you say to the owners?"

He didn't answer right away, but finally said, "Most of the owners out here are pretty tough."

"But..." she prompted, knowing there was more.

"Once in a while it's hard on them, of course. If their dog gets hit by a car or something."

She nodded, watching him. "What do you say then?"

He cleared his throat. "I tell them that I don't know what to say."

She smiled. In that moment she wanted him. Badly.

He frowned at her smile. "What?"

"That's a good answer."

"That answer is terrible."

"No." She squeezed his hand. "It's good. It's honest and it shows that you know that it's a big situation for them."

He looked at her longer this time before returning his eyes to driving. "That would have been enough at your mom's funeral?"

Allie closed her eyes, bracing for the wave of pain. A moment later, she opened them again. It had been more of a sharp twinge than a wave.

She thought about his question. "Nothing would have been enough," she finally answered. "There's nothing to say. Which makes your answer good."

Neither of them spoke for nearly a minute. Then she asked, "Is that what you would have said to me?"

She could admit that she'd thought about it. Thought about having him there. How that would have felt. If it would have helped. She liked to think so, but they had no context for this serious, sad stuff.

His fingers tightened on hers briefly, and she wondered if he was even aware of it. "No, probably not," he said, his voice gruff. "I would have taken one look at you and done what I did at your wedding."

She felt the smile spread slowly. "Really?"

"Probably," he said without hesitation. "I hate seeing you sad or hurt, Al. I would have reacted to that without really thinking. Like I did at your wedding."

She thought about that. Did she believe Gavin would have stormed into the church and carried her away from her mom's funeral?

Yeah, she did.

Coming for her at the wedding couldn't have been easy on him. Sure, he'd stormed in there like a man on a mission and she knew nothing would have stopped him—well, unless she'd said no. *She* could have stopped him. But no one else would have gotten in his way of rescuing her.

Still, Promise Harbor was a place he'd hoped to never go back to. She'd seemingly chosen another man. It had been a year since they'd said good-bye. He had no reason to think that he had any right to be there, to assume he knew what was best for her. But he'd still come, out of concern—and love—for her. No matter how hard it was to get there, no matter what demons he might face coming home to Promise Harbor or what resistance he might have gotten, he'd come. For her.

"I wanted to be anywhere but in that church that day." She didn't believe that she needed the funeral to have closure or to honor her mother. She intended to honor her mother every day. "That would have been awesome."

His frown relaxed a little. "That would have been inappropriate. In real life you sometimes have to do things that suck," he said. "But I should have been there with you. I want to be there, Al. For the sucky times and the fun times."

She pressed her lips together and sat back in her seat. This more serious Gavin was pretty damned great. She leaned her head back and closed her eyes with a smile, still holding his hand.

"Maybe she didn't have a favorite flower," Gavin said after a minute. "I think you would have known if she did."

Allie's eyes flew open. "But..." Then she thought about it. Her mom's favorite color was yellow, her favorite food was turkey and dressing, her favorite holiday was Christmas. Maybe it *was* possible that there was no right answer to the flower question. "We finally settled on tulips. And they were gorgeous."

"I'm sure they were."

She watched him for a moment, a sense of contentment flowing over her that was completely at odds with the desire to rip his clothes off.

"So, now we can have sex."

Gavin didn't answer, but he shifted on the seat.

"Because I talked and opened up," she added.

He still said nothing.

"And you said that if we talked, then we could have sex."

Still nothing. "Gavin?"

"Just trying to decide where to stop for condoms."

She sighed with relief just a second before the want slammed into her. He was giving in. "I'm on the pill."

"Four of the best words I've heard in a long time," Gavin told her. And he pushed the speedometer another ten miles an hour.

They didn't talk much for the final fifteen minutes of the drive, and Gavin simply grabbed her hand as they ran to the front door.

But they were only halfway up the stairs when they heard, "Gavin!"

They both turned to see Lydia in the doorway from the kitchen, phone in hand.

"You have a call. George needs you to take a look at a cow." She looked at Allie. "Infected udder."

Allie wrinkled her nose and Lydia smiled.

Gavin sighed. "Dammit," he muttered. Then said, "Hold that thought?"

"As long as you're not talking about the thought of an infected udder." Yep, that had worked to cool the sexual tension. For sure. "Infected" was just one of those words.

Gavin chuckled and tugged her back down the stairs. "No, not that one."

"The one where you and I are naked in your bed? Sure."

"I'd invite you on this trip too, but there won't be any cute puppies to play with."

"Infected cow parts?" she asked. "No, thanks. I'm good here." She smiled at Lydia, just to rile the girl. "I'm in the mood to make some pasta or something anyway. Comfort food, you know." At Lydia's frown Allie snuggled closer to Gavin. "You've always loved my lasagna," she reminded him.

Gavin made a sound of appreciation and Lydia's frown deepened.

"Get out to George's," Lydia said to Gavin, still watching Allie. "The sooner you get back, the less time she'll spend duct-taped to the chair for trying to put even a foot in my kitchen."

Gavin chuckled and carefully steered Allie into the living room past Lydia. "Don't worry, she'll stay out of your way. Right, Al?"

Allie sighed. Lydia was small, but she seemed tough. There was a definite frustration about her. Allie could absolutely beat her if it came to rounding up a classroom of first graders or putting together a fundraiser or reorganizing a closet, but if it came to arm wrestling or duct tape, Allie was a little afraid.

"Just hang out. Relax," he said.

There was that relaxing thing again. Not really her specialty.

"And stay out of Lydia's way," she said dryly.

He shrugged. "Not a bad idea."

She looked around the living room. "How long will you be gone?"

"It's a twenty-minute drive one way. It's going to be at least an hour."

An hour. Ugh. She'd go crazy by herself for that long.

He handed her the remote control for the TV and nudged her onto the couch. "Watch a movie."

"It's going to be porn," she told him, aiming the remote at the sixty-four-inch screen.

He coughed and reached for the TV's off button. "Maybe read."

"I've got two erotic romance novels in my bag," she said. Which was true.

His gaze went to her mouth and he swallowed. "I don't suppose you want to play solitaire."

She gave him a look that she was sure conveyed her thoughts on that idea.

"Just...relax," he repeated again, obviously out of suggestions. "And stay out of the kitchen."

She glanced toward the hallway. At least fighting with Lydia would be interesting.

"I don't think she's kidding about the duct tape," he said, reading her thoughts.

She didn't think so either.

Then he headed for the door to leave her here while he went out to work again.

She frowned and slumped back on the couch with a sigh. This was ridiculous. She was sitting in Gavin's house in Alaska, alone. A cupboard door banged in the kitchen and she amended her thought to alone with the first person to dislike her in a really, really long time.

She had nothing to do. No one to talk to. No projects to work on. A few months ago she would have given her right arm for an afternoon with nothing to do.

Now she just felt restless.

Allie pushed up off of the couch. She wasn't watching TV, porn or not. She headed for the deck again. Maybe she'd go for a walk. The sunshine and fresh air and gorgeous scenery had to be good for her.

But she was down the steps off the deck and the equivalent of a block from the house when she looked up at the mountains and thought how much her mom would have loved it here.

The pain hit her directly in the chest and she gasped for breath.

She felt her throat closing and her thoughts began spinning. Memories seemed to come from every direction—her mom taking Allie and her brothers on nature hikes in the fall to gather as many different colored leaves as they could find to make a collage, her mom at the beach, in the garden, riding bikes with Allie and her brothers. Lily had loved the outdoors and this place would have made her ooh and ah for sure. But she'd never see it, never have the chance to walk like this, never...

Allie spun on the path and ran back for the house.

She barreled in through the sliding glass door and then slammed it behind her as if she could shut the thoughts and memories out too. She concentrated on breathing, her hand pressed to her chest, willing her heart to slow.

She squeezed her eyes shut and forced herself to think about something else.

Gavin.

His face came to mind. He was grinning that grin she loved and holding her hand. She took a deep breath, feeling the air flow in more easily. She thought about his laugh, about the stupid Boston College sweatshirt that he'd worn so many times that only the B and C were readable, about the way he preferred his peanut butter and jelly sandwiches grilled.

She breathed again, fully now, her heart rate slowing.

Carefully she opened her eyes and looked around his living room. She concentrated on picking up on the details of the room, pushing the thoughts of her mom to the back of her mind.

She looked at the furniture, the bookshelves, his movie and music collection.

For the first time she noticed the framed photographs on the mantle and started forward. Did he have photos of his family? Her?

But as she got closer she saw that they were photos of him with animals. In three of the pictures, he was surrounded by gorgeous huskies. He had his arms around their necks and was grinning broadly at the camera. The final three photos were also of Gavin with animals. Polar bears, to be exact.

She stared. Polar bears again? They looked real enough, but in one photo he and two other guys were kneeling behind a huge bear lying on the snow. Definitely close enough to become the bear's lunch. The animal was either fake or dead.

Of course, looking at the way one of the guys was holding his head and Gavin was lifting the humongous paw, she thought possibly it was just sedated.

Allie lifted a finger and touched Gavin's smile.

It wasn't like she hadn't seen him smile. She had, of course. They'd laughed together a thousand times. And he did have that seductive grin that he turned on when he was getting her naked—the one that said he knew exactly how weak he made her knees and how hard her stomach flipped when he touched her.

But this seemed different somehow. In this picture he was smiling...

For a reason other than her.

She jerked her hand back as the realization hit her.

Gavin was smiling about something that had absolutely nothing to do with her. Which sounded stupid and selfish, but she realized in that moment that she truly had believed that most of Gavin's happiness, the things that really gave him joy and made him laugh, had to do with her.

Dammit.

When had she turned into such an egocentric brat?

Pissed at herself, she grabbed one of two photo albums off the mantel and took it to the couch. Gavin had been out of her life for over a year. She had some catching up to do. Had he taken some trips? He hadn't flown up to the top of Mount McKinley or landed on any glaciers, but surely he'd had some fun in his new home. Had he met some new friends? He claimed he hadn't been with any women—and Nancy had more or less confirmed that—but surely he didn't spend every night at home alone.

But the pages of the photo album weren't what she expected. They were filled with more polar bears. People too. Several different people, mostly dressed in the same cold weather gear Gavin was wearing. But the photos did tell more of the story. They showed people working with the bears, giving injections, taking measurements and other activities Allie didn't quite understand. There was also a photo that showed the people indoors, arms around each other, smiling for the camera in front of a banner that read *US Geological Survey*.

In all the photos, Gavin was grinning, clearly enjoying the hell out of what he was doing.

She felt a lump in her throat as she looked at a copy of the photo he had in the clinic of him with the twin polar bear cubs. He was really happy. Contented even. She hadn't seen that in Gavin much over the years.

He had fun. He enjoyed himself. But there had always been an underlying current of determination—like having fun even took concentration. He was so driven. Always.

Now he seemed settled. He'd always had a restless air about him, the feel that he was looking for something and would keep moving on until he found it.

She thought about what he'd told her about his dad. He'd been a cheater and a liar. Big-time. A pro. He'd practically been a male prostitute. He was paid in favors instead of money, but he was still a major slimeball.

And Gavin was nothing like his father. Not that he ever could be, but he *worked* at being the exact opposite. He worked hard and did the right things, because that was how he wanted to get what he needed.

Allie closed the book and sighed. Knowing what she did now, she couldn't blame him for distancing himself from his father. More, she couldn't expect him to ignore the things his dad had done—maybe was still doing—or really to reconcile if his father wasn't sorry. She knew his mom was a tougher case, but it was clear that Gavin had little or no respect for the decisions she'd made. It would be really hard for him to pretend there was nothing wrong, yet equally hard to make his mom face what her husband had been doing and that she deserved better.

If he didn't agree with their philosophies and choices, maybe it really was best for him to just get out and stay out of their lives.

She knew Mr. and Mrs. Montgomery and knew she'd

always have a hard time with this truth about them when she saw them on the streets of the harbor.

That thought made her sit up straighter.

If she saw them on the streets of Promise Harbor, that meant she'd be back *in* Promise Harbor.

Of course, she'd be back in Promise Harbor eventually. Wouldn't she?

She had to be. She couldn't stay away forever. She couldn't stay in Bend, Alaska, forever.

Could she?

But if she didn't stay, she wouldn't be with Gavin.

He was clearly happy here. He'd found the contentment, the respect and the success that he'd always been searching for. And the harbor had nothing for him.

Her heart started pounding and she felt like doubling over, the pain similar to what she'd felt outside thinking about her mom. Dammit.

This was what happened when she was left alone— thinking.

She shoved herself up off the couch, returning the photo album to its place on the mantel.

She needed something to *do*.

Gavin let himself into the house an hour and a half after heading for George's farm. He couldn't wait to get to Allie...and get her upstairs.

But he stepped into the kitchen to find Lydia banging pots and pans. Loudly.

"What's going on?" He hung his keys on the hook by the door.

"She's using my Wii." Lydia banged a metal pan onto the countertop.

"She?"

"Allie."

Gavin tried not to smile. Not that Lydia was looking at him

anyway. She was currently stirring something in a big pot on the stove—making an incredible amount of noise with the wooden spoon she was using—and alternately checking something on the laptop she had open on the middle island.

"Why are you letting her use your Wii?" Lydia had shown up in Bend having hitchhiked from somewhere in the States. She'd never said where exactly and he'd never asked. She had a suitcase and a big paper bag that he later discovered held a Wii and several games.

"It keeps her out of the kitchen," Lydia muttered.

He did smile then, but quickly hid it. "Did she eat anything?"

"I set pasta salad and bread out on the coffee table while she was upstairs."

"That was nice of you," Gavin said, even though he knew she hadn't done it to be nice.

"I couldn't let the pasta salad go to waste. Especially since you weren't here to eat. Again."

Lydia loved taking care of him. He just labeled their relationship "complicated" and didn't think too much about it. But he knew that Lydia took her job with him seriously and found a lot of reward in it. So, when things happened—like him not being here to take care of—she got pissy.

"But she didn't eat it," Lydia added.

Dammit, again. When was that woman going to start taking care of herself—or letting him take care of her?

"Why not?"

Lydia scowled at him. "Probably to piss me off."

Gavin thought about that and decided not to agree or disagree on that point.

"All I know is that she eventually came back downstairs. I just ignored her until I heard her swearing. Then I went to check."

"To make sure she was okay?" Gavin asked with a small smile.

"To make sure she hadn't broken a lamp or that she wasn't

bleeding on the carpet or something," Lydia said. "Blood's a bitch to get out."

Gavin *definitely* wasn't going to comment on that.

"But she was just using the stupid workout game that came with the Wii. I've never done it. It looked like yoga."

Gavin glanced toward the living room. Yoga. Yeah, Allie did yoga. He remembered it vividly. And fondly. The yoga pants made her ass look amazing and some of the poses were downright erotic—at least when it was Allie doing it in front of him. More than once he'd come home to find her working out and had been unable to keep from working her out in another way.

"Yoga, huh? I better go check on her."

"It's not gonna work to calm her down," Lydia said. "She can't relax. She's like a frickin' hummingbird. She can't sit still, she can't just chill. I liked her better when she was sleeping all day."

A hummingbird. Not a bad analogy. "She's been having a hard time."

Lydia just looked at him for a long moment. "Lots of people have hard times."

"Yep. And some of them handle it by going to bed for several days, some handle it by keeping busy, and some..." he paused meaningfully, "...handle it by running away."

Lydia turned to the stove and banged her spoon on the pan again. "Just make sure she doesn't break my machine or she's buying me a new one."

Got it. They weren't going to talk. That had been working for them for almost a year now.

He headed for the living room, hoping to find Allie in the bridge pose.

But he pulled up short in the doorway.

She was most definitely not doing yoga.

She was punching and kicking. Hard. She was gasping for air and sweating and looked like she'd been at it for a while. She also looked like she was worked up enough to keep going.

He propped his shoulder against the doorway and watched for a few minutes, not wanting to get in the way of this. It looked like kickboxing wasn't new to her. Besides, she was wearing yoga pants and an exercise bra. Only. It wasn't yoga, but he couldn't help but appreciate the view.

Finally she stopped and put her hands on her knees, bending at the waist and pulling in long breaths. Clearly she didn't know he was there, so he took time to drink in the sight of the curve of her back, the way tendrils of hair escaped her ponytail and clung to her wet skin, the way her breasts lifted and fell as she breathed.

After a minute, she lowered herself to the floor and then sprawled on her back, knees bent, still just breathing. Her eyes were squeezed tight and she flung an arm over her face. There was something about her, something about how she was pushing herself, something about all of this that felt...wrong. Something was off. He should have been concerned about her working out so hard. She'd just gotten over being sick. In fact, she wasn't even done taking her antibiotics yet. Surely she should be taking it easier than this.

He started into the room, but just then Allie pounded her fists onto the floor beside her. "Fuck!"

Eyebrows up, he watched her push to her feet, stomp to the Wii and change the game disc. A moment later, she stepped back, pushed some buttons on the controller in her hand and then started shooting the crap out of the bad guys that were jumping out from behind buildings and cars on the screen.

She blew up a couple of buildings, used a rocket launcher on a truck, and shot several more men before she got nailed by one of them.

She stood, staring at the screen, panting.

"Allie?"

She swung to face him, visibly startled to find him there.

"You okay?"

She just stared at him, breathing hard. Then she shook her head, let out a little sob and stumbled toward him.

He caught her against his chest. Her arms wound around

him tightly and she buried her face in his neck. He just held on.

Hands splayed big across her back, he held her. And when it became clear that she was crying, he held her tighter. Her tears were hot against his skin, her body shook and all he could do was stand there, squeezing his own eyes shut and rubbing up and down her back.

He had no words. And he hated it.

It felt like two years had passed by the time she loosened her hold slightly and the shaking in her body calmed.

Minutes later, the crying seemed over, but she clearly didn't want to move out of his arms. Which was just fine with him. He bent and scooped her up. She didn't protest, didn't even gasp. She just cuddled closer as he started for the stairs.

His own shaking didn't start until they stepped into the bedroom. She right here, real and alive and warm and sweet, and...he had no fucking idea what to do with her.

Having Allie in his bedroom had always been simple before. They made love all the time. There wasn't a position or a time of day they hadn't tried. And it was always fantastic. She was expressive and honest in bed and he'd quickly learned what she liked, what made it good for her, and then he made sure that every single time was incredible. Loving her, physically and emotionally, had been easy.

Now, though, everything was new. Her needs weren't as straightforward as they'd been before. He wasn't the expert at knowing what she wanted and needed now.

He hated that.

The thing, the person, he'd always been most sure of was now what he was feeling most insecure about.

In the past, he'd been well acquainted with the things he was trying to prove, the things that he felt less than amazing at. He'd been trying to make his way, make his mark, earn his place for a long time now.

In Bend, he'd done it. He really had. He belonged here because of who he was, not because of his father or some favor someone had done for his father. Gavin was accepted and liked and respected because of who *he* was. He was confident and calm and happy with himself for the first time in years.

Until now.

Confident and calm were not how he was feeling with Allie.

He'd grown up, he wanted to be serious but—he didn't even know all the details about what she needed him to be serious about.

Then his shaking got worse. What if she told him what the tears were all about and he had no idea how to fix it?

He didn't have serious conversations with anyone. He and Lydia danced around her past, he and his family didn't stay in touch, Hayley was the closest thing he had to a lifelong friend and they'd mostly just screwed around and gotten into trouble together. If there was anything serious or life-changing going on in her life, he sure didn't know about it.

And now there was Allie—who needed *something.* Something he wasn't sure he could give her.

Yeah, calm and confident were definitely not the things he was feeling here.

He glanced around and then headed for the bathroom.

He set her gently on the counter and pulled away slowly, making sure she could hold herself up. "You got it?" he asked.

She nodded.

He turned and started filling the tub. He didn't have bubble bath or scented candles or any of...whatever else girls used in the bathtub. But warm water couldn't hurt.

They didn't try to talk over the running water and he resisted looking at her. Without the tears, he was more aware of just how much skin really showed in her workout gear, and he was trying to ignore the fact that she was going to have to undress to take a bath. Hopefully she could manage that on her own and not need his help...

Her turquoise workout bra hit his shoe.

He looked up to find that she'd shimmied off the countertop and was now peeling her yoga pants off, watching him as she stripped.

Her bare breasts bounced as she moved, the tips hard,

making his mouth water.

With her pants and panties at her ankles, she kicked the clothes free and Gavin greedily took in the sight of her. She reached up and pulled her ponytail loose, shaking her hair out, and he watched as the strands floated up, then came to settle around her shoulders.

He was rock hard within seconds.

"Allie," he rasped, not really sure what he was going to say after that.

"Touch me, Gavin."

God. How could he resist that? He'd walked away from her like this already once today. How could he be expected to continually say no to what they both wanted so much?

He stood and took a step forward. He ran his hands from her shoulders to her fingertips, still battling with the wisdom of doing even that much. But Allie took his hands and lifted them to her breasts.

His air whooshed out as her nipples pressed into his palms and she rocked closer, her eyes sliding shut. "Yes. Touch me. Make me think only about you."

He wanted to help her work through it, not just distract her from it all. But even as he thought the thought, his thumbs brushed over her nipples, sending electricity skittering up his arms.

She gasped and pressed closer. "Yes, Gav."

He should say something. Something supportive and encouraging. He should tell her that he was here, for her, for so much more than this. But her hands slid under his shirt and up over his chest and the contact made everything in him tighten.

She needed this. She needed him. For this. No one else could make her feel the way he did.

And he still had no effing idea what to say or how to say it anyway.

So he kissed her instead.

And when her tongue stroked against his and her nails dug lightly into his pecs, his brain shut down and his body took over.

He knew one thing—*this* he was good at. Making Allie feel good physically was something he was very good at.

He lifted her back onto the counter and stepped between her knees, then filled his hands with her breasts again. She arched into him, kissing him hungrily, her hands in his hair, then under his shirt again, then around to his ass. She wrapped her legs around him, her heels digging into his butt, urging him closer.

The button and zipper on his jeans gave way and suddenly he realized he was still wearing what he'd been wearing to George's farm.

"Ah, dammit." He tried to pull back.

"What?" She reached for him. "I need you."

"I've been at the farm." Wow, she was really strong when she was wanted something.

"I don't care."

"I'm covered in mud and smell like cows."

"I don't *care*." She leaned back enough to strip his shirt off and toss it away.

With her leaning like that he could see everything, and he lost his train of thought.

"I just need you, Gavin. I don't care that you've been working." She ran her hands up and down his naked chest, her eyes roaming over him. "In fact, it's completely sexy. You're sweaty and..." She stopped and looked down at herself. "Ugh." She pulled her hands away and her legs dropped. "I've been working out. *I'm* sweaty and..."

He cupped her face and kissed her. When he lifted his head she was staring at him, effectively distracted. "You're gorgeous. I love seeing your body work. Seeing you sweaty and breathing hard makes me think of all the other ways to get you that way."

"But I'm..." She sighed. "I'm not feeling sexy now. Mood lost."

No way. He had to do something for her and this was it. This was all he had at the moment.

"I can fix that." He toed off his shoes and shucked out of his pants.

Allie swallowed as she took in the fact that he was naked. And very happy to see her.

"Yeah, that definitely helps," she said.

He chuckled and turned to open the drain in the tub and pull the lever to start the shower.

"This will help too." He gathered her close, slipping his hands under her butt and lifting her.

She gave a little shriek as he turned them and stepped into the shower with her. The shriek turned to a groan, though, as she slid a little and her hot, wet center came into contact with his erection.

"How we doing?" he asked huskily, hands splayed wide on her ass, moving her up and down against him again.

"Oh, yeah," she groaned.

"Thought it might." He slid her up and down again, her heat against his cock making him throb.

"More," she gasped.

"Definitely," he promised. "But I've got some more tasting and touching to do."

He set her on her feet and turned until she was under the spray. She tipped her head so that her hair fell back from her face as it got wet, and closed her eyes. The water ran over her body, her nipples hardened and she sighed. The water flowing over her skin glistened and he felt his cock harden further. He skimmed his hands over her arms, her back, down over her breasts and stomach.

Her head came up, her eyes opening. Without looking, she reached for the soap on the ledge and rubbed it in her hands, then began smoothing it over his body, starting at his shoulders, spreading over his chest and down over his abdomen. Then lower. Dropping the soap, she took him in both hands, gliding up and down his length with just the right amount of pressure to nearly bring him to his knees.

"God, Allie," he groaned.

"I just want to make sure that we get everything clean."

She ran her hands up over his chest, taking the soap from his skin and then rubbing it over her breasts, then down her stomach before leaning so the water washed the bubbles from both of them.

He was panting by the time her fingers slid between her legs. She kept her eyes on his as she circled her clit. Finally she smiled. "You can look, Gavin."

"Thank god." He not only looked, he went to his knees to get an up-close view.

She started to pull her hand away, but he caught her wrist. "Oh, no, you don't. Keep going."

She did. She parted her legs and circled the pad of her middle finger over her clit again, nice and slow. Gavin ran his hands over the back of her thighs, gaze locked on her finger. She increased the rhythm and he glanced up to see her bottom lip pulled between her teeth, her eyes hot on him.

She slid her finger deep then, moaning softly as she did. Gavin felt his heart pound and he squeezed her thighs, dragging in a deep breath. Suddenly he had to be the one making her moan.

He came to his feet in one fluid motion, lifting one of her legs as he did it, spreading her open. He turned her back to the wall and pressed close.

"You okay?"

"God, yes."

He thrust deep.

"Gavin!" she gasped.

"Allie," he groaned, dropping his forehead to the wall over her shoulder and just pausing to feel. She was tight and hot and...all his. He moved his hips, eliciting a deep moan from her.

"Gavin."

God, he loved hearing his name on her lips.

He moved again, pulling another groan from her. Then again. And again. Faster and deeper and harder.

Her fingers dug into his shoulders and her mouth went to his neck, where she sucked lightly, then licked, and he couldn't get deep enough. He thrust three times, then kicked the curtain out of the way, lifted her and stepped out of the tub. He didn't care that there was water spraying all over the bathroom, or that he was risking his neck by stepping out dripping wet. He had to be deep, as deep as he could get.

"Gavin?" she asked, just before he laid her down on the rug, knelt between her knees, spread her legs open and thrust again.

"Oh, yes," she praised. "More."

She looked so hot, spread out, dripping wet all over, begging him. He thrust fast and hard and deep and he could feel her inner muscles start to ripple. She grabbed the towel hanging from the rack over her head with both hands, using it to lift her upper body and press closer as he continued to drive into her. As her release built, she pulled harder on the towel, and the rack came loose. Gavin's hand shot out and knocked it away before it hit her in the head as her orgasm swept over her.

She called out his name and gripped his hips with her thighs, and the way she milked him and the look of absolute bliss on her face sent him quickly over the edge.

He braced his arms, keeping his weight off of her for a moment, until he felt everything sweep over him and let go.

Then he slumped to the rug beside her with a heartfelt, absolutely contented sigh.

"Thank you."

She didn't think that she'd ever been more grateful to someone. And it was for sex.

But it was fantastic sex. With Gavin. It didn't get better than that.

All of the tension and the sadness were gone. She was completely relaxed, sated, happy.

She hadn't been any of those things, and certainly not all three together, in a really long time.

He chuckled. "I could say the same."

She rolled toward him, breathing deep the scent of soap and man. "Seriously. Thank you for changing your mind about the rules. I *really* needed that."

He didn't say anything but she felt him stiffen slightly. And not in the good way.

Damn. "Gavin, I know you want this to be different..."

"It is different."

But it wasn't. He was her haven. As always. He'd made her feel all of the great things that he always made her feel, the great things that she was addicted to, that she needed in the midst of all the other crap.

It *couldn't* be different. She *needed* it to be the same.

She propped herself onto one elbow. "What we've always had is really good, Gavin. It's what I want. And need."

"You don't know what else it could be," he said, finally looking at her. He stroked his hand over her hair. "You don't know how much better it could be."

Something in his voice, or his eyes, made her heart squeeze. She just wasn't sure if it was love or panic.

Who would have guessed those two emotions could feel so similar? Heart pounding, hard to breathe, goose bumps all over.

She did love him. She always had. But he'd always panicked her too.

She knew almost from the beginning that they didn't want the same lives. By their third date they talked about Promise Harbor, and he made it clear that he wasn't going back. Ever. A smart woman would have just ended it then. At least, a smart women who knew she definitely was going back to the harbor. But by then, she was already in love and couldn't walk away. Three dates and she was in deep.

So love and panic went hand in hand. She knew it would eventually end. She knew her heart would eventually break. She lived in fear of when that would happen.

Unless she didn't think about it.

Her ability to shove her emotions down deep and ignore them had been practiced long before her mom got sick.

It was why she let him keep their relationship fun and sexy. He didn't ask deep questions, he didn't pry for information and she didn't offer much up either. She'd figured it would help her keep some distance for her heart.

She'd been wrong, of course, but that had been her philosophy.

Interestingly, she didn't need to bare her soul, or know everything he thought and felt, to fall for him. She'd fallen in love with how he'd wanted to take care of her, how he just wanted to be with her, not because he needed her like everyone else, but because he loved her. She also watched him take care of the animals he loved and how he was always there if someone needed to borrow money or needed a ride or needed to laugh. He didn't do deep conversations or sage advice, but what he did do, he did very well. Gavin was honest and loyal and always did what he said he would do. In her eyes, that made him better than most people she knew, even if serious conversations about emotions gave him hives.

And now, his aversion to all things deep and serious was supposed to be working in her favor.

"Being with you, right now, is better than anything I've had for a really long time," she told him honestly. Couldn't that be enough?

"I know."

His confidence was another thing that had always drawn her. That and his laid-back attitude.

"But I don't just want to be better. I want to be the best."

"You are—"

"No," he said, pushing himself up off the rug. "But I will be. The best thing in your life, the best thing to ever happen to you."

Okay. So the laid-back attitude had changed a little.

She scrambled to her feet too. "Gavin, I want you. I'm glad I'm here. Can't we just—"

"We can get married."

All of the oxygen in the room seemed to have disappeared. Allie felt her mouth drop open and her lungs try to expand, but nothing would happen.

He frowned at her. "Breathe."

She tried. She really did.

Finally, he took her by the shoulders and leaned in, putting him on eye level with her. "Breathe."

"Gav..."

"Jesus, did you hyperventilate when Josh proposed?"

Chapter Seven

That pulled her out of it. Allie sucked in a long breath and blinked. Dammit.

"I'm not hyperventilating," she told him, feeling breathless no matter what he called it. "That's technically breathing too fast."

"Whatever." Gavin was scowling at her. "Did Josh's proposal affect your breathing?"

She pushed him back and frowned right back at him. "That doesn't really matter now, does it?" She crossed her arms over her breasts.

He looked at her. "How'd he do it? How'd he propose?"

"Not naked on the bathroom floor out of the blue," she snapped.

Gavin wanted to *marry* her? What? How was that going to work exactly? Should she have been expecting that?

Yeah, maybe.

"No, Josh wouldn't do that, would he?" Gavin grabbed his pants and pulled them on.

Feeling even more exposed than she had in the midst of the hot sex, Allie grabbed the towel that had fallen when she pulled the towel rack down. She stared at the towel rack. Wow. She'd pulled it right off the wall.

"He asked me at dinner," she said softly, wrapping the towel around her.

"I wasn't talking about the proposal. I was talking about doing you on the bathroom floor."

"I—" She snapped her mouth shut. Damn. No, there had never been wild sex on the floor with Josh. Or wild sex anywhere else. What sex there was had been nice. Just like

Josh.

"But look at us—first time and we're already going at it on the floor." Gavin grabbed his shirt, boots and socks and stomped into the bedroom. "I sure didn't hesitate to spread you out on the hard tile, did I?"

Allie scooped her clothes up and followed him. "I *liked* it, in case you couldn't tell," she said, exasperated. What was the problem here?

"So what else will I do that Josh won't do?"

She stopped in the middle of the room, watching him strip out of his jeans again and toss them into the hamper. Distracted by the fact that he was naked again—and that naked was a really good look for him—she asked, "What do you mean?"

"I'm guessing Josh doesn't go for a weekend watching a *Big Bang Theory* marathon and doing body shots off of each other." Gavin yanked open a drawer and pulled a pair of sweatpants out.

"What the hell are you talking about?" Allie asked, pulling her shirt on without a bra, feeling the need to be covered ASAP. She'd loved that weekend.

"What about backward meals?"

She paused in pulling her pants up. Those were fun. They'd start by going out for dessert somewhere, then go to a different restaurant for the entrée, then another for soup and salad and end somewhere else with appetizers and drinks. "What about them?"

"Did Josh ever take you out for a backward dinner?"

She thought about that. She couldn't imagine Josh doing that. She could, however, picture the confused look on his face if she told him about it. "No. We mostly had dinner at his mom's or with my family. Or everyone all together." And Allie had done a lot of the cooking.

She tugged her pants up the rest of the way and zipped them. It was absolutely no surprise to her that she had more fun with Gavin than she did with Josh.

Duh.

That was a huge reason why she was currently standing in the middle of Gavin's bedroom in Alaska in postcoital bliss.

Though his crabby mood was quickly ruining that bliss.

"I also don't see Josh as the type to take you roller-skating, or sneak into a high school prom or have a water balloon fight with you."

She shook her head, her heart flipping as the memories paraded through her mind. "No, he never did any of those things." She swallowed. Suddenly she felt the need to defend Josh. Or her choice in saying yes to Josh. Or both. "But there's more to getting married than—"

"Exactly."

"Exactly?" She frowned. "I thought you were trying to talk me into you."

"I'm trying to talk you into letting me show you that there's more to me than roller-skating and eating dessert first."

He wasn't looking at her but she could see the strain in his face. She'd always loved the roller-skating and dessert part of being with Gavin. But...this seemed important to him.

Josh wasn't a big dessert eater, period. "But I love dessert," she said weakly.

"You think of me for fun, but I don't want to just be the extra stuff. I want to be...the main meal, what you need most. Hell, I want to be your *vegetables.*"

He wanted to be her vegetables. Great. That sounded ridiculous, of course, but she couldn't smile. She knew what he meant, and before her mom got sick she would have been thrilled.

But she didn't want that now. Her life was full of vegetables—so to speak. She had lots of things in her life that were good for her. Teaching, taking care of her family, marrying Josh. All good for her, all important in her life, all just a little...unexciting.

It wasn't that she disliked any of those things. She liked some vegetables, too. She could eat asparagus and carrots on a regular basis and be just fine, and she happened to love broccoli. But there were also some she really hated. Brussels sprouts, for instance.

The truth was, good for her or not, she wanted more than broccoli.

Like ice cream. Chocolate syrup. Whipped cream. Candy sprinkles.

Dessert.

Gavin was her ice cream sundae. She didn't want to trade that in on broccoli. No way.

"I need you, Gavin. That's why I'm here."

"Let me show you that I can be good husband material, Allie," he said gruffly.

Her stomach hurt. She didn't want husband material. She'd had that—or at least, she could have had that. She needed Gavin. Just the way he had always been.

Why couldn't they seem to get to the same place at the same time?

"How?" she finally asked, trying not to sound skeptical or resigned.

Gavin opened another dresser drawer, pulled out a T-shirt and tossed it to her. "Put this on. Then we're going downstairs to eat dinner and watch TV and talk. We're going to have an evening like a normal couple."

Oh, boy. She held the shirt against her. A normal couple.

There was that love-panic combination fluttering in her chest again.

But she exchanged her shirt for Gavin's T-shirt.

"Lose the pants," he said.

Now *that* sounded promising. "You got it." She stripped the pants off.

"Now let's go."

"Go?"

He took her hand and headed for the stairs. Him in only his sweatpants—and she'd noticed he was going commando—and her in his T-shirt and a pair of panties.

Okay, at least it was sexy.

"Lyd! We're here!" he called.

The first floor smelled amazing once Allie actually paid attention. Garlic and tomato sauce and... Her stomach rumbled.

"Yeah, and no more skipping meals," Gavin said, leading her to the couch.

She started to reply and then thought better of it. It wasn't worth arguing with him. She had skipped lunch and he really wanted her to eat and have healthy habits. Fine.

Lydia came in with a big tray. There were two plates, a bread basket, and a bottle of wine with glasses. She set it down in the middle of the coffee table without a word and headed back for the kitchen.

"Thanks, Lyd," Gavin called after her.

Allie watched her go with a frown. She didn't need to be Lydia's friend, but she did kind of wish that she didn't annoy the girl so much.

Then she looked at the tray.

They were having lasagna.

And if it tasted even half as good as it smelled and looked, it was way better than Allie's.

Score one for the moody assistant.

Allie took a seat, then pulled her feet up onto the couch, tucking her knees under the shirt. Gavin handed her a plate, poured the wine and settled back, flipping the TV on. "I know you like this movie," he said, cutting into his own dinner.

Allie had her first bite of lasagna in her mouth and wouldn't have cared if he turned on a war documentary. The lasagna was that good.

But it wasn't a documentary. It was *The Bodyguard.*

She looked at him. "Ha-ha."

He grinned. "What? Obviously this movie means something to you."

"You just love that I called and sang that song, don't you?" she asked, reaching for the wine.

"I do. It was a stirring rendition." He chewed with a smug look on his face.

Allie drank, then said, "I was drunk, you know."

"Oh, I know. But the fact that you were thinking of me, when your inhibitions were down and with everything going on around you, meant a lot." His eyes were on the screen.

She studied his profile. He was so damned good-looking. Sexy. And talented with that mouth that was now closing around his fork tines.

They'd spent plenty of time perfecting their skills on one another, and he knew exactly how to get her going exactly where he wanted her.

She knew his buttons too—though today she'd been wondering if she'd lost her touch. Earlier that morning she'd stood naked in front of him and begged him to take her to bed and he'd said no. Because of her tears. Because she'd lost her mind and cried after an orgasm.

Then again, just a little bit ago, the tears had moved him. She drank again and thought about that. No, it hadn't been the tears. Well, they'd started it. She'd been fighting them all afternoon, and then when she'd turned and seen him standing there all she could think about was being in his arms. The moment she'd felt his strong, solid body against hers, she'd lost it again. She'd cried on his shoulder for the first time ever. And wow, it had felt good.

And speaking of feeling good...the bathroom counter and shower and floor had all felt pretty damned good too.

Thank god, he'd relaxed his rules about talking first. Or forgotten his rules. Or said "to hell with the rules". Whatever had happened, she was thankful.

Looking at him now, she felt that tug in her chest. He wanted to be a "normal couple" with her. He wanted to get married. He wanted to show her he wanted all of that.

How was that going to work? Alaska was a long way from Promise Harbor. Was he saying he'd consider moving home now?

Her heart tripped at that. Could she really have Gavin? Her chest felt tight as the hope welled up. Hope she hadn't even realized she'd had deep down.

"My brothers are a mess," she said, watching carefully for Gavin's reaction.

He looked over at her. "What?"

She took another drink of wine and then set the glass on the table. "You asked about my dad and brothers earlier," she said. "They're a mess." She took a bite of lasagna and watched Gavin process that.

He muted the TV and turned to face her, and it hit her that he was taking this very seriously. "How much of a mess?"

"Charlie's quit five jobs in the past year. Danny's failed three classes and is considering taking a year off. Which will mean he'll never go back to college." She hated that her brothers were constantly taking the easy way out. Charlie quit jobs when he didn't want to show up on time anymore. Danny dropped classes if they required more homework than he felt he was able to fit into his very busy social calendar.

"They've had a tough year," Gavin said.

"Yes," she agreed. Her mom had done everything for the boys. Allie was trying to help them out, but there was only so much she could do. "But they're making things even tougher with their choices. Charlie doesn't have health insurance or money for his bills, so he moved back in with Dad and I. Danny will have a hard time finding anything over minimum wage without a college degree, and he's already lost his girlfriend because she got sick of him slacking. And he's living with us too."

"I'm...sorry," Gavin offered.

She was too. "I just wanted to...tell you something. Since you asked."

He leaned in. "Thanks."

"Yeah." She took another bite of the best lasagna in the world and admitted that telling Gavin that much hadn't hurt at all.

"How about your dad?"

Now that was a more painful subject. She swallowed and pushed a piece of pasta around her plate. "He's a mess too," she said. "Of course." He and her mom had been married for thirty-four years.

"Of course," Gavin echoed. "I guess that's a dumb question."

She looked up. "No. It's not."

Her dad had been completely lost when her mom first got sick. It had taken Allie a week or so to fully and competently take over organizing his routine—something he hadn't been able to do since the motorcycle accident twelve years before. But once Allie understood Lily's method for keeping Owen on track, he did okay. By the time Lily had passed away, Allie had taken over the bill paying, the scheduling, the shopping, the laundry and...everything. "He misses her terribly but..." She trailed off, realizing where she'd been about to go with the conversation.

"But what?" Gavin pressed.

"Nothing. Things have been getting better."

Because of the wedding.

Allie put her hand against her chest and focused on not freaking out. Josh was there. And Greta was back for a little while now. And Sophie. They would make sure Owen was okay. Yeah, Charlie and Danny might be on their own—and in some trouble—but at least Owen had people to lean on. Josh knew the details, he knew the things Allie took care of. He'd step in, she knew it. Yeah, he might be mad at her, but he'd never let Owen down.

"Allie?" Gavin leaned closer, his eyes full of concern. "What is it?"

"Nothing. Just..." She wanted to say it. She wanted to tell him. It would be the first time she'd said it out loud and suddenly she wanted to tell someone.

"Just?" Gavin prompted.

She bit her lip, then said quickly, "I said yes to Josh because he can like my family when I can't."

Gavin watched her, considering that. He didn't seem shocked by her confession. "What's that mean?"

She sighed. "I love my family but..." She shrugged, trying to ignore the twinge of guilt over what she was about to say.

"Sometimes it's hard to like them. Josh gets that and he kind of takes over for me sometimes. He'll take my dad out to do something or listen to my brothers whine. He just...makes things easier."

Gavin worked on not swearing. Or scowling.

Josh had been there, helping Allie. That was good. At least *someone* had.

But it had, obviously, helped win her heart.

More than that, it was something Gavin had never done.

He'd helped her, but not with her family issues. Not only did they not interact with each other's families, they didn't talk about them much. Gavin knew that Allie and her mom took care of her dad and the boys, but he didn't know the details. He'd never asked.

The details hadn't mattered.

Or he hadn't realized they mattered. Or maybe they hadn't mattered until about the time Josh decided to propose.

Gavin ran his hand over his face and let out a breath. "I'm glad you had someone on your side."

He was glad. Of course, he would have preferred it be a girlfriend who took her shoe shopping and out for margaritas when things got tough. Instead, it had to be a good-looking, successful guy whom everyone loved and who had a history with Allie's family.

Of course she'd said yes to his proposal.

"Josh helped pull me—all of us—through a really bad time," she said.

Gavin glanced over to find that she'd exchanged her plate for her wineglass and was studying the merlot solemnly.

Yeah, he sucked at this. He wanted her to talk to him, to open up, to tell him all about her struggles. Then when she did, he ended up wanting to punch Josh Brewster. And for what? For being there for Allie? Being what she needed?

Yes.

Because it was easier to want to punch Josh than to be

pissed at himself.

Josh had been there for her because Gavin hadn't been.

"I wouldn't have known what to say," he finally said into the silence. "I would have wanted to say the perfect thing and it would have killed me to not be able to. I would have seen how sad you were and I would have wanted to make you smile and I would have done something stupid."

She looked up from her wine. "Something like what?"

He sighed. "It doesn't matter. I wouldn't have known how to step in, I wouldn't have known what to say."

"What would you have done, Gavin?" Allie pressed. "Give me an example."

He blew out a breath and pictured Allie sitting in the front pew of the church at her mom's funeral. "I would have picked you up, carried you out of there and taken you to my house, made you get into flannel pajamas, sat you in front of a *Looney Tunes* marathon and made you eat Froot Loops."

She stared at him, her lips parted in a surprised O.

Josh had probably given her a locket with her mom's picture inside and held her hand through the service. Or something equally annoyingly perfect.

"Sorry," he said with a shrug when she still didn't speak. "My instinct would have been to take you away from all of it instead of being there beside you through it."

Allie cleared her throat. "I know. And it sounds..."

"Stupid."

"Wonderful."

He raised an eyebrow. "Do you mean crazy?"

She shook her head. "You don't get it. No one else in my entire life would ever think of feeding me Froot Loops after my mother's funeral, but I'll take sugary kids' cereal over ham sandwiches and potato salad any day."

Gavin didn't know what to do. Should he hug her? Say something eloquent?

Hell, probably the eloquent thing, which was what he really sucked at.

"Al—"

"That's what they fed us. Ham sandwiches and potato salad. In the social hall at the church. Which ticks me off because I liked ham sandwiches and potato salad before that. Now I'll never be able to look at them again without thinking of the day my mother was buried."

Jesus. Gavin swallowed hard. Being eloquent was beyond him even without a huge lump in his throat. This wasn't getting any easier. Why had he thought talking was such a great idea?

"Do you have any idea how many casseroles we got after the funeral?" Allie asked him.

Gavin just shook his head.

"Twenty-two." She shook her head. "Can you believe that?"

If giving casseroles was the way to show someone that they were cared for, then yes, he could believe that. Not only had Lily Ralston been beloved, but she, Owen and all their children had been born and raised in Promise Harbor. They knew everyone.

"Even if we ate one every night, it would have taken almost a month to go through them," Allie said. "I didn't have room in the freezer. It was nuts."

"People were trying to help you out," Gavin said, thinking that was a pretty good thing to say at the moment.

"I know." Allie reached to set her wineglass down. "And it did help. Dinner was one less thing to mess with some nights anyway." She looked up at him again. "But a bowl of Froot Loops would have been perfect. Simple to make, always turns out right, and it would have reminded me of building forts with the furniture and blankets in the living room Saturday mornings with my brothers. Nice memories."

Gavin couldn't believe that he'd gotten that right. Who knew that Froot Loops could be the simple answer to such a complex issue?

"What else?" she asked.

"What else what?"

"What else would you have done?"

Other than avoiding the whole thing and staying on the other side of the United States? Gavin shoved his hand through

162

his hair. He hadn't let himself imagine Allie and what she was going through. It was too hard. It was too...unfixable. And he hated that.

But to answer the question he made himself think about how Allie might have looked or felt or acted on the Mother's Day after her mom was gone. His chest ached and he scrubbed at the spot over his heart. "I would have covered your bathroom mirror with comic strips and jokes."

Her lips curled into a half smile. "Any dirty jokes?"

"Of course."

The smile grew into a full smile and her eyes were brighter. "What else?"

To make her go from sad to happy like that? Anything. He thought hard, digging for creativity. "I would have rented a snow machine and had a snowball fight with you in the middle of June."

She sat up straight, her eyes wide with interest. "What else?"

His imagination was revved up now. He loved not only making her smile, but also surprising her with how he did it.

"I would have set up a scavenger hunt where you had to go around town and collect packages from me. When you had them all together you'd realize it was a new outfit. Then a limo would have picked you up outside the last stop and brought you to me."

She was sitting up on her knees on the couch now, her wine abandoned on the table. "Where would you have been?"

"I'm thinking...carnival."

She grinned. "Yes. A carnival would be perfect." She leaned forward. "What else?"

"I would have whisked you off to a beach where you could just lie around in the sun with umbrella drinks."

"Would you have been there?"

"Definitely. I'd be the one rubbing the suntan lotion all over you."

She gave him a sly smile. "A nude beach?"

"Only if it was private." His imagination *really* liked that idea, and preferred this talk and teasing to the talk of how to take her mind off of her mom.

"I like that. What else?" she asked.

"Really anywhere far away where I could pamper you and keep you away from everything sad."

Their gazes held for a moment. Then she said softly, "You did that."

His gut clenched at that. "Better late than never?" he asked.

"See?" She sat back, her smile much less bright. "No one else would have done any of that. That's why I like you, Gavin. Things aren't serious and sad when you're around."

He knew she wasn't trying to insult him, but there was something about the words that made him want to deny them. But it would sound incredibly stupid to insist that things *could be* serious and sad when he was around.

She started to crawl toward him and Gavin could see the intent in her eyes. All thoughts of sadness disappeared. But this could be serious. She was going to seduce him.

And he was going to let her.

She'd just climbed onto his lap and was leaning to kiss him when he heard, "Gavin!"

It was Lydia, but he could tell she was yelling from the kitchen.

"Yeah?" He had to clear his throat and try again when his answer came out gruff.

"Yeah?"

"Dave Wilson needs you."

Gavin dropped his head to the back of the couch with a groan. "Why?"

"He said..."

But he couldn't catch the rest. "Lyd, get in here!" he called.

"Are you naked?"

"Not yet," Allie called with a big grin.

Gavin grabbed her hips and tossed her to one side. "Let's

not teach her anything she doesn't already know."

Allie rolled her eyes. "That girl is a lot of things, but stupid is not one of them."

"Thanks."

They both turned to find Lydia in the doorway, holding a piece of paper.

"Dave's horse is in labor and having some trouble."

Gavin sighed. This was the one drawback to being the only vet for almost a hundred miles. He looked at Allie. "Sorry. This could take a while."

She waved him away. "No worries. Go. I'm fine."

"You sure?" "Fine" was not exactly the word he'd use to describe her lately. Bipolar, maybe. But not fine.

She glanced at the clock. "I'll probably go to bed."

Bed. It was just one word, and she hadn't even said it with any sexual intention, but desire hit him hard and hot in the gut. God, he wanted to join her. He'd had lots of plans for having her in his bed now that she was healthy and happy.

She gave him a wink that told him she knew precisely what he was thinking.

"I'll be home as soon as I can."

"Feel free to take advantage of me when you get back."

Gavin coughed and glanced at Lydia. She looked bored.

He knew that she probably wasn't as innocent as he liked to assume. She'd run away from home, after all. That took guts, if nothing else, and generally didn't happen when things were happy and rosy. Still, she seemed so young to him, and he wanted only to be a positive influence in her life.

And for some reason, Allie seemed to like to rile her up.

"Don't worry," Allie said, reading his hesitation in his eyes. "Lydia and I will be fine."

"Two words," Lydia said, watching Allie. "Duct. Tape."

Yeah. Gavin headed for the door.

He might be willing to storm into a wedding and carry the bride away, but he wasn't about to play into this...whatever it was between the girls. A guy had to have *some* sense of self-preservation.

He didn't take advantage of her. He didn't even wake her up.

Allie rolled over and blinked at the beam of sunlight that seemed determined that she be conscious at nine the next morning.

Nine.

She couldn't remember the last time she'd slept that late. The days since coming to Alaska not considered, of course.

She rolled to her back and stretched. Gavin had been there. She wasn't sure how she knew, but she did. But he definitely wasn't now.

He was probably already working.

He did a lot of that. And he seemed to love every minute of it.

Frowning, she pushed herself up out of bed. She didn't want to think about how much Gavin seemed to love Alaska and Bend. Nancy had said that he was still basically a newcomer, that everyone was waiting to see if he'd stick. But she knew Gavin. This was an adventure, a challenge. He'd stick. She knew it.

But he said he wanted to marry her. What did that mean? What was she supposed to do with that? If she said yes...well, she couldn't think about that. That was *way* too complicated.

Thinking about the puppies and polar bears in Gavin's life instead, she showered and dressed. This time when she pulled on an outfit that she'd bought just for her honeymoon, she felt only a tiny twinge of guilt. She counted that as progress. The truth was, she'd said yes to Josh for the wrong reasons, but he'd also asked her to marry him for the wrong reasons. They were equally wrong, she figured, and overall it was a good thing they hadn't gone through with it.

She brushed through her hair, letting her thoughts go to Josh and the Wedding That Wasn't. She didn't try to cut them off before the guilt took over. She just let her mind wander.

Knowing Josh, he was pissed. Not so much that she'd left him at the altar—she winced anyway, knowing that it had to be embarrassing if nothing else—but that she hadn't done what she'd promised to do. Josh Brewster had never made a promise in his life that he hadn't kept. She was pretty sure that Josh had lost all respect for her. Which hurt a little. She'd known Josh forever and he really had been there for her through the worst time in her life. But he deserved to be with someone who loved him...*really* loved him.

That made her thoughts drift to Devon.

And that made her sad.

She and Devon had been tight at one time. Allie didn't have a lot of girlfriends. She knew it was because she didn't have time to maintain another relationship in her life and she regretted that at times. But she wouldn't have traded the time she spent with her mom for a bunch of gab sessions over chai lattes with anyone. Her relationship with Gavin had cut into other relationships too. She was often busy or gone on evenings or weekends. But again, she wouldn't trade those times.

Still, it would be wonderful to have someone she could talk to about Gavin. A woman who could understand the love-panic thing he caused in her. A woman who'd maybe been there herself.

Devon had been crazy about Josh. And vice versa. Had Josh mixed Devon up the way Gavin did her? Well, he *had* been on the verge of marrying someone else. That had to have been tough.

Then again, Allie had called Devon when she and Josh started officially dating and again after Josh proposed. Both times Devon had said it was fine, that she was over Josh. Which meant Allie could *really* use her advice. How did someone get over the love of her life?

But did she want to be over Gavin? That was where things got tricky again and Allie forced her thoughts back to Devon. It wasn't like she was going to win any Best Friend of The Year awards, but thinking about her screwed-up relationship with Devon was easier than thinking about her whatever-the-hell-it-was relationship with Gavin.

Okay. Devon.

Devon was awesome. Devon was beautiful and smart and fun and...the perfect woman for Josh, frankly.

Maybe when she got back to the harbor, she'd invite Devon out for a chai latte and she could nudge them together. They probably wouldn't go out unless Allie told them it was okay. Sure, she'd gone off with Gavin, but Josh and Devon were better people than she was.

She'd be sure to tell them that she wouldn't mind a bit if they dated again.

That might even help Josh forgive her.

Allie frowned at that. Would Josh forgive her? Did she deserve to be forgiven?

Allie tossed her brush back into her bag and headed downstairs.

She was really getting into this whole I-don't-like-this-topic-so-I-just-won't-think-about-it thing.

Not sure where else to start looking for Gavin, she headed for the kitchen. Lydia was there, of course, and her back was to Allie as she stirred something in a big pot on the stove.

But Allie had no more stepped onto the ceramic tile and the girl said, "Don't even think about it."

"Geez, you have eyes in the back of your head?" Allie groused.

"I know all," Lydia said, not even turning.

"Where's Gavin?"

"Out."

"Out working?"

"Yeah." Lydia leaned to grab a bowl of what looked like chopped onions.

"For how long?"

"A while."

"I suppose you packed his schedule full in an attempt to keep him away from the house and drive me crazy."

"Pretty much."

Allie sighed. Loudly. "You're clearly a natural, but I've had more practice being annoying than you have." She guessed Lydia to be nineteen or twenty at the most. "I can do this all day. I've got nowhere to go and nothing to do."

Lydia finally glared at her over her shoulder. "What do you want?"

What *did* she want? She could *not* stay here while Gavin was out most of the day. If it was just her and that Wii in the other room, one of them was going to get hurt. And it might well be her. She was more out of shape than she'd realized. "I need something to do."

"So?"

"So, I figure either you tell me how to get to town, or you move over."

"Move over?"

"I was thinking about making cornbread."

Lydia turned to face her fully. "You're not making cornbread."

"It goes great with soup."

"Stew," Lydia said flatly.

"That too."

"My sourdough rolls are better."

Dang, that sounded good.

"My mom's cornbread was award winning," Allie said. Lily had won the Promise Harbor bake-off five years straight. "I know the recipe by heart."

Lydia crossed to the door that led in the opposite direction from the one that went to the clinic. She pulled a set of keys from a hook by the door. "Gavin bought the work truck when he got here, but kept his car." She tossed the keys to Allie and pulled the door open.

Allie caught the keys. Okay, she was going to town. Big surprise. "I need directions too. And," she pointed a finger at Lydia, "no getting me lost on purpose. I *will* make you regret that."

"Take a left at the end of the driveway. Go three miles. Take

169

a right and drive until you hit town. If you get lost, you're stupid."

Wow, Lydia *really* didn't want her around. At the moment, that was a good thing.

Allie started for the door, but Lydia didn't move. She was watching Allie contemplatively. Which made Allie nervous.

She stopped a good five feet away. "What?"

"There's something you need to hear."

Crap, what was this going to be? How happy Gavin was here in Alaska? How she was just using him to feel better but deep down she knew she had to go back to Massachusetts eventually? Yeah, she knew all of that.

She was also doing a really good job at ignoring it and would not appreciate Lydia bringing it all to the forefront of her consciousness, where she'd have to deal with it.

Allie crossed her arms and narrowed her eyes. Maybe she could intimidate Lydia into *not* telling her. "Oh, really?"

"Your mom wasn't perfect."

Okay, then. Definitely not intimidated. Allie dropped her defensive stance and drew up straight, staring at Lydia. "*What?*"

"She made your dad codependent, your brothers lazy and gave you a guilt complex." Lydia said it all coolly and evenly. There wasn't a mean tone in her voice or a resentful glare on her face. She just met Allie's gaze steadily.

Allie swallowed hard. "*How* do you possibly know all of that?"

"I've been Skyping with your brother."

If Allie had been shocked to hear this near-stranger talking—somewhat accurately—about her mother, she nearly fell over to hear mention of her brother. "*Excuse me?*"

"He got Gavin's number and called, but that was while you were still in bed." It was clear from Lydia's tone of voice that she thought that was a major sign of weakness.

Allie bit her tongue.

"He called again the next day, but not for you that time. We moved to Skype the next day."

"You've been talking to my brother since I got here?"

"Yeah."

"Which one?"

"The one that can't hold a job."

Allie gaped at her, Lydia's negative judgment of her forgotten, then glanced at the laptop that was never far from the girl. Clearly she'd overheard some of Allie's conversation about her family with Gavin last night.

"What have you talked about?"

"I told him he's too hot to be a loser."

"Um...wow." Lydia thought Charlie was hot? Charlie was twenty-five to Lydia's maybe-twenty. Then again, the girl was more grown up than some people twice her age. And Charlie definitely *wasn't* grown up.

"I also told him that everyone has a mom and that sometimes they die. It doesn't get to be his excuse for everything."

Allie had *no* idea what to say to that. There was definitely something not-all-that-subtle under Lydia's words...

"And he should be thankful for what he does have—a sister who gives a shit and a father who doesn't smack him around."

Allie worked on not wincing. Not all that subtle, for sure. That explained some, if not all, of the running away.

"And I told him that sometimes you have to make things happen the way you want them to if they don't happen that way on their own."

Allie shook her head. "I have no idea what to say."

"When we talked this morning he told me he'd gone to a job interview and he got it."

Allie looked at the clock. It was just after ten here, which made it two o'clock in the harbor. "How long did you talk last night?"

"About four hours," Lydia said.

Based on when she and Gavin had been talking on the couch, that had to have extended Lydia's conversation with Charlie well past midnight in Massachusetts. And he'd gotten up for an interview? And impressed someone?

"What's the job?" Maybe flipping burgers didn't require being fully awake.

"It's at the bank. It's entry level but there's a management program he can apply to after six months and start moving up."

Allie knew she was staring at Lydia like she was speaking a foreign language but...wow.

"I don't suppose you could work on getting Danny back in school."

Lydia nodded. "Charlie's going to talk to him."

Maybe the girl could cure cancer and end worldwide hunger while she was at it.

"I don't know what to say," Allie said for the second time.

"Well, I prefer you speechless," Lydia said. She swung the door wide open and then headed back for the stove.

Allie moved for the garage, feeling strangely dazed.

She got into Gavin's car, still processing all the information Lydia—of all people—had just given her. Lydia's mom had died, she had an asshole father and she was counseling Allie's brother. Charlie was a role model—for better or worse—for Danny. If Charlie got his act together, Danny really might follow.

But why was Charlie listening to a stranger on the computer?

Maybe because she was talking straight with him. Her mom had died too. She knew how that felt. Maybe because she was living what she said—if things didn't work out the way you wanted them to, you *made* them work out. She hadn't liked her home life so she'd left.

Running away wasn't always the answer but—Allie looked around at the Alaskan landscape as she followed the directions to town—she certainly couldn't throw stones here.

Gavin's driveway was really just a long dirt road—a long, bumpy dirt road. It went for at least two miles through the birch and spruce trees, and she took it slow over the bumps and dips. The road leading into Bend was wider. That was about the only improvement.

She finally got to town and decided to drive around and see what Bend had to offer.

That took five minutes.

The businesses all lined the main street and sported old-fashioned storefronts with painted wooden signs and wood-slatted front porches. It looked very much like it probably had back in the early nineteen hundreds.

She wasn't sure if the main street through town was actually called Main Street because there were no street signs. Then again, giving a specific address wasn't necessary to find a business. You just drove until you saw it. You'd eventually find everything—as long as you didn't blink.

It was clearly tourist season in Bend. Even though it was early in the day, people strolled up and down in front of the main shops. The farther down the street she went, the more the crowds thinned, until she reached the end and turned around. Visitors didn't have as much need for the hardware store, grocery store and bar at the end of the street as they did for the main cluster of shops that included the Outdoor Adventures office, the Alaskan Gifts shop, and the coffee shop. The main street boasted everything from bike rentals to rafting to helicopter rides to hiking tours, hunting and fishing suppliers, outdoor gear shops and local artists, including painters, jewelry makers and clothing.

Allie's destination, Denali Adventures Climbing School, was right in the middle of the west side of the street.

Climbing up a solid, unmoving, unchanging mountain still sounded like a great idea. Fun even. That's what she wanted and if it didn't just happen, or Gavin didn't set it up for her, she'd follow Lydia's advice and make it happen.

"Hi," she greeted the guy behind the counter of Denali Adventures with enough enthusiasm to make the good-looking twentysomething chuckle.

"Hi. Can I help you?"

"I want to climb a mountain."

"Well, I like you already."

She smiled. "What now?"

"How much experience to you have?"

"None. Well, rock walls," she said.

"You have any equipment?" he asked.

"Nope."

He grinned. "So we need a few classes."

Right. Probably. But she frowned slightly. Classes? "How many are you thinking?"

"That depends on how good you are and how fast you catch on."

Well, how hard could it be? You held on tight and headed in the general direction of "up". Seemed simple enough to understand.

An hour later, Allie was frustrated and sore. She'd forgotten—or had chosen not to remember—that she hadn't been very good at climbing rock walls.

"I think we have some work to do," Scott, as he'd introduced himself before the lesson started, said good-naturedly as he helped her down off of the small wall behind Denali Adventures.

It was a real, outdoor, honest-to-goodness rock wall, not manmade. And it was amazingly difficult. Or she sucked. Or both.

"How much work do you think?" she asked, trying not to breathe so hard. "I want to *actually* mountain climb. It sounds really fun."

Or at least it had an hour ago.

Scott smiled. "Some definite work. Climbing takes training, Allie. It's a fantastic sport, but you have to know what you're doing so you're safe, and you have to be in shape."

She pulled in a deep breath and wiped the sweat, that she shouldn't have even worked up at this point, off her forehead.

"You're fresh," he went on. "And I like your enthusiasm, but we're gonna have to take some time."

"I wanted to climb *today*," she said, unreasonably.

"Well, you did. Kind of." Scott gestured to the wall they used to train beginners. *Real* beginners. Like people who had never seen a mountain before. And her.

Yeah, she'd climbed today. Kind of. And it hadn't been all that fun.

Scott helped her get out of the equipment—something else she hadn't considered—and she said, "I'll let you know about the lessons."

It was going to be a big expense, for one thing. And, though she'd never admit it to him, Gavin might have been right about it being too soon after the pneumonia. She was way more tired than she should have been and it had taken way too long to catch her breath. And her shoulder hurt now.

"Hey, don't let today discourage you. It just takes some time and planning."

Planning. Planning was the antithesis of spontaneous. She knew all too well about planning.

She gave Scott her credit card and took his business card. If she decided to sit down ahead of time and plot and plan her next fun outing, she'd give him a call.

But it wasn't likely.

She'd plotted and planned enough to last her a lifetime. Her mom had been too busy taking care of everyone else to take care of things for herself—like funeral plans. And Allie's dad couldn't handle any of that. Hell, Allie planned out the week for her dad and brothers from meals to appointments to chores she needed help with around the house. Which was part of the reason she'd been unable to work up any interest or energy to plan her wedding.

She was *not* going to plot and plan for *fun*.

On that note, she stepped out onto the sidewalk, looking around. What sounded good? What was something she could just go *do*? Something that required no prethought, no reservations, no special equipment. Just something that felt good at the moment.

One sign on a storefront two blocks down, away from the touristy shops, caught her eye. It was another of the businesses that the people of Bend frequented but that was too rustic for visitors. It wasn't exactly new, but it did sound good at the moment.

The sign read simply *Saloon.*

Chapter Eight

Gavin took only one step between his truck and Denali Adventures before Scott Travis pointed down the street. He was grinning.

Gavin didn't have to look to know where Scott was pointing. The sign read *Saloon* in big red letters, but that was to keep up with the old-fashioned feel of the restored main street storefronts. The locals always had and always would call it The Hub.

It only took a second for his eyes to adjust to the dim light inside the bar.

Nick, the bartender, pointed to the table by the jukebox, but Gavin didn't need Nick to tell him where Allie was. He found her immediately.

For one thing, he was always incredibly aware of her, wherever they were. For another, there were only four other people in the place and none of them were female. Jack and Dodger were on their regular stools—which meant it was after ten a.m. The other two were twentysomethings from out of town. Gavin knew almost everyone in Bend—all eight hundred and sixty-two of them—and he'd never seen these guys before.

They looked from him to Allie, and Gavin figured they'd been paying attention to her since she'd walked in.

The fact that they sat three tables away told Gavin they either hadn't made a move yet, or they'd been shot down. He was good with either scenario.

"Tequila with a straw?" he asked, taking the chair across the tiny table from Allie.

She seemed to be brooding. "Sprite," she told him, stirring the clear liquid in her glass with the straw.

"Hard to get liquored up with no liquor," he commented.

She shrugged. "Knew I wouldn't be able to find my way back to your house sauced and knew Lydia wouldn't come for me."

She had a point.

"You okay?" he asked.

"Well, it's official. I can't have any fun without you."

"Glad to hear it." And he was. He loved being the one to make her smile.

She sighed heavily. "Yeah, but now you want to be all serious—not fun anymore. So where's that leave me?"

"I don't want to *just* be fun," he corrected.

"You said you wanted to be my vegetables," she reminded him.

"And vegetables aren't fun?" He sounded like an idiot, but she'd started this.

"Vegetables are an analogy," she said.

"Thank god."

"Vegetables are the serious stuff in life. That stuff that you have to deal with, even if you don't want to. And the fun stuff is...chocolate frosting. It's not *necessary*, it's extra, but it's wonderful." She stirred her soda again, seeming lost in thought. "Given the choice, ninety-five percent of people would pick chocolate frosting over broccoli any day."

He frowned. "And I'm the broccoli and you're in that ninety-five percent?"

She looked up. "No. *I'm* the broccoli."

Now he was confused. "What am I?"

"You're like carrot cake. A little bit of both."

He smiled. "Do you like carrot cake?"

She gave him a sad smile. "Love it."

Surprise rocked through him. He'd been working on the assumption that all of the emotions—including love—that they'd always freely talked about were still there. He'd heard her sing that she'd always love him. But she hadn't actually said it, until now.

He reached out and took her hand. "What am I missing

here?" he asked, sensing there was something. "I'm both good for you and fun. What's the problem?"

"*I'm* the broccoli," she said again. "And I can't be chocolate frosting."

"Then I'll be enough for both of us."

She shook her head. "What about my brothers, Dad, Josh, everyone?"

Gavin decided that he could happily live to age one hundred and twenty-seven and never hear Josh Brewster's name again. Ever.

"They need..." he prompted.

"Fun stuff, sweet stuff that's just *good*, not only what's good for them. But I'm broccoli. They put up with me because they do need me, but I'm not fun. They wouldn't pick me."

Okay, this was one of those moments he pretty much sucked at. He'd really rather go get her a can of frosting and a giant spoon and hope she'd feel better, but he knew he needed to say something. Something good.

"You could be frosting, Al." He wanted to be more broccoli-ish, himself. If he could do that, Allie could be more dessert-ish. Maybe.

She was serious. A worrier. An organizer. It was how she was wired. And there was nothing wrong with that. Unless she felt like there was.

"I don't know," she said. "Chocolate frosting is a lot to ask of broccoli."

"Well, how about you start with something smaller," he said with a smile. "Like whipped cream. Or even sprinkles. And work up to the frosting."

She thought about that—with an expression that was way more serious than a discussion about dessert toppings called for.

"Stop overthinking," he told her. "That would be a good start."

She wet her lips and nodded, then got up and held out her hand. "I'm going to practice on you."

He shoved his chair back and took her hand. "Happy to help." He had no idea what this was going to entail, but he was ready and willing.

She led him to the parking lot and stopped beside his truck. It wasn't hard to find. It was one of five trucks in the parking lot.

Gavin dug in his pocket for his keys.

"Do you remember Tim Carlson's party?" Allie asked.

He dropped the keys.

He stared at her. Did he remember her suddenly pulling him into the kitchen and going down on him in the corner, regardless of the fact that there was a houseful of people coming and going from the room?

"Um...yeah."

"That was pretty chocolate-frosting-like, don't you think?"

Jesus. Gavin closed his eyes and sucked a breath in through his nose. That had been chocolate frosting, whipped cream *and* sprinkles. With a cherry on top.

"Yeah. I'd say," he choked out, looking at her again. "Definitely chocolate-frosting-like."

She stepped close. "I'm in the mood for more. Right now."

She ran her hand up and down over his fly. The semi-erection he had going from just the mention of that near-public blow job surged fully to life.

"We almost got caught," she said, stroking him again.

Almost. Gavin gave a hoarse chuckle. Three guys had walked in on them, seen what was going on and left with huge grins. "No one stayed to watch, but we definitely got caught, babe," he told her.

Her eyes widened and her pupils dilated. "Really?"

"The whole party knew how lucky I was that night."

She pressed harder against the hard length behind his zipper and Gavin groaned. Did the idea of being seen like that turn her on?

She unsnapped and unzipped him before he could complete the thought—or even his next breath.

"How many people saw us?" she asked, slipping her hand inside the denim and cotton.

Her bare hand against him knocked the rest of the air out of his lungs.

"You never told me," she went on, stroking him as she spoke. "Did you like that they saw me doing that to you? Because the idea of someone watching me suck on you and lick you, seeing how much I want you, what I'm willing to do to please you, makes me hot, Gavin."

He grew harder in her hand and she smiled up at him slyly, clearly noticing.

"You kind of like it too, huh? You'd like for people to see what we do to each other." She looked down. "Let me do it here, Gavin. Just like this."

The woman he loved and wanted more than anything was begging to give him a blow job?

Was he an idiot?

He cupped the back of her head, staring into her eyes. "You want that, Allie? You want someone to come by and see what you do to me?"

She licked her lips. "Yes," she said breathlessly. "I want them to see how much I want you, how I'm willing to do anything, anywhere."

He kissed her roughly, his heart pounding and his cock throbbing. Then, still holding the back of her head with his hand in her hair, he looked up and down Main Street. Bend didn't even have—or need—a stoplight on their main drag. There simply wasn't enough traffic to pose a threat. The tourists mostly stayed on the east end of Main, but they occasionally wandered down here. They definitely could get caught.

He looked back at Allie. She was watching him, her eyes hot, her bottom lip caught between her teeth. "Tim's party was a little less of a risk," he reminded her.

She swallowed hard. "I know."

He looked deeply into her eyes. She was totally turned on. Gavin shook his head. "I didn't know this was a fantasy. I would have let the guys watch back then. I know they would have gladly stayed."

She gave him a naughty smile. "Sounds fun, doesn't it?"

He groaned. Turning Allie on was fun.

"Would you have wanted them to get involved?" He had no idea what he'd do with an answer of yes, but watching her breath catch was worth asking. He'd never been into sharing women and sincerely doubted he'd be *able* to share Allie, but he asked anyway.

She shook her head. "No. Not that. Just the watching. And it's just a fantasy. You're all I need or want. But the idea of showing the world that I'm all yours makes me..." her eyes dropped to where her hand was still in his pants, then back to meet his gaze, "...hot. And wet."

Gavin coughed as want swept over him.

Well, who was he to argue with that? Watching her eyes sparkle like they were now was irresistible. Even without knowing about the hot and wet part.

They were on the far side of the truck. Yes, they could get caught, but it was unlikely anyone would really *see* anything. They might assume a lot—but Gavin could definitely live with that. And even if they did see something—even everything—he wasn't so sure he'd mind that either. Having Allie want him like this was addictive. Addiction made people do crazy things.

His fingers curled gently into her scalp and his eyes met hers as he pressed just enough to encourage her to go to her knees in front of him.

They both moaned as she complied. Her hands went eagerly to his pants, tugging his fly open and pushing his briefs out of her way. He wasn't fully exposed—that was the one drawback to public sex, he supposed. Well, that and the risk of arrest, of course. But Allie didn't let his clothes slow her down. On her knees in the soft dirt outside The Hub, she took the head of his cock in her mouth without hesitation.

He grabbed for the rearview mirror to stay upright.

She licked up and down his length, swirled her tongue over the tip and then sucked him into her mouth again. The wet heat of her mouth was amazing all by itself, but Gavin couldn't lie—that she was on her knees in the parking lot made it even hotter.

He moved just enough to thrust in and out a few times, just enough to have heat racing through him from his cock to his toes. But he had no intention of finishing that way—or even going any further. When he hauled her to her feet, she protested and he shook his head. "You want more?"

She smiled and licked her lips. "You make me wanton."

"Happy to hear it." He spun her to face the truck and tucked himself back in, but didn't try to zip over his painfully hard erection that would probably just get worse here in a minute.

"Brace yourself," he whispered hoarsely in her ear.

She put her hands on the side of the truck, palms flat, a shiver going through her body.

He gathered her hair to one side, exposing her neck. He kissed along the sensitive skin behind her ear to the spot where it curved into her shoulder, then he bit down gently.

She gasped, her hips wiggling against his groin. He was already hard, but that friction made him suck in a quick breath. He settled one hand on her hip to keep her still. He was going to drive her crazy but had to keep his own cool.

The truck was parked so that anyone coming out the front door of The Hub could see them. They'd be able to see the way he slid his hand up under her shirt to palm her breast, the way she arched into him, the way her head fell back when he played with her nipple.

Of course, there weren't many people in Bend who came to The Hub this early. Still...

"Someone could walk out at any minute," he said gruffly as he tugged on her right nipple.

"I know," she gasped. But she definitely didn't try to pull away. Her breathing was ragged.

He lifted her shirt, exposing the left cup of her bra. The air wasn't cool, but she shivered and Gavin grinned. He pulled the cup down and she moaned.

"The next person to come out will see all of this," he

reminded her, fueling the fantasy—that could be quite real at any moment. He rolled her nipple between thumb and forefinger.

She moaned again, louder.

"They'll see how gorgeous you are, how much you love having my hands on you, how hot I make you."

She looked toward the door, nearly panting.

"You really do love this, don't you?" he asked, actually surprised.

She shook her head but she made no move to cover up.

"I didn't know you were an exhibitionist." He didn't mind. He hadn't known *he* was an exhibitionist either, but he suddenly didn't care if a crowd gathered. He wouldn't mind if the whole town saw this gorgeous, amazing woman pleasuring him and letting him have her body however he wanted it. He felt like a fucking king. Even more, he wanted the *world* to know that *he* was the guy she let close, let touch her, who brought out the lust in her, made her wild. Allie was coming apart in *his* hands. They could put that on national TV if they wanted to.

"I didn't know I was either," she whispered back to him. "But..."

He moved his free hand to the front of her jeans and unsnapped and unzipped. "I have to feel how hot you are."

She moved her feet further apart and he smiled. He slipped his hand in front of her jeans, past the silk of her panties and down into the wet heat that proved she was right with him.

Her head dropped forward as he slid his finger in and out, then up over her clit.

"*Gavin*," she groaned.

He slid his finger deep, stroking long and slow, pressing his erection against her butt. He felt her clench around his finger and knew she was thinking about being watched.

"Damn." He stroked over her clit again and thumbed her nipple. "You want to have spectators, Al?" He growled. "'Cause I'll take you back in there and lay you out on the pool table and fuck you in front of everyone if it will make you scream."

Her muscles clenched again and she gasped. He had no

idea she had this fantasy. Would *he* really do something like that? He wasn't sure. It would definitely push his boundaries, but if it made Allie happy, he'd consider it.

"Maybe I should just call the guys out here?"

She pressed back against him, breathing faster.

"Those young guys could stand right over there on the porch," he said huskily. "They would be able to see your nipple, see my fingers stroking you, see the way you spread your legs for me and the way you beg me for more."

Her breathing grew choppy and he felt her grow hotter and wetter.

"They could watch me get you off just like this. Or," he said against her neck, "I could strip you down, open my fly and thrust into you from behind. I could make you come around my cock instead while they stroke themselves, watching you lose your mind right here against my truck."

Allie cried out, clenching around his fingers, her orgasm making her whole body tremble.

After she went completely stiff, she slumped forward, her forearms on the edge of the truck bed, her head on her arms, breathing hard.

Gavin slipped his hand from her jeans and pulled the cup of her bra to cover her before letting her shirt fall back into place.

"Home. Now," he said. Jerking the truck door open and practically throwing her onto the seat before jogging to the driver's side. They'd get his car later. He wasn't letting her get more than an arm's length away from him right now.

They didn't make it even two miles. Gavin pulled over—well off the road so no one would think they'd had car trouble this time—and pulled Allie into his lap. After only a minute of fumbling with clothes, he pushed up into her.

She rode him until they came together seemingly moments later.

"Holy crap," Allie said after she'd caught her breath.

He chuckled, stroking his hand over her hair. "Guess we'll have to start over for the guys."

She pulled back and grinned at him. "I appreciate the offer. But I'm good with keeping that just in my imagination."

She climbed back into her own seat so they could have some space to readjust their clothing. As she'd needed to pull one entire leg of her jeans off, it took some time and squirming to get everything back in place.

Watching her bend and wiggle made Gavin eager to get home. It was about time he made love to her in his bed.

He shifted the truck into gear and said, "You know—we just chocolate frosting-ed the hell out of each other."

She looked up from rebuttoning and grinned proudly. "And I started it."

Gavin laughed. "You most certainly did." He pulled the truck back onto the road. "In fact, I don't know that I'll ever be able to eat another piece of cake without getting an erection."

But her laughter and the way she took his hand as they drove was what really got to him. That was better than sex *with* chocolate frosting.

And that was saying something.

They fell into a routine for the next few days that seemed just about perfect.

Allie slept late while Gavin got up and went into the clinic for patients. When she finally wandered downstairs she always found breakfast waiting for her—muffins, yogurt parfaits, and, of course, oatmeal. Lydia was never around—probably a good thing—but Allie had decided to make a truce with the girl. She went into the kitchen only for food Lydia had prepared specifically for her—she knew because there was always a piece of paper that said "Allie" beside the plate or bowl—and she tidied up when she left the room.

After breakfast she made a habit of taking a long walk on Gavin's land. She explored hills—definitely no mountains—and the stream that ran through his property. The views were gorgeous, the air clean and the quiet and solitude restful.

Until one evening when Lydia mentioned the possibility of

running across a bear.

Allie stayed a lot closer to the house after that.

At lunchtime she and Gavin would meet up in the kitchen. Lydia was generally there, preparing the salads and sandwiches and soups and starting dinner, so they didn't have time to get too frisky. There were some stolen kisses, some sexy innuendos, even a few less-than-innocent touches when Lydia wasn't looking, but the one time they tried to make a good excuse to go up to the bedroom together, Lydia put her foot down.

"If you're going to have sex in the middle of the day, tell me so I can bump the patients back to two o'clock," she said sternly.

"I don't need two hours," Gavin had protested with a grin.

Lydia had looked from him to Allie and said, "Sorry to hear that."

After that, sex in the middle of the day was off the table. So to speak.

Allie spent the first afternoon around the house. But, predictably, that drove her crazy. So the next two days, she explored Bend. She checked out the bookstore, the antique shop, the sewing and craft shop, and the coffee shop/ice cream parlor.

She did yoga when she returned to the house and then read until Gavin was finished in the clinic. Then they spent the rest of the evening together—unless Gavin got called out to see a patient, which happened three of the five nights—and then made love until they fell asleep, exhausted and happy.

The following Tuesday, Allie awoke with a smile for the sixth morning in a row. She stared up at the ceiling. She'd never slept this much. Or this well. She hadn't eaten this well or exercised this much or relaxed this much in...ever.

She stretched, feeling amazing.

That was followed by the jab of guilt, then worry, before she succeeded in stuffing those emotions down deep.

She couldn't feel guilty about not being at home to make breakfast and organize everyone's days. Lydia said Charlie and Danny were doing great and their dad was "fine".

Fine.

She frowned. What did that mean exactly? Fine wasn't bad. But it also wasn't great.

She rolled and pushed herself out of bed. Her dad hadn't called her. He could have easily gotten Gavin's number from Charlie. He was clearly not worried and didn't need to ask her how much soap to put in the washing machine or where he'd put the checkbook. Either he really was fine or he wasn't washing clothes or paying bills.

Maybe he wasn't calling because he hadn't paid his phone bill and his service had been canceled.

Allie was still stubbornly avoiding her cell phone and the texts and voice mails waiting for her. Gavin said he'd told Hayley to let everyone know she was all right, and Lydia kept Charlie updated. That was good enough. Apparently for her father too.

Allie forced herself to calm down as she pulled her hair up and stepped into the shower. She wasn't actually worried about the laundry or bills. If something happened, Charlie would ask Lydia and she'd tell him how to fix it.

Allie had walked into the kitchen two nights ago to find Lydia on the computer with Charlie. She was showing him and Danny how to put together a PowerPoint presentation.

She'd said a quick hi to her brothers and heard that Dad was "fine" again, before she completely lost their interest to the younger, cute, nonsister girl in the room.

So Lydia could take care of whatever they needed.

That was fine.

Kind of.

Trying to come up with something that Lydia couldn't coach her intelligent-in-spite-of-how-they-act-brothers in, she almost ran the girl over.

Lydia was standing at the bottom of the stairs—did she have Allie under video surveillance or something?—holding a plate.

Allie stopped on the bottom step, literally unable to pass.

She couldn't believe Lydia and Charlie had started up a

friendship. Or whatever it was. But, strangely, since learning they were talking and that he had a new job, Allie realized she wasn't really worried about her brothers. She was—*annoyed* she supposed was the best term—that they seemed to suddenly need someone they barely knew more than they needed their own sister. But there was something to be said for having the attention of a non-relative girl their age. Who was cute. Even when she wasn't smiling. Of course, Allie had noticed that Lydia smiled a lot when she was on the computer with Charlie.

Truthfully, though, it was nice that someone was keeping track of them. And it felt nice for it not to be her.

"What's this?" Allie indicated the plate.

"Spinach, mushroom and Swiss omelet."

Allie's stomach growled on cue. She checked out the breakfast. There was a side of fruit—oranges, grapes and strawberries—and a toasted English muffin too.

Allie crossed her arms. If Lydia got her all excited about the food, then said it wasn't for Allie, she might have to smack her.

"Sounds good."

Lydia handed her the plate. "Here."

"Why so nice this morning?" But Allie took the plate, then stepped up two steps, out of Lydia's reach.

"Gavin's upset."

Allie was prepared for a smart-ass comment, so it took her a second to process Lydia's words. "Upset?"

Lydia nodded, looking worried. Not annoyed, not bored, not irritated, not resigned. Worried.

"What's he upset about? And what does that have to do with my breakfast?"

The food Lydia left her every morning was delicious, but this was beyond anything she'd done so far.

"He got a call this morning," Lydia said.

Was he upset *at* Lydia? If Lydia was kissing up to Allie, hoping she'd put in a good word, it was probably too little too late. Still, Allie would hear her out.

"You need to talk to him," Lydia added.

"About what?"

"The call. Make him feel better."

Allie looked closer at the younger girl. She was worried, but maybe not about her fate. She was worried about Gavin.

"Have you talked to him?" Allie asked. "What's going on?"

Lydia shook her head. "Gavin and I don't do that."

"You don't talk?"

"Not about serious personal stuff."

Allie's eyes widened. "This is personal?"

"I guess. I don't know." Lydia actually seemed shaken up by the whole thing. "The call was from the zoo."

"The zoo?"

"In Anchorage. He does some work there sometimes. That's where the bears are."

Allie stepped down the two bottom steps. "The bears?"

Lydia rolled her eyes—well, that was more in character at least—and said, "The polar bears. The twins."

Ah. The polar bear cubs. Right. They were at the Anchorage zoo. "What did Gavin say after the call?"

"Nothing. But he threw his coffee cup against the kitchen wall, swore and stomped off to his office."

Allie's gaze flew to the door to the clinic. That image worried her a little too. Gavin never really got pissed off like that. He didn't *throw* things, anyway.

"Nancy tried to talk to him but he told her to leave him alone. And *I'm* not going in there. But someone should."

Allie looked back to Lydia. "Me?"

"Who better?"

Allie narrowed her eyes suspiciously. "Because I might get yelled at and you'd enjoy that?"

"Because you make him happy," Lydia said in a tone that indicated Allie was being particularly dumb. "He's a lot happier since you've been here."

Allie blinked. That was almost a compliment. From Lydia. "Wow. Saying stuff like that makes it less likely you'll need bribes to get me in there," Allie said, holding up the plate of eggs.

"It's not a bribe," Lydia said, turning back to the kitchen. "You might need the sustenance. I've never seen him like this and you're kind of puny."

Allie started to protest, then thought better of it and took two big bites of the best omelet ever made before pulling in a deep breath and starting for the hallway to the clinic. She set the plate on the counter for Lydia, wiped her palms on her pants and opened the door.

Gavin's friend, Carter, was on the other side, also reaching for the door.

"Allie. Hi."

"Hi, Doc."

"How are you feeling?" he asked.

"Better. Not quite up to mountain climbing, but better."

He smiled. "I heard you started lessons."

Lord, Bend was faster on the grapevine than Promise Harbor could ever hope to be.

Of course, it was one-twentieth the size.

"One lesson. I think I'm good for now."

"Scott's usually able to charm everyone into at least the basic package."

"Yeah?"

"He's good-looking, funny...you didn't notice?" Carter gave her a knowing smile.

Huh. She hadn't.

Well, she'd noticed he was good-looking in a matter-of-fact kind of way. Not in a wow-he's-good-looking way.

"Guess not."

"Good."

She smiled. She could tell Carter that she noticed and remembered every sigh, smile and kiss from Gavin. But instead she asked, "Did you talk to him?"

Carter shook his head. "Nancy called me after he locked his office door but he told me to fuck off."

"What could this be about?" she asked.

This was so not the Gavin she was used to.

"I'm guessing the twins aren't doing well. They were pretty sick when the team brought them in and they are, after all, wild animals. Survival of the fittest and all. They wouldn't have made it in the wild, but this was a gamble too."

Allie pressed her hand over her heart. "What was wrong with them?"

"They'd been orphaned," Carter said with a shrug. "They were starving to death when Gavin found them. Some of the team tried to talk him out of bringing them in, but he insisted and convinced the zoo to try to rehab them."

Allie blew out a long breath. Okay, *that* was the Gavin she knew and loved.

And now the tables were turned. Gavin needed her now. She could do this.

She just wished she knew if he needed broccoli or chocolate frosting at the moment.

She knocked on the door to his office, remembering Lydia's words about Allie making him happy.

Whether she'd meant it as a pep talk or not, it did help when he bellowed, "Just leave me the fuck alone, Carter."

She cleared her throat. "It's me."

There was a long pause with no sound. Then the door swung open. She started to smile, but couldn't do it as she looked into his face. She knew how it *felt* to look like he did.

She also knew exactly what he meant about not knowing what to say.

So she just stepped forward and wrapped her arms around him.

He caught her to him, holding tight, his nose in her hair, breathing deep.

She just held him, wracking her brain for words and coming up with nothing.

Finally, he pulled back. She hated the look of sadness in his eyes. "What happened?"

"One of the twins died," he said.

Her heart ached for him. "I'm sorry." She kept her arms around him.

He gave a humorless laugh. "It's stupid to be this upset. Especially compared to—"

"No," she cut in, "it's not stupid."

"But your mom—"

"Gavin, it's okay for you to be sad about this. It doesn't have anything to do with my mom."

He pulled her fully against him again and just breathed.

They stood like that for a couple of minutes, until Gavin said, "Go away, Carter."

"So, you're okay?" his friend asked from behind Allie.

"Yes."

Then Carter said simply, "You got it."

The door swung shut and Gavin pulled back. "I'm okay."

"You sure?" She felt very inadequate. She had no words, no way to make this better.

"It was mostly just a surprise," he said, pushing his hand through his hair. "I called down to arrange to take you behind the scenes to meet the bears when we go for the festival. The zoo stays open late that night and has some stuff going on for the public, but I wasn't sure who'd be there and if they'd let me in if they didn't know me. I figured Dr. Thompson could make the arrangements ahead of time for us to get our hands on the girls."

It must have hit him that he wasn't going to be able to do that again with one of them. He sucked in a shaky breath and Allie knew exactly the stab of pain he was feeling. Those moments when the truth snuck up and smacked her really sucked.

"You want to talk about it?" she asked.

She was fine if he *didn't*. If he did...hell, she had no idea what to say or do in that case. Damn.

This really was hard. She felt a new sympathy for all the people who'd tried to be sensitive to her and her family.

He shrugged. "Not too much to say. It was a risk from day

one. I knew that."

He looked at his desk. The scrapbook she'd looked at the other day was laid out on top.

"Knowing it doesn't make it less painful," she said. "Sometimes people think that it's easier when you can plan for it, but when they're gone, they're gone. That still hurts like hell."

He was watching her intently, his hands in his pockets. "Do you think about her all the time?"

Allie nodded. "Every day. But it's at weird times now. Like I'll think of how much she liked something or wonder what she'd think of something."

"I'm really sorry she's gone." The sincerity in his voice caused an instant lump in her throat.

But this was supposed to be about *him*. She wanted to make him feel better. "What can I do?" she asked. "You want to go to Anchorage?" That had been the plan for after lunch.

He shook his head. "Nah. There's nothing I can do there. I'm going to...work." He gestured toward the door. "I'll probably talk to one of my team members later and let her know what happened to Allie."

Allie pulled up tall. "Who?"

He gave her a rueful smile. "Mandy and I found the twins so we each got to name one. I named mine Allie."

She was strangely touched by that. And strangely jealous of Mandy. She'd be able to truly share this with Gavin. She might even know the right thing to say or do to make him feel better.

"I have a couple things to do in the clinic, then I'll come find you. Maybe we can go out."

"Sure, whatever you want," she said.

He smoothed a hand over her hair. "Thanks. You make me feel better."

She gave him a bright, fake smile and headed for the house.

What a bunch of crap, she thought as she walked away. She hadn't done one thing to help him or make him feel better.

She paced into the kitchen, slamming the door behind her.

"What happened?" Lydia asked, immediately more attentive to Allie than she'd ever been.

"Nothing." Allie slumped onto a kitchen stool. "I hugged him and told him I was sorry."

"He let you in," Lydia pointed out. "That's good."

"Big deal." Allie scowled at the floor.

"Just being there made him feel better," Lydia told her confidently.

"Oh, sure, my magical healing powers," Allie scoffed. She hadn't been on this side of this stuff before. Certainly never with Gavin. As they'd talked about before, they didn't do this stuff. She got stressed out and Gavin made her have fun. That was their recipe for—everything.

Lydia frowned at her. "You don't think someone can make you feel better just by being there?"

Allie shrugged. She wanted to *do* something for him, somehow give him something he needed.

Was this how he'd always felt? Like just being there wasn't enough? That there had to be some *action*, some effort, some gesture?

And was it true? If he'd just been there and held her and listened to her talk it out, would that have been enough?

Possibly. But she wasn't *sure*. They just hadn't tried it that way.

"It happens," Lydia said firmly. "Just knowing someone *wants* you to feel better can help."

"Well, that makes me feel pretty damned helpless."

Lydia nodded. "I think that's part of the deal."

"The deal?"

"Loving someone."

Allie stared at the girl. Lydia was studying the countertop with fierce concentration. "What about loving someone?"

"I think feeling helpless sometimes makes you realize how much you care. When you want to help them so damned bad but can't...makes you think of all the things you'd be willing to do if you could. And when you realize what's on that list, you realize how much you love them."

Allie swallowed hard. "What was on your list with your mom, Lydia?"

She looked up, not seeming surprised Allie knew she'd been talking about her mom. "I would have taken her place," she said without hesitation. "The surgery, the chemo, the whole thing."

Emotions slammed into Allie. Chemo. It had been cancer for Lydia's mom too. Allie blew out a breath. She knew those emotions well—that clawing need in her gut to fix things, to save her mom, to *do* something.

And now Gavin.

"Think about it," Lydia said. "If we *could* fix everything, we'd never understand how far we'd be willing to go. And I think that's a good thing to know."

Allie nodded. She had to. Lydia was right.

The need to protect everyone she loved all the time still burned deep down and always would, she was sure. She'd never be able to fix it all. No one could. But being willing to do everything *in her power* to make it better mattered.

It mattered to her that Gavin had done that for her. She'd always known that he'd do everything he could, anything she asked. It hadn't fixed it all. But it had mattered that he tried.

And now more than ever, she understood his need to try.

"Do we have any Froot Loops?" she asked Lydia.

Lydia looked surprised. "Um, yeah. Gavin just asked me to get some the other day."

"Perfect. We won't need lunch."

"But—"

"Lydia," Allie said, finally putting her foot down. "He's mine to take care of. He needs Froot Loops right now and you're just gonna have to get over it."

Lydia pressed her lips together. Then finally gave Allie a nod. "Okay."

Chapter Nine

By the time Gavin made it back to the house, Allie had logged on to his laptop and into her Netflix account and found some old TV episodes on demand. She met him at the door in her pj's. She handed him a spoon and a bowl and then took his other hand.

He looked down at the cereal, then back to her. Then to the tent she'd constructed in the living room by pushing furniture together and draping blankets over the couches, chairs and tables.

And finally, he smiled.

The relief was crazy. Was this how he'd felt all those times she'd come home from the harbor? The rush of *Thank god*? The thrill of being the one to get the smile? The burn to do anything and everything necessary to fix whatever was wrong?

Wow. It really could be addictive.

"Thanks," was his simple response.

She held up the side of the tent and gestured for him to crawl in.

"Just a warning," she said, following him on hands and knees, "when Lydia helped me get the blankets, I promised we wouldn't have sex under here."

He grinned and started to respond, but the TV screen, paused on the first episode of his favorite TV show, caught his attention.

"*Big Bang Theory*?"

She laughed. Looked like there was no risk of grossing Lydia out now that his attention was firmly on episode one, season one.

"I know you said cartoons, but that's me. You need this."

Gavin settled back against the pillows she'd propped along the front of the couch for that purpose.

"Ah," he sighed. "This really is a great idea."

He took a big bite of cereal and she hit play, then settled in next to him and munched on her own Froot Loops.

They were starting the third episode when Allie realized what had happened. This was a lot like the scenario Gavin had wanted to create the night with the movie and lasagna—the quiet time together, just *being*, like a normal couple.

She thought about it as he chuckled at the show, and she felt that same relief and contentment she had before. He was okay, good even, in part because of her. She liked this. And just sitting here doing nothing in particular was also good.

Allie leaned into him, running her hand over his chest as she soaked up the emotions of the moment, along with the feel, smell and sound of Gavin.

She liked the idea of being there when Gavin's day, week or just life in general went sucky. Or maybe it was more that she hated the idea of *not* being there. When he was sad, upset, hurt...or even happy. It had definitely felt good to be the one he'd opened the door for.

She wanted to do this forever.

Forever.

For*ever.*

The thought sank in slowly, but when it—and all it really meant—hit her consciousness, she sat up quickly, knocking the corner of the sheet off the arm of the chair.

Just like that, the outside world flooded into their cocoon.

"Al?"

His husky voice made her press her lips together.

"Yeah?"

"You okay?"

How did he know that she might not be? He had been absorbed in the show.

She turned to look at him and knew immediately how he sensed something had changed—he was in tune with her and she with him. They were connected. Somehow. Inexplicably. On a level she hadn't even known existed until Gavin.

How could she not be with him forever?

But how could she?

His life was here. This was vacation for her. A few days ago he'd insisted that wasn't true, but she'd just—typically—ignored that rather than deal with it. Now it was right in front of her and...she didn't know what to do.

"I have to...get a refill," she said, scrambling to her feet before he could detain her—or do something that would make her want to stay even more. She made an even bigger mess of the blankets, tripping over one that wrapped around her ankle as if trying to keep her in place.

"Allie—"

But she didn't stop, didn't even look back—because that was all it would have taken for her to dive right back in and never leave.

She was shaking a little as she headed into the kitchen. She couldn't stay. She *couldn't* stay. This was *Alaska*. On a map, two places didn't get much farther apart than Bend and Promise Harbor. And she wanted to be in Promise Harbor.

Swallowing hard, she made herself at least admit the truth to *herself*—she *needed* to be in Promise Harbor. Not so much wanted to be.

The question became—could she more easily live with the guilt of *not* going home or the heartbreak of leaving Gavin?

Lost in thought, she didn't notice Lydia sitting at the center island in the kitchen until she heard her brother's voice.

Allie spun to find Charlie's face filling up Lydia's laptop screen. Lydia's back was to her, and for the girl who was aware of everything—especially Allie's moves—to not notice that Allie had set foot on sacred ground meant that she was completely absorbed in her conversation with Charlie.

Knowing she was eavesdropping, but unable to stop, Allie watched them for a minute.

"I have three," Lydia said.

"Where?" Charlie asked.

There was something light and teasing in his tone. Something that Allie hadn't heard in his voice for a very long time. Of course, there hadn't been a lot to be light and teasing about for a long time.

And maybe that was partly her fault. The thought hit her suddenly and Allie frowned. She knew she'd ridden both Charlie and Danny hard in the past year, but...she glanced toward the living room...had anyone made sure they also smiled and laughed and let go of the sad, serious stuff?

Allie leaned slightly, wanting to see her brother's face, but not wanting him to notice her in the background. He was clearly in their kitchen in the harbor—she'd recognize the bright white cupboards with glass fronts anywhere. In fact, those cupboards brought a lump to her throat.

Damn.

Lydia giggled and Allie drew upright. A *giggle*?

"I don't think I should tell you."

Charlie grinned, obviously focused enough on Lydia to not notice Allie—or anything else.

"Why not? I'm going to wonder and use my imagination if you don't."

Lydia laughed again. "Okay, where do you think they are?"

"I hope there's one on your hip," he said without pause.

Allie's eyes widened.

"You hope so?" Lydia asked. "Why?"

"'Cause that's sexy as hell."

Allie's eyes got wider and her mouth opened. She'd never heard her brother use the word "sexy" in her life.

"And it fits you," he added.

"It does?" Lydia asked.

It *did*?

"Definitely. If you don't have a sexy little angel tattooed on your hip, I want you to go out and get one tomorrow."

There was that giggle again, but Allie hardly noticed.

Her *brother* was talking to *Lydia* about being sexy and having tattoos? And imagining where they were on her body?

"An angel?" Lydia asked.

"Yeah," Charlie said, his voice a little gruff. "A cute little innocent cartoon angel girl...completely at odds with the naughty stuff you like."

Oh god. Enough eavesdropping. *Clearly* this was more than Lydia talking to Charlie about their dead mothers and his lack of ambition. However it had started, it was now at a very new and different level. One that Allie did *not* need to know about.

She backtracked outside the kitchen, then made a lot more noise coming in this time.

Lydia spun on the stool to face Allie. "Oh, hi!" she said too brightly.

Way too brightly considering she rarely smiled at Allie.

"Hi."

"Allie, that you?"

She leaned in, trying to pretend she was surprised to see her brother—and pretend she was not aware that he was aware that Lydia had a naughty streak. "Charlie?"

"Hey, girl."

"How are you?" She resisted asking about the job, asking about how messy the house was, and asking what grade Danny had in his English class.

"Great. I'm great," Charlie said.

And she believed him.

"You look great," he said with mild surprise.

"I...do?" That gave her pause. Charlie didn't say stuff like that to her. It must mean she looked *different.*

"Definitely. You're not pale and skinny. You looked like crap at the wedding."

Ah, well, leave it to a little brother to take the shine off of a compliment quickly.

"Thanks," she said wryly.

He chuckled and she found herself smiling at the sound.

"No, seriously. You look good. Lydia said you've been taking it easy."

Lydia coughed and Allie narrowed her eyes. So they had

been discussing *her* as well. And Lydia commented she was "taking it easy"? She might like to know that Allie routinely got up at five a.m., went to bed at midnight and barely sat down during the hours between.

"I've been sleeping in, working out and eating well." There, that was as close as she was going to get to giving Lydia any credit. She also left off the lots-of-great-sex and falling-in-love-all-over-again part of the equation. He was her little brother. He didn't need *every* detail.

"Good for you. Keep it up," Charlie said.

Then she couldn't resist one question. "How's Dad?"

"He's great too, I guess."

Uh-huh. It was the "I guess" that got her. "Is he eating?"

"I'm sure he is," Charlie said with a chuckle.

"Are you doing laundry?"

"You've only been gone a little over a week," Charlie pointed out.

"Meaning?"

"I've got enough clothes to go a couple weeks."

Allie gritted her teeth and tried to tell herself it didn't matter. She didn't need to get on him. He was the one who'd be smelling bad—or going naked—if he didn't take care of the laundry. But she just couldn't let it go. "What about Dad?"

Charlie sighed. "He's *fine*, Allie. I talked to him on Sunday and they were having a nice time."

"*Sunday?*" Allie repeated. "Why haven't you talked to Dad in three days?"

"They left on Saturday."

"They *left*? Who left?"

"Dad and Sophie."

Allie was sure her expression was comical, but she felt her heart stop and then restart with a hard thump that she felt through her whole body. "Dad and Sophie are...where did they go...why?" She stumbled through all her questions at once.

"They went up to Greenbush Island. They were just going to spend a few days, getting away."

She took a deep breath. It wasn't like they'd run away and not told anyone. Obviously her dad had his cell phone if he and Charlie had talked. He was with someone who knew him well and cared about him. She told herself all of those reasonable, rational things. But her blood pressure continued to rise. "Josh thought this was okay?" She was *so* calling her ex-fiancé. If he *did* think this was okay, she was going to have to yell at him. If he didn't, she was still going to yell at him for not stopping them.

"I don't know if Josh knows. He wasn't here when they left."

She froze. "*What?*"

"Josh wasn't here when Dad and Sophie decided to go," Charlie repeated.

"Where was he?" Surely Charlie meant that Josh hadn't been there at the exact minute they'd decided to take off. He wouldn't really be *gone*.

"He took off the same day you did, sis," Charlie said. "He's been gone. Just got home Saturday."

Allie felt a little dizzy. Josh hadn't been there to take care of things? And something was going on with her dad and Sophie. And Charlie was having cybersex with Lydia.

Allie put a hand to her forehead.

All hell was breaking loose.

Because of course it was.

Allie had been gone far longer than it took to get a drink refill, and Gavin had finally waited long enough.

There'd been something going through her mind when she suddenly sat up and bolted. He had no idea what, but after a reasonable amount of time without her returning, he knew he needed to go after her. Either something was going on in her head, or she and Lydia were destroying his kitchen.

She was in the kitchen with Lydia, all right, but they weren't fighting.

Lydia was chewing on her bottom lip, watching Allie worriedly.

And he saw immediately why—Allie looked like she was going to faint, throw up or throw *something*. Or all three.

"Al?" He went straight for her.

"Bye, Charlie," he heard Lydia say quickly.

He glanced over to watch her close her computer screen, grab the laptop off the counter and head for her bedroom.

Uh-oh.

"I have to go home."

Allie's voice wavered and he stopped with several feet still between them.

The words were not at all what he'd been expecting. Gavin had to concentrate so hard on what she'd said that he couldn't even put one foot in front of the other. He drew up short and just stared at her.

"Gavin? Did you hear me?" she asked, coming forward. "I have to go. To Promise Harbor. Right away."

"What's going on?" Concern finally overrode his shock.

"Dad's gone." She looked like she was equally pissed and worried.

"What do you mean gone?"

"He left town. With Sophie."

"Sophie? Josh's mom? Are they...involved?" Okay, that could be a little awkward for Allie.

"I don't know!" She paced a few steps, then turned back to him. "I don't know anything. Charlie just said they were gone. He doesn't even know for how long. And apparently Josh took off after the wedding." Now she looked more pissed.

Um, yeah, actually Gavin knew that. Hayley had told him that Josh had left shortly after the wedding fiasco. Telling Allie her fiancé had run off with his ex might not be a good move at the moment. Telling Allie he'd known about that all along would definitely not be a good move at the moment. Shit.

She ran a hand over her forehead. "I assumed he was there with Dad, making sure things were okay. And now Josh is back in town, but Dad's gone. Now...I don't know. No one's really making sure anything's okay."

"Your brothers are there."

"I told you that they're *not* holding things together," she said. "I have to go."

Fuck.

Promise Harbor. How could such a small place—relatively speaking—so far away cause him so many problems?

"Allie, you don't have to go. They'll figure it out. They need to learn to cope without you."

She focused on him with a frown. "Why? Why do they need to learn to cope without me?"

"Because..." he suddenly felt like maybe he needed to proceed with caution here, "...you're not there."

"Which is why I need to *go*."

"But..." Okay, he was about to sound like a jackass. He figured knowing that made it slightly better. Slightly. Maybe. "You're here. With me."

She narrowed her eyes. "Yes. At the moment."

At the moment. That sounded a lot less permanent than he wanted it to. He gritted his teeth, then said, "When are you going to let go of them?"

She sucked in a quick breath, her eyes going wide. Several seconds passed with no sound. Then she said, "Let go of them?"

He knew he should just shut up. If he didn't, they were going to fight. But this had been the elephant in the room since she'd gotten here. He'd even talked about marrying her without talking about this directly.

He couldn't shut up.

He wanted her. She wanted him. Life here was good and good *for* her. God knew, having her here with him was what he needed more than anything.

He couldn't just shut up and let her leave. If what he was going to say made it hard for her to choose, then good. He didn't want it to be easy. Unless she chose him, of course.

"They're not your responsibility, Al. They're your family. They're your dad and your brothers—your life isn't supposed to revolve around them. If you go home to them, you're giving up what you really want and need. You shouldn't have to do that. You have a right to a happy, fulfilling life."

"What am I giving up if I go home to them?" she asked, her voice gruff. She was holding herself stiffly, her arms crossed tightly across her stomach.

He knew that she knew what his answer was going to be, but she was going to make him say it.

"Me."

"Because if I go home, we're done, right?" she asked.

"My life is here," he said stubbornly, sounding like an ass but seemingly unable to help it.

Yes, he had bad feelings about his hometown. He kept in touch with his mom, heard from his brothers at times, but he didn't expect to reconcile with his father. His past, for better or worse, was in Promise Harbor, but his future was...somewhere else. He'd accepted that a long time ago.

But even more, he was concerned about Allie going home. If it was a visit, if it was a few days, maybe even a few weeks, that was different. But she wouldn't be able to leave Promise Harbor again. Or rather, she wouldn't *choose* to leave again. They would *need* her so much, purely out of habit, that she wouldn't be able to cut the strings.

Her time in Alaska with him had, however, proven that she needed to get away from there. She was healthier in just the few days she'd been here than she had been in over a year. Her skin had a faint tan from her long walks outside, she'd put on a little weight, and her skin, hair and eyes shone from eating well and sleeping deep and long. And—if he did say so himself—the great sex couldn't be hurting anything either.

She was happy. She was relaxed. She felt good. She wasn't running on empty physically and emotionally here.

Two days ago, she had finally let herself sit down and just be. Once she realized it wasn't anything to be afraid of, she'd found sitting still was quite conducive to reading and watching movies, and—since she did love cooking and Lydia had yet to concede her spot in the kitchen—she'd gotten hooked on the Food Network. She'd also mastered eight of the twelve levels in the video game she'd "borrowed" from Lydia's stash.

Lydia was just so happy to not have her underfoot that she

didn't make noise about Allie using her stuff—much.

Bend was good for her. Promise Harbor wasn't. How could he let her just go back without a fight?

Allie hadn't said anything and Gavin stepped forward. "I love you, Allie."

She bit her bottom lip. And didn't say she loved him too.

"I want you to stay," Gavin went on. "This is where you belong. You're happy here. *We're* happy here. Marry me."

"And if I stay," she finally said. "I'll feel guilty every single day. Is that what you want?"

"Guilty about what? Making your dad and brothers do things for themselves for a change?"

She was clearly fighting tears and it hurt to watch her hurt like that. But he had to do it.

"You don't understand," she argued. "My dad needs help, Gavin. His...injury... He can't..."

Gavin frowned. "Injury?"

She sighed. "He was in a motorcycle accident when I was seventeen. He has a mild brain injury. He has trouble remembering things and making appointments and...stuff."

Gavin's frown deepened. Mr. Ralston had been a teacher at the high school until their junior year in high school. Gavin had never had him for class, but knew that he'd been well-liked. Gavin remembered the accident, and he knew there had been some injuries that had resulted in Mr. Ralston no longer being able to teach full time, but Gavin had assumed that the trauma had been physical only. No one in town ever talked about any other issues—and in Promise Harbor that was incredible. "I didn't know about that." But it made *a lot* of sense.

"I know. I...we...tried to keep it pretty private. Mom was obsessive about covering things up for him. The school—and the town—thought he quit teaching so he could help the Brewsters with their business and the Brewsters helped protect him too."

"Including Josh. And you."

She nodded.

Of course.

Gavin shoved his hand through his hair. "Dammit, Allie." He looked into her eyes. She looked worried and sad and frustrated. And in the midst of being pissed at her, he still wanted to hug her and make it okay. "You don't think that's something I might have wanted to know?" he asked, feeling his gut knot. "This is a big part of your life. It explains a lot of things. Why wouldn't you tell me?"

She met his frown with one of her own. "We didn't do the serious stuff, Gavin. We didn't talk about our families. It was all just fun and good times. Remember?"

He did and he suddenly wanted to throw something. Fuck. It was all backfiring. He'd done those things because he loved her, because he didn't want to see her hurting or sad. But what it had done was engrain in her the idea that that was all he had to give. And it was all his fault.

"That's why you always had to be there?" he asked.

She nodded. "My mom took care of things, but she took on so much that I felt like I had to be there when I could to take some of the load."

Gavin felt his chest tighten. God, she'd been there for all of them. How could he...

Despair swept over him and he felt like he was being suffocated. He clenched his fists and worked on breathing. Despair because he couldn't keep her.

He couldn't make her stay. In fact, he should probably encourage her to go. It was the right thing, in many ways. If she stayed, her mind and heart would be four thousand miles away in Promise Harbor anyway.

Did he want to live that way? Knowing that her life with him made her feel guilty?

"My dad's basically alone, Gavin," she said. Her tone had lost its intensity. Now she just sounded...tired. "If Josh isn't looking out for him and I'm not there, there's really no one. My brothers are too wrapped up and honestly..." she took a deep breath, "...it's not all their fault. Mom and I kept things from them too. We've covered Dad's deficits up for so long, I doubt my brothers really understand there are problems."

"Is he in danger?" Gavin asked. "I'll call Hayley."

She squeezed her eyes shut and sniffed. "I don't think so, but...I don't know." She pulled in a long breath. "No, he's safe. He won't wander off or have a car accident or burn the house down. Not stuff like that."

She seemed to be trying to calm herself. "He'll just forget stuff. Not take care of himself. If I'm not there to cook dinner, he'll think about making something for dinner but not remember all the ingredients to use. So he'll try to find it in a cookbook, but he won't remember which one so he'll pull them all out. He'll look through them and get distracted looking at other recipes and the whole thing will take him so long that he'll completely miss dinnertime. Then he'll finally be so frustrated and hungry he'll just eat a can of soup and go to bed.

"Oh," she added, "and he won't put any of the cookbooks away. They'll stay spread out on the dining room table for days. He'll also not think about doing any laundry until he has no clothes left. Then he'll go to work in some old ratty thing he pulls out of his drawers and embarrass himself."

She stopped and pressed her lips together, hugging herself. "That's what I really hate—the idea that he might embarrass himself. Forget a meeting or not pay a bill or not remember to pick someone up when he promised to." She rubbed her forehead. "And I hate talking about him like this. None of it's intentional. He has damage to the part of his brain that helps him remember things and organize and plan."

Gavin was watching her, literally aching all over.

Fuck. She had to go.

Even if it weren't for her dad—and he obviously needed her—she would never really settle here. She'd always be torn, always think she needed to be there.

He couldn't keep her like that.

He cleared his throat. "I'll call Major. He can fly you home as soon as he's free."

"I can get a flight—"

"Major can get you there sooner and easier," Gavin cut her

off. He was also going to call Hayley and have her check on Owen and Sophie's trip. She'd make it seem casual, but she could dig up the details, he was sure.

"I, um..." She licked her lips and looked at him. "I don't know what to say. I..."

"You have to go."

She didn't answer right away, but finally she nodded. "Yeah."

"I get it. I understand. Hell, Allie," he shoved his hand through his hair, "I would have understood all along if you'd told me."

"We didn't do that."

She'd said the same thing before and it pissed Gavin off more each time.

"Yeah, I know," he snapped. "We had some fun, but none of this. I know."

"I don't want to hurt you," she said quietly.

"How can I be hurt by this?" he asked, actually asking himself the same question. How could he actually be *mad* at her here? "It's not like you're going home to marry some other guy."

He'd meant it as a joke, but as he heard the words out loud, his chest tightened again. Maybe she wasn't going home to get married, but at some point in the future another guy would come along, another Josh, and he'd help her out, take some of her burden, and she'd decide that it was pretty great to have someone on her side like that, and when he asked her to marry him—because, of course, he would—she'd say yes.

Fuck.

Could he live with that? Could he keep himself out of *that* church and *that* wedding?

Only if he cut himself off again. Only if he didn't hear or see or know anything about her and her life.

"I'll call Major." He stepped around her, careful not to touch her—because he knew he'd never stop—and went to find a phone as far away from her as he could get.

Three hours later, Allie was on her way to the Bend airport to get in his plane. Major had agreed to pick her up since they were going the same way. Which worked out great for Gavin because he'd rather cut off his arm than say good-bye to her at another airport. He'd done that more times than any man should have to say good-bye to the woman he loved.

In fact, he hadn't said good-bye to her at all this time.

It was the asshole way out, but he was okay with that at the moment.

He was now in his office, staring at the photograph of him and the cubs and hating everything. Absolutely everything.

It had been just over a week. He was being dramatic thinking his whole life had changed in that time.

It wasn't actually possible that he was *devastated*. They'd broken up more than once before. The last time had been big. And he'd survived.

Barely.

Fuck. He sure as hell *felt* devastated.

He spun away from the photo and paced to the window.

This was what they did. They hung out, had fun, until her family needed her and she went home.

So why did it feel so fucking bad this time?

He rubbed a hand over his face. He knew exactly why it felt so bad. Being more than the fun guy she hung out with meant going to Promise Harbor.

It meant doing the things that he sucked at—talking, supporting, knowing what she needed, being there even when he had no idea what to say or do.

Going to Promise Harbor with her, for her, also meant he could very possibly fail spectacularly.

Letting her come home to him in Boston all those times was a hell of a lot easier than being in the throes of the chaos and crap with her. Talking about all the things he *would have* done *if* he'd been there when her mom was sick and when she passed away was a hell of a lot easier than actually sitting in the hospital and the funeral home.

He growled in frustration and turned from the window.

He was going to have to go. They both deserved to know if he could man up when needed.

He hadn't had a great role model for manning up and doing the right thing and being there. It was an excuse, and one he hated himself for, but he'd seen firsthand the heartbreak in a woman who had been let down by the man she loved and trusted. Gavin would *never* cheat, but not being supportive, not understanding what she needed, not being able to deliver what she *really* needed would be letting Allie down in another way. He didn't need to involve another woman to disappoint and hurt Allie—he could do that all on his own.

So he'd just never really tried. It was weak and pathetic and childish, but never trying seemed to feel better than trying and failing, and it protected Allie from heartbreak.

Until now.

He couldn't let Allie go to Promise Harbor alone.

He didn't want her trying to handle all of this on her own, and if he was completely honest, he didn't want her running back into Josh Brewster's arms when she needed someone on her side.

Allison Ralston was the only woman—the only *person*—in the world who could get him back to Promise Harbor. She was also the only reason that he would ever do what he did next.

He called his father.

"Hello?"

Hearing the deep voice on the other end of the phone for the first time in ten years made Gavin close his eyes and just breathe for a moment. He wasn't nervous, exactly. But he was definitely anxious about the conversation and anxious to have it over with.

"It's Gavin."

There was a long, not surprisingly shocked silence. Then he heard his dad say, "Gavin?" His voice was gruff.

"Yeah."

"Son. I..."

"I'm calling to tell you something and I really need you to just listen," Gavin said. He couldn't listen to his father call him "son" or say anything that might set off his temper. He didn't want to fight. That wasn't what this was about.

"Okay," Greg Montgomery said. "Go ahead." There was a touch of apprehension in his voice.

Which made sense. Gavin had said some not very nice things to his dad in the past.

"I'm coming back to Promise Harbor, but I need you to not think this has anything to do with you," Gavin told him. "It doesn't, at all. This doesn't mean I forgive you or want to have a relationship. And you will absolutely not call in any favors for me."

Again, there was a long, tense silence. Then his dad said simply, "All right."

"I'd be willing to see you," Gavin said, surprising even himself with the words as they came to him, "if it's for a family dinner or something. If Mom and Garrett and Gabe are there. Maybe a lunch with Garrett and Gabe sometime."

"All right," Greg said again, almost carefully.

"And tell Mom that I'd like to see her. But I'm not sure I can see you alone. Or even just you and Mom. You need to know that."

Greg cleared his throat. "All right."

Gavin couldn't describe the feelings churning through him. It felt...okay...to talk to his dad again. He didn't feel angry, he didn't feel resentful, he wasn't waiting to jump on something to criticize like he'd done those last two years living at home. He'd...moved on. Maybe. He could still get plenty pissed off if he thought about things too hard, but he could maybe, possibly, let it go. A little.

"Is it a girl?" Greg finally asked.

"What?" Gavin pulled himself back to the moment.

"The reason you're coming ho...to the harbor?"

Gavin realized his dad had almost said "home" but had corrected himself. Gavin thought about that. His dad realized he'd made a life, a home, somewhere else. But the thing was—if Allie was in Promise Harbor, then that *was* Gavin's home.

"Yeah," he admitted, "it's because of a girl."

"She's a good one," Greg said.

Gavin knew his parents and brothers had been at the wedding. Obviously Greg knew which girl.

"Yeah," Gavin said, agreeing with his father for the first time in over a decade. "She's more than good."

"Well," Greg said with a sigh, "nothing will tear you apart and put you back together better than you were before like loving a woman you don't deserve."

Gavin felt his breath lodge in his throat and had to swallow three times before he could speak. It wasn't exactly fatherly advice, but it was a shared experience. And that was more than he and his dad had shared in a really long time.

"Yeah. Well...tell Mom I'll be over to see her." He'd call his brothers himself but he didn't think he could quite handle his mom crying right now. Which she would do. Without question.

He loved his mom, but there was another woman in Promise Harbor he needed to concentrate on.

"I'm going to Promise Harbor," he announced as he strode into his kitchen. He knew that Nancy and Carter would be there with Lydia. Concerned, maybe. Curious, definitely.

"Thank goodness," Lydia breathed.

Gavin looked at her in surprise, but Carter jumped in with, "You staying there?"

"I don't know. Maybe," he said honestly. There was a lot to consider. Upending his life here without any warning wouldn't work. But right now, he just needed to be with Allie.

"I'll cover things here," Nancy said. "Call as soon as you can."

Gavin was surprised at their easy acceptance. Then he noticed there were suitcases packed by the door. "What's this?"

"I packed for you," Carter said.

"I supervised," Lydia said.

There were three suitcases though. He couldn't just take

everything with him in one trip and never come back. "Look, no matter what happens, I'll have to come back here and tie up loose ends. I only need one suitcase."

"Those two are mine."

He turned to stare at Lydia. "Yours?"

She lifted her chin. "I'm coming too."

"And staying for a while," he observed.

"Maybe."

Okay. He really didn't know what to say or do with that, so he just nodded. "Let's go."

He got a hold of Major before they'd even stowed Allie's suitcase, so the plane was still sitting on the tarmac when Gavin and Lydia pulled up.

Gavin climbed on board to find Allie sitting in one of the window seats, legs crossed, arms crossed, staring out the window. She didn't even acknowledge him.

Yeah, well, he wasn't exactly thrilled about this either.

He took the seat right next to her and reached for her hand. He had to tug a little, but he finally linked her smaller fingers with his and sat back in his seat, trying to relax. He was here, with her. That was the first step. That was what mattered.

"What are you doing?" she finally asked, turning to him. "You don't want to go to Promise Harbor."

"No, I don't," he said honestly.

"Then why are you here?"

The first words that came to mind made the most sense. "Because I need to hold your hand, and I can't do that unless I'm in Promise Harbor with you."

She clearly didn't know what to say to that. She pulled a breath in and then said, "That's it? That's all you want to do? Hold my hand?"

He thought about it. That he could do. That he wouldn't fuck up. So that seemed a good plan. "Yeah," he finally said. "That's it."

She didn't say anything more, but she finally sat back in her seat, leaned her head back and rolled it to look out the window. She did, however, keep her hand in his.

As they sat and waited for Major to finish his preflight check, Gavin thought about what Allie would need when she got home. He could make sure she slept, ate something decent, didn't drive distracted.

But what she'd most need was to know that everyone was all right. She needed some answers. She needed to be reassured.

His heart lurched as he realized that he couldn't do that for her. He didn't know what was going on any more than she did.

He knew exactly who would though.

Fuck.

He pulled out his phone and fumbled to text Hayley with one thumb. It was a simple message: *I need to get a hold of Josh Brewster.*

Like a true friend, Hayley didn't ask questions. She just replied with Josh's cell phone number.

His text to Josh was simple too—*Allie needs you. She'll be in the harbor early tomorrow morning.*

He didn't get an immediate response and he made himself close his phone and turn it off for the flight. Not that it mattered. As much as he hated to admit it, he knew Josh would be there for Allie when she needed him.

Gavin glanced over at Lydia. She was curled up in her seat, sleeping.

He knew she'd been talking with Allie's brothers, especially Charlie, but he was still surprised how quickly she'd jumped to come to Promise Harbor with him.

Of course, no one knew better than he did how twisted up someone could get because of a Ralston.

Chapter Ten

Allie awoke three hours into the flight and turned her head to find that Gavin really was beside her. For a moment, she'd thought maybe she'd dreamed it.

He was sleeping too, his head turned toward her, his hand still holding hers.

She felt her throat tighten at the warmth and strength that seemed to spread from her hand up.

He just wanted to hold her hand.

That had been sweet. Just what she'd needed to hear.

She hoped like hell it was true.

She sighed, her gaze running over his face. Every feature was so familiar—the laugh lines around his eyes, the little flip of hair at the crown of his head that didn't like to lie flat, the lips that said and did the most wonderful things to her.

And he was here, really here, with her, beside her, heading for Promise Harbor.

For what?

She couldn't stop the thought or the frown that accompanied it. He was coming with her to...what, exactly? Help her? That was nice, but *how*?

She sighed. Gavin wanted a relationship. He wanted to be a "normal couple". That meant being involved with her family and seeing her every day and being a part of everything she did.

She wasn't sure she had it in her. Mostly because she wasn't doing a great job with the people who already depended on her. She wasn't sure she should add anyone to the list.

But she also couldn't imagine her life without him.

Josh was the only guy who'd ever been involved with her family. That had been easy though—he'd already been there, a part of things, understanding the ins and outs, not being frustrated or impatient or...jealous. That was one advantage to being with a guy who wasn't madly, deeply, head over heels for her. He didn't mind when her family came first. All the time.

Allie looked down at Gavin's hand. When they'd been talking—okay, arguing—earlier he'd asked when she was going to let them go. The answer to that was never. They were her family. She would be there as long as they needed her to be.

That was going to frustrate Gavin at best. It was going to run him off to Alaska again at worst. If that happened, it would be for good this time.

Of course, if he stayed, there was no guarantee that things would work out either.

They were both from the harbor, but had never been a couple there. They didn't know each other's families, didn't hang out with their friends together, and didn't show up at Barney's Chowder House together. They hadn't done the sharing-everything-no-matter-what thing.

It could very well blow up in their faces.

Yeah, this was a great idea.

A great idea that she couldn't quite let go of.

Seven hours and sixteen minutes later, Allie, Gavin and Lydia landed in Boston. Lydia, bless her heart, curled up in the backseat of the rental car and went back to sleep. Or pretended to anyway.

Gavin insisted on paying for the car and then driving. Every mile they traveled closer seemed to wind them both tighter.

When Allie had pulled her wallet out to pay for the fast food they picked up, he'd snapped, "Let me do it."

"You don't have to do everything," she'd snapped back.

"Let me at least fucking do what I can," he'd said, with a scowl at the girl in the drive-through.

"What's that mean?" Allie had demanded.

"It means that I don't know what the hell's gonna happen in Promise Harbor so I'm gonna at least pay for the damned burgers."

Okay, clearly she wasn't the only one feeling anxious about what was coming.

They pulled into Promise Harbor an hour later.

"You need to find a place to stay," she said to Gavin as they passed the sign that said *Welcome to Promise Harbor*.

He didn't answer and was frowning again—or still—when she looked over at him.

"You can't stay at my house." Surely he understood that.

"Fine." The word was flat and delivered with a deeper frown.

"Well, really, what did you think?" she asked, exasperated and knowing that it wasn't all about Gavin.

"I didn't think about it period." Same flat tone.

"I can't bring you to my dad's," she pointed out. "For one, he barely knows you." In fact, she wasn't sure her dad knew him at all beyond his name. "For another..." Shit, she couldn't say that. She bit her lip.

"For another?" he asked, glancing over at her.

"Nothing."

"Allie," he said warningly.

"Never mind. It's my dad's house and I can't just bring some guy to stay."

"What," he bit off, "were you going to say?"

She sighed. Fine. "Josh will be around."

Gavin growled. Her eyes widened.

But it was true. She couldn't really bring the guy who'd broken up their wedding home to stay right in front of everyone, could she?

"Well, he will."

"You sure? Thought he was out of town," Gavin sneered.

"He was," she acknowledged. "But he's back."

"Great." Gavin's tone was even more clipped, if that was possible.

"So you'll stay—"

"Jesus, Allie, I'll stay out of precious Josh's fuckin' way, okay?"

She glared at him. "That's not what I meant."

"Wasn't it?"

She opened her mouth, shut it, then said, "I just don't want to rub his nose in it."

"I do," Gavin muttered.

She huffed out a breath. This was a ridiculous fight. "You don't have to be jealous of Josh."

Josh wasn't going to be the man she needed to concentrate on.

But neither was Gavin.

"I'm not jealous of Josh," Gavin said firmly. "You're in love with me and in my bed. I'm not worried about Josh."

His words made her heart trip even as her frustration bubbled higher. "I'm not in your bed right now." That was the least of the things she needed to worry about. Even if staying cocooned in bed with Gavin, shutting the real world out, sounded absolutely perfect. And so familiar.

They'd done that as a substitute for a real relationship for so long that now they were jumping in without any practice.

Now it was sink or swim.

He looked over at her, his expression full of challenge and possession. "You *are* in my bed right now, Allison. In every way that it matters, you are."

Okay, so figuratively that was true.

She swallowed, liking that more than she should. It was all a moot point right now anyway.

Except that it wasn't.

There was something about knowing that no matter how bitchy or unreasonable or unfocused she was, he still wanted her, still knew she was his. That made her breathe easier.

He reached across the seat and took her hand. "Listen, this is new for us. But here's the deal. In the past, I let you leave, let you deal with all of this alone. That's over. I don't know what the hell I'm doing, but I'm going to be there."

She liked that a lot too. "Be where?"

"*There*," he said again. "I don't know. Wherever I need to

be."

That sounded really nice. She didn't know where she needed him to be either, but knowing he was willing was...nice.

Josh had always been there. He'd taken a lot of weight off her shoulders, but this felt different. Bigger. For Josh it was natural and he barely gave it a second thought. In fact, she wasn't sure he gave it any real thought. He just did it. He'd take her dad for coffee, or give Danny twenty bucks, or ride Charlie about his latest resignation. But it wasn't a big deal.

For Gavin it was. This wasn't natural for him. This wasn't easy. In fact, he looked pretty damned uncomfortable thinking about it. But he was here, doing it anyway.

She squeezed his hand. "Okay."

He glanced over quickly. "Okay? As in, you'll call me if you need something?"

She thought about that, then slowly nodded. "Okay."

That wasn't natural for her either. She just took care of things. Except for the things Josh took care of. But she never really asked him. She didn't need to, and she'd always chalked that up to proof of what a good match they were—he knew how to help her without her asking.

But...she wasn't sure she would have asked him. Leaning wasn't easy for her. She would have worried about what he'd think if she couldn't handle something.

With Gavin she didn't. Gavin would like her—love her—even if she broke down sobbing for no apparent reason. Or stayed in bed for three days straight.

She sighed. No, she didn't need to worry about seeming weak or Gavin seeing her at her worst.

Been there, done that.

Gavin pulled the car up to the curb in front of a big old house at the end of the dead-end street next to the lake.

It wasn't his parents' place.

"Who lives here?"

"Hayley. This was her grandfather's place. She owns it now."

Allie was so grateful he had somewhere to go. "Does she know you're coming?"

"Nah, but it won't matter." Gavin put the car into park and turned to look back at Lydia. "Lyd. We're here."

As Lydia was yawning and stretching, Gavin turned his attention fully on Allie.

"You will call me," he said firmly. "I might suck at this at first, but you will call me and give me a chance. And I'll get better at it."

Something warm spread through her chest, and she felt the vise that had been squeezing her heart loosen. She smiled. "A chance at what?" she teased lightly. She actually really appreciated his honesty about not knowing what he was doing exactly.

The bumbling attempt outside his comfort zone meant more than all the perfect words and actions from everyone else in the past two years.

"The chance to be there," he said with a little grimace.

"And 'there' is...?" she prompted.

"Hell if I know." He gave her a half smile. "We might both need to work up to the big stuff. You don't ask for help well and I don't give it well."

She smiled. "I'll try."

"Like changing a lightbulb, or something," he said. "Or running to the grocery store for something you forgot."

Her smile grew and she nodded. "Okay. When a lightbulb goes out or I run out of milk, you're my guy."

He leaned in and rested his forehead against hers. "I'm your guy anyway, Al," he said huskily. "Any time for anything. Promise."

"I promise," she said softly. "But you have to promise not to get all upset or offended if I *don't* call too. I have...stuff to figure out."

"You need to talk to Josh," he interpreted. With a sigh, he leaned back.

She nodded. "I do. I need to figure out what's going on. And

I just think maybe it would be best if you weren't there. At least at first."

He just looked at her for three heartbeats. Then he leaned in and kissed her sweetly.

Lydia slamming the door as she got out pulled them apart.

"I will see you," he said, firmly.

She nodded.

Allie watched them lug their suitcases up to the door and Gavin pound on the door. Then wait. Then pound again. It was just barely six a.m., so it was understandable that it might take Hayley some time to wake up and get to the door.

Allie just hoped Hayley was a morning person and didn't Taser people who showed up uninvited.

Finally the big door swung open. There was a moment when Allie couldn't see anyone else before suddenly Gavin caught Hayley in his arms in a tight hug. Allie swallowed hard and put the car in drive. Thank god for Hayley. She'd take care of Gavin until Allie could.

She turned the car toward the Promise Harbor fire station and speed-dialed the sixth number in her cell phone, hoping Josh was at work. She'd be less likely to use expletives if there were other people around.

He wasn't there. And no one—predictably—answered at Sophie's or at Allie's dad's house.

Five minutes later, Allie pulled the rental up in front of the house that would have been her address if Gavin had been ten minutes later in getting to the church.

She shivered at that thought—how close she'd come to making such a huge mistake. Then she put that in the maybe-I'll-think-about-that-later box—which was getting damned full of stuff, frankly.

Instead, she got out and headed for Josh's front door, hoping he was home. It was Wednesday, so if he wasn't at work, typically he'd be at his mom's for breakfast. But his mom wasn't in Promise Harbor.

She was *gone*. With Allie's *father*.

The world was going crazy.

Allie pounded on Josh's door for a full minute, but there was no answer and she had to accept that this wasn't going to be as easy as she'd hoped.

She had Greta's cell number. She supposed she could try to get a hold of her. What would Greta think about Sophie and Owen getting it on?

Allie frowned and dropped onto Josh's top front step.

Sophie and Owen? Getting it on?

She made herself breathe. They could just be antiquing, she supposed. Maybe they just both needed to get away. They were friends, after all, and they'd both had a child starring in the Wedding That Wasn't. Maybe they were just drinking mai tais and shopping.

And maybe they were getting it on.

"Argh!" Allie covered her face with her hands, propping her elbows on her knees. It was true that not knowing was the hard part.

She didn't really care if they were involved, she realized. She loved Sophie and neither of them should be alone. They'd known each other forever.

Good for them.

But she'd like to know what the *hell* was going on.

Was Owen okay? Was Sophie reminding him to take his blood pressure meds and to watch his salt intake? Did she know that he was allergic to mangos?

More, did she know that he watched NCIS nonstop? And that he'd tell her about the same story he'd read in the newspaper three or four times? And that she'd have to physically take him to get his haircut or he'd never remember?

Yeah, there was more to being involved with Owen than Sophie might realize.

He might drive her nuts.

This little getaway might be the first and last.

Allie looked up at the sound of a car pulling in to Josh's driveway. Josh got out a moment later. Then the passenger side opened. And Devon Grant stepped out.

Allie got to her feet.

Um...

"Allie, Jesus, I went to your dad's. What are you doing *here*?" Josh asked, rounding the car and coming toward her.

He didn't seem surprised to see her, exactly. "Why'd you go to my dad's? He's not there." She put her hands on her hips. "Did you know he was with your mom?"

Josh stopped at the bottom of the steps. "Gavin told me you were back and needed me. What's going on?"

That tripped her up. "Gavin told you I was here? And *needed* you?"

"Yes. What's going on?"

"What's going on?" She stomped down the steps. "My father is *gone*. And you weren't here. *I'm* the one who needs to know what's going on."

"Mom and Owen went up to Greenbush Island for a few days. Everyone's fine."

Allie waited for him to continue. "*And?*" she finally demanded.

Josh frowned. "And nothing."

"Did you talk to them?"

"I..." He cleared his throat and glanced over at Devon, who had come up beside him. "Briefly on the phone. I just got back Saturday. We just missed them."

Allie narrowed her eyes. "Yeah, heard you were gone too."

"And you wouldn't think of being pissed about that, everything considered, right?" he said, eyebrows up as if daring her.

Allie blew out a breath and crossed her arms. She'd love to be self-righteous here and yell at Josh for letting all of this happen. But, of course, she couldn't. It was her fault.

All of it.

Losing what little energy she'd pulled together with adrenaline and ire, Allie let her shoulders slump. "Sorry about the wedding."

That was a really stupid way to apologize, of course, but

she didn't know what else to say.

"Me too."

She looked up. "*You're* sorry? You didn't run out on me."

"No, but," Josh glanced at Devon again, "I never should have proposed in the first place."

Allie looked at her ex-best friend too. Then she nodded. It was true. "Okay."

"Okay," Josh repeated. "Now why is Gavin texting me about you?"

Allie felt her heart cramp. She lifted a shoulder. "He's worried about me."

"But he's not here with you?"

"He's here. He's just not *here*."

"Why not?"

"Because I thought it might make you uncomfortable."

"Oh. Right." Josh looked a little uncomfortable that he clearly wasn't all that uncomfortable seeing his ex-fiancée for the first time since she'd left him at the altar.

Suddenly, the whole thing hit Allie as really funny.

Allie started laughing. And couldn't stop.

She was here with her ex-fiancé and her ex-best friend, who were obviously now a couple—again—talking about her father and her ex-almost-mother-in-law, who may or may not be a couple, and telling them that she was now home with the guy who'd stolen her away from the wedding that neither her nor her ex-fiancé were upset hadn't happened.

She had no idea what was going on with anyone—including herself.

And that was actually...okay.

Not knowing what was going on was *never* okay with her. Except that now, suddenly, for some reason, it was.

She laughed until her eyes watered and she had to sit down on the steps again.

"Oh god," she finally gasped. "This is the craziest situation."

Josh was looking at her like he was afraid she might actually be crazy, but Devon was smiling.

"Okay." Composed again, Allie stretched to her feet. "I'm going...home. I guess."

Her mind flickered briefly to a house with a huge back window that looked out on the highest mountain peak in North America. Home.

Yeah. She was going to her dad's house.

"Call if you need anything," Josh said.

Allie paused halfway down the sidewalk and gave her friend and almost-husband a smile. "Sure. Thanks." But Josh couldn't give her what she needed anymore.

A few minutes later, Allie let herself into her dad's house.

It was quiet. But that wasn't what she noticed first.

It smelled good.

And it was tidy. Clean even.

She dropped her bags by the door, staring at the living room she hadn't been in for over a week. How was it possible that there weren't dishes and mail everywhere?

She turned on two lamps and looked around. The only good explanation was that her dad had forgotten to get the mail. Or eat. For over a week.

She frowned. No way had her brothers gone without eating for that long. There should at least be empty chip bags and soda cans sitting around. She swore they acted more like they were thirteen than twenty-five and twenty-four.

Dreading what she'd find, she headed for the kitchen.

But it too was clean and neat.

If her wedding invitation hadn't been hanging on the fridge door next to the white dry-erase board where she left her dad reminders, she would have gone back outside and checked the house number. But this was the right house.

Kind of.

Allie turned in a full circle. Everything was put away, the sink was clean and, sure enough, there was a pile of mail on the table. But it was neatly stacked and she could see that it had been opened. Flipping through it quickly showed that none of it was bills to be paid. So someone had paid the bills or tossed them. And even Danny wouldn't toss the bills.

Mostly because Danny didn't ever throw anything away.

Huh.

She checked the fridge, but there was no expired or rotten food and there were even a couple of containers of leftovers that were new. So someone had cooked? Sophie? Maybe.

There was only one last place she needed to check in this *Twilight Zone* house.

Taking the steps two at a time, she went to her brothers' rooms.

They were messier than the rest of the house but they weren't disasters. There were clean clothes in their drawers and no dirty dishes that she could find. And she tried.

Feeling very confused, she pulled her cell phone out and called Charlie.

"Hey, Al," he greeted. "What's up?"

"Where'd the leftovers come from?" she asked without preamble.

"What leftovers?"

"The ones in the fridge."

"The fri... You're at home?"

She frowned as she headed back for the kitchen. "Yes, I'm home. You told me Dad was gone. So I came home."

"Jesus."

She heard some bangs and rustling on Charlie's end of the phone.

Then he said, "He's not *gone*. He's on a trip."

"Yeah. He's not here."

"And hopefully he's having a great time."

"Charlie, you don't understand..."

"I do, Allie," he interrupted. "I do understand. You're usually in charge. But when you left, we made do. And that might surprise you. It might even piss you off. But we're okay."

She narrowed her eyes. "Why would that piss me off?" Surprise her? Definitely. But was she mad? She didn't think so.

"You like being in charge. It was the way you bonded with

Mom, and now that she's gone it's your way of staying close to her. But our world didn't fall apart without you."

She opened her mouth to respond and then closed it again. The world didn't fall apart without her? Huh.

"Where'd you get that insight?" she asked.

Charlie sighed. "I always knew that you were trying to be like Mom."

"And who pointed out that it was my way of staying close to her?" Because Allie hadn't actually realized that herself. At least not in so many words. She'd felt the need to fill her mom's shoes, to pick up where Lily left off, but she hadn't realized that she was actually comforted by it. She was, though. It was the routine, the familiarity, looking through her mom's files, reading notes in her mom's handwriting—it had all kept Lily close.

"Lydia," Charlie finally said.

Ah. Of course. "And she talked you through making dinner a couple of nights," Allie guessed. "That's where the leftovers came from."

"Yeah," Charlie muttered.

Allie took a deep breath. A million things were flying through her mind, but one thought seemed to sum it all up— *Holy crap.*

Her world really had changed in just over a week.

"Did the dinners turn out well?" Charlie didn't have a lot of kitchen experience, so even with a live chat with a fantastic cook, they might have been less than perfect.

"Edible," he said. Then he chuckled.

Allie couldn't help but smile. He sounded...good.

"And how's Danny?"

"Fine. He got an apartment with some guys he met in class."

Well, at least he was in class.

"And Dad's with Sophie."

"Yeah."

"Are they..."

"Hell, Allie, I don't know," Charlie said quickly. "I've decided it doesn't matter."

"It doesn't matter?" But in the next moment, Allie couldn't really come up with a reason why it *did* matter.

"Sophie's fantastic. She and Dad get along. Let's just leave it at that."

Sophie was definitely fantastic. Okay. Allie was going to take some advice from her brother for a change. "Okay, we'll just leave it at that."

"Okay. Now I have to get back to work."

"Work?"

"Yes. It's how I spend some of my time now." Charlie paused, then said, "And it's not so bad."

They disconnected and Allie stood staring at the phone. Her dad was okay, Charlie was okay, Danny was okay. What the *hell* was going on?

A knock at the kitchen door made Allie jump, then her heart pounded as she thought it might be Gavin. She quickly crossed the room and pulled the door open.

The person on the other side hadn't even made the list of the top ten possibilities in her mind.

"Devon?"

The other woman wet her lips and gave Allie a smile that seemed nervous. "Hi."

"Wh...what are you doing here?"

"I...um...think we should talk."

Well, sure why not? Everything else was crazy. Allie propped her shoulder against the doorjamb and crossed her arms. "Okay, go ahead."

The familiar fatigue was starting to settle in. She hated that Promise Harbor did that to her, but it did. She felt heavier here.

"Are you okay?" Devon asked.

"Well, my mom's still dead, my dad's missing, and half—or more—of my hometown hates me. I've been better."

"You're the one that left."

Allie blinked at her. Okay. Wow. "That's true."

"Are you sorry you left with Gavin?"

That was easy. "No."

"I hope you're not upset that Josh and I are together. Because...we are, Allie. We're together. And that's just the way it is."

"I'm not upset about Josh at all." That too was an easy answer.

Devon didn't say anything for a few seconds. Then she said, "I was really pissed at you for a long time."

Allie lifted an eyebrow. "Pissed at me?"

"For dating Josh. For *marrying* Josh."

Allie straightened from the doorframe. "If you recall, I didn't marry Josh."

"You said yes to his proposal. Then you left him at the altar. In front of everyone."

"Which should make *you* happy." Crap. She really couldn't handle this too.

"It does. It just..." Devon sighed. "I don't know. It hurt me to see him embarrassed and confused and hurt like that."

"Seems like he got over it pretty well," Allie said dryly.

Devon's gaze flew back to her face. She even blushed a little. "Nothing happened between us until we were both sure he was over you."

Allie's shoulders slumped. "I'm sure that didn't take long. It's not like he was head over heels, Devon."

Devon nodded. "Yeah. I know that now. He never *really* loved you."

Right. Totally true. Still not exactly something she needed rubbed in her face at the moment.

"Okay." Allie clapped her hands together. "So, if this pep talk is over..."

Devon reached out and clasped Allie's hand, seeming as surprised as Allie was at the gesture. She looked from their hands to Allie's face. "I got so wrapped up in how I was feeling about Josh and losing him and him being here with you...I didn't think about how hard the past year must have been for you."

Allie didn't pull away. She swallowed hard.

She and Devon had been close. She knew this woman, and right in that moment she could look into her eyes and see that, deep down, they were still the same people they'd been when they stayed up late eating raw cookie dough and talking about their plans and dreams...and, of course, guys. That had been before Josh and Gavin, but she could see the funny, sweet, intelligent woman she'd loved like a sister.

"Yeah. The past year has sucked."

"I wish...I wish I hadn't pulled away. I should have been there to help you through it."

"Devon," Allie said, feeling exhausted at the idea of there being one more thing that had gone terribly wrong, "you said you were over Josh. You said it was okay with you that we dated."

"I know." Devon's eyes glistened. "But I didn't mean it. It tore me up. I love him so much, Allie."

Allie pulled in a long breath. Should she have known that? Should she have somehow sensed that her best friend was hurting? "I couldn't see or feel anything past what I was going through," she finally admitted. "I just took you at your word."

"I know." Devon let go of Allie and wiped at her eyes. "And it's all okay now."

Allie thought about that. Then she felt a smile threaten and she didn't try to fight it or hide it.

"I guess that makes you one of Gavin's biggest fans."

Devon frowned, then slowly smiled. "I guess it does."

"I thought of you while I was in Alaska," Allie told her.

"You did?"

"Yeah. I was thinking how nice it would be to have a friend to talk to about everything that was going on with the damned wedding, and Josh, and Gavin, and my family."

Devon sniffed a little as she smiled. "I know what you mean."

They hadn't been friends for a long time. They hadn't had a

heart-to-heart in forever. But suddenly Allie wanted Devon with her—if Devon agreed.

"So, there's something I was thinking I needed to do. I could use a friend. Want to come?"

Devon nodded quickly. "Yes."

"Okay. I just need to grab something," Allie said, thinking through her spontaneous plan quickly. "Will you get the tequila out of the cupboard above the fridge?"

Devon's eyes got a little wide, but she agreed and Allie headed for the stairs.

She threw blankets and sweaters off of the cardboard box in the corner of her closet. It was full of stuff from her college dorm room that she'd decided wasn't quite appropriate for her "grown up" apartment. In that box was proof that there had been a few fun times that she *had* initiated. It had been her freshman year of college, her first time away from home for extended periods, the first—and only—time that she'd been out from under the roof where all her responsibilities and her mother's expectations collected. It had felt free and, yes, for a few months, she'd been fun.

Halfway through photos and things like Mardi Gras beads from a campus party, a green tank that said *I'm Not Irish But Kiss Me Anyway,* a plastic luau lei, a couple of champagne corks from New Year's Eve and other mementos, she found the shot glasses.

She met Devon back in the kitchen a minute later. "Okay, let's go."

Chapter Eleven

To her credit, Devon just got in the car without argument or question. In fact, neither said a word as Allie drove. Even when they pulled up at the cemetery, Devon didn't balk. She accompanied Allie to her mother's grave, clutching the bottle of tequila tightly against her stomach.

Allie stopped in front of her mom's headstone and finally took a deep breath.

She'd visited every week since the funeral. She'd been there the day before her wedding.

It still felt like it had been a long time.

She pulled in another breath.

Probably because things had changed so much since she'd last been here.

"Okay, I'm gonna need a shot," Allie said.

Devon thrust the bottle toward her.

"Hang on." Allie dug the shot glasses from her purse and handed one to Devon. "Remember these?"

Devon took the glass and looked at it, then lifted her gaze to Allie's. "Are these from the Cinderella night?"

Allie grinned. "Yep." They were the souvenirs from a masquerade party hosted by a sorority on Allie's campus on one of the weekends when Devon had been visiting. They had easily snuck in and mingled without anyone knowing that they didn't belong. They'd danced, drunk champagne, and both had been kissed on the veranda. Since they couldn't take the frat guys with them, Allie had swiped the shot glasses off of a table on their way out.

Devon finally relaxed and smiled too. "I can't believe you still have them."

"We had some good times, huh?" Allie poured tequila into Devon's glass, then her own.

"We had a ton of good times," Devon said.

Allie had to swallow hard before she raised her glass. "Here's to having good people to have good times with."

Devon looked like she was blinking back tears, but she clinked her glass against Allie's and they tipped the liquor back simultaneously.

Allie felt the fire burn down her throat and shook her head, then focused on her mom's name carved into the stone.

"Do you think my mom ever had any fun?" she asked without looking at Devon.

"Um...I'm sure she did."

Allie nodded. "Probably. Maybe before Dad's accident."

She really mostly remembered her mom working hard and being insanely busy. She remembered Lily smiling and laughing, but she didn't remember her parents ever sitting on the couch just watching a movie together, or dancing together in the living room, or making out in the kitchen. She also knew her mom hadn't had any girls' nights out, or even a girlfriend over for margaritas and manicures.

"Your mom was a great lady," Devon said quietly.

Allie nodded. "Definitely." She poured another shot for each of them. Then she lifted hers toward her mom's headstone. "I love you, Mom. You did a lot of great things. And in a lot of ways I want to be like you. But you weren't perfect, and I don't want to do things exactly the way you did."

Devon said nothing—she just drank. Allie couldn't blame her.

Allie poured again. "My mom wanted to take care of everyone, but she took *too much* care of them. My brothers don't know how to make things happen for themselves, my dad needs someone to make him scrambled eggs—*eggs*, Devon, the easiest thing in the world to make—and no one in this town knows how to organize a fundraiser. Because Mom always did all of it. And she almost *needed* to. I think that maybe it was more about her than the people she was helping, you know?"

"Maybe," Devon said quietly. "Being important to people could be hard to give up."

Allie nodded. "I wish I knew for sure that she'd had some fun."

She felt Devon's arm wrap around her waist and give her a half hug. "I'm sure she had fun, sweetie."

Allie's eyes filled. "Maybe. I hope so. But I'm not sure she ever realized that fun isn't really like chocolate frosting."

She had just realized it. Getting back into her real world had made her realize that if she was going to have some silly times and enjoy things, *she* was now going to have to make it happen. It was easy to let the not-perfect things get to her and it was easy to focus on the negative. Being happy, appreciating her life, was on her. No one else was in charge of making those things happen.

"Chocolate frosting?" Devon asked, pulling away slightly to look into Allie's face. "What's that mean?"

"I've realized that having fun with people you love isn't an indulgence—like chocolate frosting—it's a necessity. Like broccoli. Not sure Mom ever got that."

Devon took the tequila bottle and filled their glasses again. "It's never too late. She's here with us, so let's show her how it's done."

They toasted and drank again and then Devon kicked off her shoes and headed for Allie's car. She started the engine and rolled down the windows, then cranked the radio.

For the next thirty minutes, they danced and sang and drank tequila.

Too much tequila.

Eventually they found themselves lying in the grass behind Lily's headstone, holding their sides from laughing.

"My head is spinning," Devon groaned.

"Yeah, fucking tequila," Allie agreed.

Never would she have imagined saying the word "fucking" at her mother's grave site. Still, she kind of wished she and her mom had maybe drunk too much tequila together just once.

They'd been mother and daughter. Partners in taking care of everyone around them. Mentor and student, to some extent. But they'd never been friends.

Allie rolled her head to the side to look at Devon. She let the dizziness pass, then said, "Want to talk about boys?"

Devon looked over and grinned. "Sure."

"I'm madly in love with Gavin."

"I'm madly in love with Josh."

They both smiled stupidly for a moment, not sure what else to say. "We're gonna have to practice this," Allie said. "We need to be able to give better details than that."

"Details like sex?" Devon asked.

"Right. Definitely." She supposed. "Hell, I don't know. You were my last really good girlfriend and it's been awhile."

Devon reached over and touched Allie's arm. "We can get back there, right?"

"Yeah." She was sure they could. Why not? There was nothing keeping them apart now. "But we need to go to the bar and just hang out and listen to other girls talk so we know how to do this. They talk about sex, don't they?"

Devon laughed. "I'm sure it depends on the girls."

"Well, if you're worried that it will be awkward talking about sex with Josh..." Allie thought about that. "Okay, it might be. At first. But we'll work it out. Maybe we can refer to him as Ryan Reynolds and that will help."

Devon snorted again. "It won't hurt. And we'll call Gavin Ryan Gosling."

"Awesome," Allie agreed. "Ryans all around."

They laughed, then lay there staring up at the blue sky. Finally, Allie rolled and pushed herself up to sitting, instantly regretting it. "Oh, boy, we shouldn't have made that last toast to Jimmy Buffet."

"Yeah." Devon also made her way into a sitting position. And groaned. "But you can't really drink and sing *without* Jimmy Buffet, you know?"

"Good point."

"Maybe we should've stopped toasting back when we were talking about my shoes."

Allie looked at Devon's shoes. "No, those are awesome. Toast-worthy. And I *know* girlfriends talk about shoes."

She carefully pushed herself to standing. "But speaking of drinking and sex and singing...I want to call Gavin."

Devon struggled to her feet as well. "He came back with you, right?"

Allie felt the pain of that jab her in the center of her chest and spread. "Yeah. But..."

Was he really going to stay? Was this just a visit, an attempt to show her what he was willing to do for her? But what about when things settled down again—as much as they ever did? He had a life in Alaska.

"But?" Devon asked.

"I don't know what's going to happen."

Devon gave her a small smile before she stepped forward and hugged her. "I know that not knowing and not being in control are hard for you, but I think it's a good thing."

"Yeah?" Allie sniffed. "How?" She pulled back and wiped the tears.

"You're willing to try it with him anyway. You're outside your comfort zone for him. That's good."

Allie stared at her. She sure was. Gavin was outside his comfort zone for her too and it *was* good. "Do you think that just being there for someone can be enough? Like, not really doing anything or fixing anything but just being there?" she asked, thinking about Lydia's words when Allie had felt so helpless to do something for Gavin.

Devon looked around the cemetery, "Well, what exactly am *I* doing right now except being here?"

Allie thought about that, then nodded slowly. "Okay. You're good."

Devon laughed. Then nudged Allie's arm, "You could call him. Just tell him you need him."

She wanted to. She *really* wanted to.

She reached into her pocket for her phone and realized she didn't have it.

"Phone's in the car." She took a step forward and the ground wobbled. "Oh, boy." She grabbed Devon's arm. "I could not pass a sobriety test right now."

Devon laughed. "That's because you're not sober."

"Neither are you."

Devon grabbed Allie's arm as she tried to head for the car. "In our defense, there's a slight incline here."

"Yep, I'm sure that's the problem."

They looked at each other and burst out laughing.

"'Kay, let's try that again," Allie said, still chuckling.

Holding on to one another they proceeded carefully down the—albeit *very* slight—hill toward the car.

Devon's phone was ringing as they opened the door. She grabbed it from her purse. "Hi, Josh."

Allie froze. How was Josh going to feel about her and Devon renewing their friendship? More, how was he going to feel about Allie getting Devon drunk in the graveyard within an hour of that renewal?

"I'm fine," Devon said, too loudly. "Just fine."

Her eyes widened as she listened to Josh. Then she covered the mouthpiece with her hand and asked in a whisper—a loud whisper—"Am I slurring my words?"

She definitely slurred the word *slurred*.

"Yes. Pull it together," Allie told her, pointing at her nose. "I don't need him mad at me for something new."

Devon frowned and asked Josh, "You're not mad at Allie, are you?"

She listened, then smiled.

"He's not mad at you," she told Allie. Then she frowned again and said into the phone, "Yes, I'm with Allie." She paused. "At the cemetery."

Allie groaned. Josh was so coming to the cemetery. She knew him. He'd be concerned. He'd be here to check on them.

And there was no way they could hide that they were

drunk.

Allie only half listened to Devon try to assure Josh they were both fine. It wouldn't matter. He was still coming.

It wasn't a horrible idea, of course. They could use a ride. Neither of them should be driving.

Devon hung up a moment later and Allie leaned back against the car.

"He's on his way," Devon said, leaning next to her.

"I know." Allie sighed. "Is he going to be weird about you and me being friends?"

"No." Devon shook her head adamantly, then closed her eyes and groaned. When she opened her eyes again, she refrained from shaking or nodding and simply said, "He's happy about it."

"Until you puke in his car," Allie said with a chuckle, more relieved than she'd expected to know that Josh would be okay with her friendship with Devon. It had only been an hour and she already felt like she'd be pretty devastated if it didn't work out.

"Ah, I'll make it up to him."

Allie looked at her with surprise. Devon was grinning slyly.

"Now, see, *that's* what I'm talking about," Allie said, happily. "Hinting about blow jobs. That's a nice start."

Devon coughed. "How do you know I was thinking blow jobs specifically?"

Allie grinned. "Yeah, maybe that's just *my* favorite get-out-of-jail-free card."

Devon laughed. "This girl-talk thing is fun."

It was. But the talk of sexual innuendos and blow jobs had her mind very firmly back on Gavin. She pushed herself off the car resignedly and leaned through the open driver's window to grab her phone.

Flipping it open she was startled to see four new voice messages waiting for her.

She'd been home for three hours and everyone was already calling?

Yeah, that was about right.

That damned heaviness settled on her again.

Reluctantly she opened the screen to see who the calls were from.

They were all from Gavin.

Her heart sped up. That was a lot of calls. She certainly hoped he missed her, but... She hit the redial button and waited, holding her breath.

Eight rings later, it went to voice mail.

What the hell?

She snapped her phone shut.

"So he's..." Devon started.

But Allie's phone rang just then. It was Gavin.

"Gavin, are you okay?"

"Josh said you're at the cemetery."

She blinked. "Um, yeah. Josh told you?"

"Yeah. We've been calling back and forth trying to figure out where you girls are since you weren't answering your phones. He just called and said you were at the cemetery with Devon."

"Oh. I am. He's on the way."

"Me too."

"You are?"

He sighed heavily in her ear. "Allison, the whole call-me-if-you-need-anything bit definitely includes going with you to the cemetery."

She shook her head and immediately thought she was going to lose what little food she'd had. She gave in to her body's urge to sit down—quickly—and slumped to the curb, burying her face in her hands.

"Allie?" Gavin said in her ear. His voice was husky. "Are you okay?"

"Actually, I'm drunk," she admitted.

"You're *drunk*?" he repeated. "I thought you were at the cemetery."

"We are."

"You're drunk at the cemetery?" he clarified.

"With the woman who ran off with my fiancé," she said wryly.

He chuckled and the sound washed over her, making the heaviness lift a little. "You're drunk and you didn't call me to sing?"

"Actually, I was considering it," she said. "But I couldn't think of something dirty enough. I was just considering Kelly Clarkson's 'My Life Would Suck Without You'."

There was a long pause on the other end of the phone. Then he said, "I'm on my way."

"Just meet me at Dad's." She disconnected and then lay back in the grass by the curb. "I'm screwed," she told Devon.

"Gavin will be at your dad's?" Devon asked.

"Yep."

"And that's bad?"

"This whole thing is going to be hard on you." Allie pushed up and braced herself with her hands on the grass behind her. Devon still leaned on the car.

"On me?" Devon asked. "How so?"

"Either this is just a visit and he'll leave again—which will tear my heart out—or he thinks he's going to stay to be with me—which will also suck because it's not what he really wants." She scowled at the pavement as she said the truth out loud. "He's not happy here. And that's going to tear me up, because I love him and want him to be happy. Either way, I'm going to need a lot more tequila, a lot more often, and it's pathetic to drink alone." She looked back up at Devon. "So, since you're my best friend, you'll be drinking with me. It could be hard on you. Cirrhosis of the liver is nothing to sneeze at."

And she wasn't even joking.

It wasn't a healthy way to handle it—physically or mentally—but she didn't see a way around it.

Devon sat down next to her, taking her hand. "First of all, being your best friend, I'm determined to ration your tequila from this point on. Second of all, there are other options, Allie. Gavin could find a job in Boston. Or somewhere else where you can be together, but be close enough to home that you could come often."

Yeah. It sounded good when Devon said it. Allie just wasn't sure she could turn it into reality.

"He likes polar bears," she said, pushing up from the curb and brushing the seat of her pants off. "There are only seven polar bear populations in the world and only two in North America. So, it's Alaska or Canada. Both far away from the harbor."

Devon couldn't reply to that because Josh pulled up just then.

Josh stepped out and looked at them with a bemused expression over the top of the car.

Allie looked at Devon and she looked at Allie. Devon's clothes and hair were rumpled, there were blades of grass clinging to her pants and she had that funny, dazed look in her eyes that came from too much tequila in too short a period.

Allie probably looked even worse.

"Can you take me home?" Allie asked Josh, knowing he'd say yes.

"Yes," he said simply. "I can even buy you coffee on the way."

"I don't want coffee," she told him, gathering her shoes—that she'd kicked off at some point—and shot glasses and mostly empty tequila bottle. "That might sober me up."

"So you did get drunk on purpose." He reached out to help her into the backseat of the car, probably afraid she'd break the bottle on the door.

"I drank on purpose," she told him. "The amount snuck up on me."

"Gavin's on his way."

"He's going to Dad's." She frowned at Josh. "Why'd you call him anyway?"

"He came four thousand miles from Alaska for you. Twice. Pretty sure he'd want to be with you right now."

The truth—and sweetness—of that hit her in the chest.

"But I can't believe *you* called *Gavin* to come be with me. Doesn't that strike you as a little odd?" she asked him.

"I want a front-row seat," Josh said. "The last time you mixed tequila and Gavin's return to the harbor, things got really interesting."

Allie squinted up at him. "Did you just make a joke about the Wedding That Wasn't?"

He chuckled. "Yes."

"So we really are both over it."

"Seems that way." He reached out and put an arm around Devon.

"Okay." Allie sat back in her seat and rested her head back as Josh shut the door and helped Devon into the front. Allie closed her eyes and kept them that way until she felt the car stop.

"I should go in with her," Devon said.

"No need," Allie assured her, somehow sitting upright without feeling like puking. "I'm fine."

Josh, being Josh, insisted they walk her into the house anyway. Which turned out to be a good idea. The steps were a little taller than she'd remembered.

Gavin met them at the top step of the porch, clearly torn between being gracious about Josh helping her and wanting to grab her away from the man she'd almost married.

In the end, Josh handed her over to Gavin without a word.

Gavin swept her up into his arms and she cuddled close, thinking that was exactly where she wanted to be. He headed straight for the bedroom, Josh and Devon following.

"Wow, I'm really jet-lagged," she said with a huge yawn.

"Yeah, I'm sure *that's* the problem," Josh said.

"You okay, sweetie?" Devon asked.

"Fine." Allie yawned again as Gavin set her on the edge of the bed.

Without thinking, she stripped her top T-shirt off, leaving her in only a tank top.

"Time to go," Gavin announced, turning Josh out the door.

Devon crossed to Allie and hugged her quick. "Call if you need anything."

"You bet," Allie agreed, lying back, watching her ceiling spin. "I'll need more tequila tomorrow. I'll call as soon as I wake up."

"No more tequila," Gavin and Josh both said firmly from the hallway, but Devon pulled the door shut behind her.

Allie shut her eyes. She had a BFF again. That was going to come in handy if Gavin ended up breaking her heart.

Allie awoke several hours later, completely disoriented.

One look at the wallpaper in her childhood bedroom—the tiny yellow flowers on the white background that she'd picked out when she was twelve—reminded her where she was.

Her body insisted it was early afternoon.

In Alaska, it was. In Promise Harbor, it was—she squinted at the clock—five-oh-four. She groaned. This was going to take some adjusting.

And the tequila definitely hadn't helped.

She swung her legs over the edge of the bed and sighed. It wasn't the time that had awakened her. It was the noise downstairs. Which meant there were people here.

She really didn't want to see, or deal with, people.

Especially the ones she was related to.

She stepped into the kitchen, yawning, but she stopped in the doorway, blinked rapidly and rubbed her eyes. She still didn't believe what she saw.

Danny was at the stove. Cooking.

"What's going on?"

"Hey," he greeted her over his shoulder.

That didn't answer her question. She wandered farther into the room. "What are you doing?"

There were voices coming from the dining room just through the doorway.

"Making dinner."

"*You're* making dinner?"

"Pasta."

That was suspicious. "What kind?"

"Fettuccini with asparagus and salmon." He gave her a cocky grin. "I'm a natural in the kitchen."

"Lydia told you that?"

"Yep."

Allie couldn't believe that Lydia had been coaching her brothers to cook via Skype. "How would she know? She can't smell it or taste it."

"She just did. Said it was awesome."

"She..." Allie's attention was pulled from the fettuccini— that did look pretty good, especially considering she'd been asleep for a little over seven hours and was starving. "What do you mean she just did?"

"Like ten minutes ago."

Allie's gaze flew to the doorway leading to the dining room. "Lydia's *here*?"

"Yeah, got here like a half hour ago."

Allie headed for the dining room.

"Allie!" Devon was the first person she saw and the first to see her. Devon was out of her chair, a big red purse thrown over her shoulder, and at Allie's side seemingly in milliseconds. She grabbed Allie by the arm and tugged her down the hallway to the bathroom.

"What are you doing?"

"This is why I'm here," Devon said. She upended her purse on the countertop. Makeup, hair accessories and other items rolled, bounced and clattered on the Formica.

"To give me a makeover?"

Devon took her shoulders and turned her toward the mirror. "I figured you'd get out of bed, realize everyone was here, and you'd come running without realizing *this*." She gestured toward Allie's reflection.

Allie focused on her face. And winced.

"Ah."

"Yeah."

She'd gone straight to bed without taking her makeup off, brushing her hair or even changing out of her capris.

"Okay. Maybe I could freshen up."

"Start with this." Devon handed her a brand-new toothbrush, still in the package.

"You know," Allie grumbled as she took the brush and opened it. "It's a good thing we're best friends. I don't take that from just anyone."

Devon hugged her around the shoulders. "I know."

With Devon's help and red purse, Allie was presentable within fifteen minutes.

"So what do you think of Lydia?" The girl hadn't been very high on Allie's list of Things To Worry About for the past several hours, but now she wondered how Lydia was doing.

"Charlie seemed to be expecting her because he was right there at the door and whisked her off to his bedroom."

Allie sighed. "Great."

"He's twenty-five, hon," Devon said, applying blush to Allie's cheeks. "And they've obviously taken some time to get to know each other."

"I know. And she's *probably* twenty so it's legal," Allie said, trying to be glass half-full.

Devon laughed. "Josh asked Charlie about her. She's twenty-two."

"Oh." That made Allie feel better. If she just ignored the fact that her brother and Lydia were probably in his bedroom having sex right now, she'd feel even better.

When she and Devon emerged, Allie had to take a deep breath. The dining room was full of people. Lydia and Charlie were sitting at one end of the table with Josh and, thankfully, they didn't look particularly disheveled. Gavin sat at the other end, cradling a coffee cup in his hand and talking with Hayley Stone and Jackson Knight, Josh's best man—who had his arm across the back of Hayley's chair. Okay. That was weird. Gavin met her eyes and gave her a warm smile, but didn't move otherwise. He didn't rush to her side or ask how she was. He was just *there* and his smile told her he was fine. She didn't have to rush to his side or ask how he was either.

She could concentrate on everyone else.

But looking around the room, no one seemed to need a thing. Devon had joined Josh, perching on his lap and wrapping her arms around his neck. Hayley and Jackson were laughing—and sitting really close. Charlie whispered something in Lydia's ear that made her smile and blush. Danny had just carried another plate of pasta and a basket of garlic bread into the room.

Then things got really weird.

"We're home!"

Allie swung toward her father's booming voice. He and Sophie came through the kitchen with wide smiles and suitcases.

"Dad!" She went to him immediately. "Are you okay?"

Her dad dropped his suitcase and wrapped her in his arms. "Of course. *You?*"

"I'm…" She had to swallow and take a moment to just hug him before she said, "I'm fine."

"Charlie said so," Owen said, pulling back and smiling down at her. "Missed you."

Her dad spoke in simple sentences, sometimes with words left out here and there, since his accident. He often found it hard to talk quickly or with big words. But he'd always been quiet, more of an observer, so most people didn't notice. She wondered if Gavin would catch it now.

Allie studied her dad's face. He certainly looked fine. Maybe even good. "I—"

But her father had turned to Danny. "Smells great."

"Here, this one's yours," Danny said, setting two plates on the table.

"*You* make great pasta," Owen said to Allie as he let her go and pulled out a chair for Sophie. "So I never learned myself."

Allie stared at her father, then found Gavin's eyes. He looked concerned, but gave her a little smile.

She looked back at her dad. So she said she was fine and that was all there was to it? She'd run out of her wedding and been gone for almost two weeks, but that only took a few seconds of attention when there were noodles? And he hadn't learned to make pasta because she was so good at it? Was she so magically talented in sewing buttons and keeping track of dental appointments that he just couldn't bear to do those for himself either?

"She's good at pork chops too," Danny commented. "Don't know how she does it."

Because he'd never set foot in the kitchen as long as she was in there. Danny wandered in only for ready-made food—chips, cereal, and, of course, anything she made.

"You could read a recipe to find out how I do it," she muttered.

No one seemed to hear.

"And I love her pecan caramel rolls," Charlie added. "You should do some of those for tomorrow, sis.".

"No pecans for me," Owen said, taking a huge bite of Danny's pasta. He gave a groan of appreciation that she'd *never* heard for her cooking.

And he was reminding her to keep the nuts out of his rolls? She didn't forget stuff like that. He didn't like nuts. Right. She knew that. And, apparently, he couldn't pick them out of his rolls by himself. "If I forget, I'll stand there and pick them out for you," she said.

Her dad missed her sarcasm completely. He just smiled at her. "I know."

Allie stared at him and it hit her—he didn't miss her sarcasm because he was slow or because she hadn't been clear. Sarcasm simply wasn't a possibility in his mind. Her mother had never used sarcasm, she'd never been snotty, never joked around. She was sweet, but she was also serious and conventional. So why would her dad expect anything else from Allie? She had modeled everything she said and did here, with him and the boys, after her mom.

Allie pulled herself up tall and took a deep breath.

From here on, she was doing things differently. As she'd said to her mom yesterday at the cemetery, Allie loved and missed Lily, but she didn't want to *be* Lily.

"Dad," she said, stopping the conversation around the table, "there is no way in hell—"

"I need to talk to you." Gavin was out of his seat, his hand clamped around her wrist, dragging her from the room in seconds.

"Hey." She tugged against his hold. "I was just—"

"About to say something you'd regret," he said, stopping and turning to face her. They were in the entryway by the back door off the kitchen. Far enough from the dining room that no one would hear them.

She pulled free and crossed her arms. She wanted to deny it, but couldn't. So she just frowned at him.

"Listen, if you really want to tell your dad and brothers to go to hell, go for it. I won't stop you again. But just think about it for a second before you do. Make sure that's what you want."

"Why wouldn't I want to?" she asked, defiantly. "They're driving me crazy."

"But are you frustrated with them...or with yourself?"

That stopped her. She frowned. "I don't know what you're talking about."

Gavin lifted an eyebrow that said he wasn't buying that, but replied, "Just be sure."

"Well, what if I am frustrated with them?" she asked. "I came running home when I found out things were falling apart, gave up the trip and you."

He shrugged. "Maybe you're frustrated because things aren't actually falling apart."

"But..."

Dammit.

He was right. They weren't falling apart.

Her dad was going on trips with Sophie, obviously having a great time and managing everything in the house. Whether or not he'd had help, it hadn't been *her* help. Danny was doing fine, not only with class but cooking, and cooking *well* for god's sake. And Charlie was in love. Working. Smiling.

Hell, they were all doing more than *she* was. She hadn't cleaned a house, paid a bill or cooked a meal in almost two weeks, thanks to Lydia.

Which frustrated her *more*. "That means I've spent all this time doing stuff for them they didn't need."

Gavin reached for her and pulled her close. "Maybe *you* needed it."

She sniffed, and as his arms went around her, she felt something let go inside of her. She hugged him close and finally admitted what she'd been denying all this time. "I did," she said hoarsely. "I needed to do something to remember her and to keep from losing my mind."

Gavin held her tighter. "It's okay, Allie."

"But..." she sniffed, "now what?"

Gavin didn't know the answer to that.

Allie and her family had established some...interesting...patterns. What did they do now?

"Positive family dynamics are hardly my forte," he said with a little laugh. "I don't know."

She studied his face, then said quietly, "Thanks."

"For *not* having an answer for you?"

"For pulling me out of there before I swore at my father."

He shrugged. "Instinct."

"Well, it was good. Having you here is good."

He thought about that. It did feel good. In fact, he couldn't imagine being anywhere else. Which meant...he was staying as long as she was. Even if it was forever. And *that* didn't feel quite as good.

He gave her a smile though, somehow. "I have a question for you," he said, as something—amazingly—came to him.

"Okay."

"You know how none of you knew your mom's favorite flower?" he asked.

"Yeah."

"Do your brothers know *your* favorite flower?"

Her eyebrows pulled together slightly. "Probably not."

"How about your favorite cookie?"

She shook her head. "I doubt it."

"Your favorite movie?"

"No."

"Is it possible," he asked, "that it's because you've never told them? Not because they don't care or wouldn't care if they did know, but simply that you've been so busy taking care of them that the things *you* like have never come up?"

Allie just swallowed hard.

"Lydia compared you to a hummingbird," he said, remembering. Lydia had been frustrated with Allie at the time—big surprise—but it had been an accurate analogy.

"She did?" Allie seemed genuinely puzzled by that.

"A few days ago," he said with a nod.

"Why?"

"Have you ever watched a hummingbird?"

"I guess."

"They're hard to focus on," Gavin said, rubbing his hands up and down her upper arms. "They flit around and go so fast that's it hard to *really* see them." He took a breath and decided to go ahead and make his point. "Kind of like your mom," he said gently. "She was always moving, always doing something, so focused on everyone else that no one could focus on her. Kind of like you."

He watched the thoughts and emotions play across her face. She went from confused to surprised to thoughtful to, finally, understanding. She wet her lips. "I suppose it's possible," she admitted. "We've never really talked about that kind of stuff."

"You mean, you've never really talked about *you*. Who you are, what you like."

"Okay," she said softly. "Maybe."

"Do that," he said simply.

"Just go sit down and start talking about myself?" she asked.

"Kind of. Do you know Danny's favorite cookie?"

"Danny likes all cookies," she said.

"But surely he has a favorite," Gavin pressed.

It was amazing, but he actually saw her eyes lighten and the lines around her mouth that showed how tense she was ease. "He probably does."

"And Charlie probably has a favorite movie."

"Probably."

"There you go."

She stood just looking at him for a long moment and he finally asked, "What?"

"I thought you said you were just coming along to hold my hand."

"Allie, I just..." Acted without thinking. He'd just needed to do something to protect her—even if it was from herself.

"You're doing great," she said with a smile.

He felt relief wash through him. "Maybe we should go back in the other room while I'm ahead."

Chapter Twelve

He kept hold of her hand as they stepped out of the little alcove into the kitchen. Josh was leaning back against the sink, clearly waiting for them.

Gavin drew up short, keeping a shoulder in front of Allie, putting him between her and her ex.

Josh noticed. He lifted an eyebrow and straightened from his slouch. "Everything okay?"

Gavin didn't do the everyone-in-his-business thing well and he was hardly ready for Josh, of all people, to act possessive or concerned. "You've *got* to be kidding me."

Josh seemed unruffled. Typical. And annoying. "I'm not kidding." He looked at Allie. "You okay?"

Gavin stepped forward before she could answer. "Her being okay is *my* job." He said it firmly, meeting Josh's gaze directly. He knew the other man would know what he meant.

Josh's jaw tightened. "We just care about her."

"Now it's even 'we'?" Gavin asked. Of course. They were all her bodyguards as long as she was here doing what they wanted her to do.

"It's always been 'we'." Josh's words were steady and sure. "We're a family. Whether Allie and I are married or not, our families and our lives are mixed together. It will always be that way."

Gavin worked on not reacting. He wasn't going to let Josh get to him. He wasn't even entirely sure that Josh was *trying* to get to him.

Gavin recognized that he was likely riled up, at least in part, because he was damned uncomfortable here. There were a lot of people here at once who knew each other too frickin' well and had for a long frickin' time. They were at ease being in each other's personal space as well as each other's business.

In Gavin's life, people knew what he wanted them to know and he asked only about the things he wanted to know from them. There wasn't a lot of deep-dark-secret-sharing in his life, he didn't have a lot of history with anyone he spent time with, and there definitely wasn't a lot of touchy-feely-hugging going on. It certainly never got to whatever-this-was between the Ralstons and the Brewsters. Here it was really hard to tell where one family stopped and the other started. Watching Josh with Danny and Charlie, he was sure most people would assume they were all brothers. Seeing how Sophie watched Allie, with pride and affection clear on her face, a stranger would very likely believe that Allie was Sophie's own. And watching Owen and Sophie together, it was *very* hard to believe they weren't more than friends and neighbors.

So Josh felt protective and concerned. Fine. Gavin wasn't going to tell Josh to fuck off. He also wasn't going to punch him in the face. If the other man was testing him, he'd try to understand. If Josh was warning him, Gavin would probably be smart to heed it. But he would not back down, he would not tuck tail and run and he would not show Josh—or Allie—how Josh's words about family stabbed Gavin in the gut.

Family was something Gavin wasn't good at. That and being there for Allie when she needed him. But he was working on it. All of it. And it was none of Josh Brewster's business anyway.

Fuck. He *really* wanted to punch Josh, though.

"I appreciate you looking out for her," Gavin made himself say.

Not that he thought Josh had done a very damned good job of it, considering how sick and exhausted she was when Gavin got to her. He could just fucking keep on looking out for her the way he'd done after she left the wedding with Gavin—from afar.

"I'm not just looking out for her," Josh said. "Family goes deeper than that. It's forever, no matter what."

"I'm good with forever, no matter what," Gavin said, trying not to growl. "We'll just have to put another chair at the family dinner table. Because where Allie is, I am."

Josh didn't look impressed. He moved his attention to Allie. "So you are okay?"

Gavin heard her sigh. "Yes, Josh, I'm fine."

"Your dad doesn't realize—"

"I know," she broke in. "I'm fine."

Gavin felt satisfaction course through him and barely kept from grinning smugly. He'd talked to her about her dad and she'd listened. She'd cut Josh off. Ha.

"If you need—"

"She's good," Gavin said.

"Everything okay in here?"

Jackson strolled into the room, looking casual, but Gavin knew he was there as Josh's backup.

"We're fine," Gavin said tightly.

"Completely fine," Allie agreed.

Josh even nodded. "Yeah."

"You sure? You've been in here a while. The three of you are kinda full of surprises lately, so we were wondering."

There was that "we" again. Gavin gritted his teeth.

"Just talking," Allie said.

"Just making sure everyone is good," Josh added.

"Brewster," Gavin said with warning, "I think we're straight on that, don't you?"

Josh hesitated and Gavin came that much closer to hitting him.

Then Hayley Stone came through the doorway. "Everything okay in here?"

"For fuck's sake," Gavin muttered, starting toward the living room with Allie in tow.

It was anyone's guess if Hayley had come in because of Jackson, because of Gavin or just because she was the only one who carried a gun, but Gavin was done reassuring anyone about anything. He was still trying to get used to having five conversations going on around him all at the same time and having so many people in one space at one time that he couldn't keep track of which coffee cup was his.

Having everyone constantly making sure everyone else was "okay" and "fine" and "good" was really getting on his nerves.

He strode past Josh, Jackson and Hayley and headed straight for the couch, where he deposited Allie next to her father while he sat on her other side. There was no room for anyone else, and here he could just sit back, touch Allie and *not talk* for five frickin' minutes.

Forty minutes later, his head was pounding. It was so loud and chaotic in the room, and, he could admit, he was tense. His neck and shoulders for sure—feeding his headache—but he felt the tension all the way to his gut.

Looking over at Lydia, expecting a similar reaction from the girl who made keeping to herself an art form, he was surprised to see her grinning and talking and laughing right along with them. She'd never be as animated as Charlie, but he seemed to bring something out in her that Gavin hadn't seen until now.

He glanced at Allie. He knew the feeling.

Never would he have imagined sitting in her father's living room with her entire family plus the Brewster embellishments, *plus* the embellishments of the embellishments. He suspected that Hayley and Jackson were here equally for Josh and for Gavin himself. Hayley knew him well. She had to have known this would be so far out of his comfort zone he'd need GPS to find his way back.

She gave him a wink and saluted him with her coffee cup.

He rolled his eyes at her.

Then he tuned in to Allie again. She was doing a good job just *being*. She hadn't refilled any coffee cups, hadn't cleared the dishes off the dining room table—Devon and Jackson had done that actually—and hadn't unpacked her father's suitcase that still sat in the corner. It might be driving her crazy, but she was putting true effort into just sitting and talking with her family.

He kept his hand on her knee though. He'd only needed to squeeze three times and say "let it go" twice.

He glanced over at Josh. He had his hand on the back of

Devon's neck and was laughing at something Danny was saying, but Gavin knew Josh was keeping his eye on him and Allie.

Or maybe he wasn't and Gavin was just paranoid.

Yeah, maybe that.

Josh glanced over just then and Gavin wanted to flip him off.

And it wasn't even really Josh's fault. He was in love with Devon. Obviously. And why not? Devon was gorgeous, smart, sweet and clearly loved him back.

No, it wasn't that Gavin was worried about Josh wanting Allie. Or vice versa.

It was more that Josh fit with her better than Gavin did.

Gavin lived in Alaska. Josh lived here. Gavin didn't know Allie's family. Josh was part of them. Gavin could barely say the right thing while Josh couldn't do anything wrong.

He wasn't worried about Allie wanting Josh or vice versa. But Brewster was like a big old reminder of the things Allie needed.

Which made Gavin very tense.

And that was even without thinking about the fact that Josh had seen Allie naked.

Gavin rolled his neck and tried hard not to squeeze Allie's knee too hard as his tension ratcheted up. He was going to have to get over the urge to hit Josh. Allie and Devon had apparently made amends and Gavin's best friend was with Josh's best friend. It seemed inevitable that he'd be spending time with the guy.

Truthfully, Josh might have a few reasons for wanting to punch him too, Gavin admitted. Like the whole ruining-his-wedding thing. For instance.

Gavin rubbed a hand over his face. God almighty. He was sitting in the middle of the living room, literally surrounded by everyone who had been most affected by him storming into the wedding. Suddenly he felt like the biggest ass in the world. He was drinking coffee with the people whose lives he'd turned upside down.

Sure, it might have been for the best and everyone here might even admit that—but he still felt like an ass.

He quickly stretched to his feet, causing Allie to jump slightly. He strode to the kitchen, knowing she'd follow. He concentrated on breathing deep. He just needed a break. This was all a lot to deal with at once.

He downed a glass of water and turned in time to see Allie enter the kitchen.

"You okay?" She looked...like she didn't want to be here.

"Yeah. Sure."

She sighed and came forward, wrapping her arms around him.

Gavin buried his nose in her hair, breathing deep and absorbing the feel of her. Her warmth, her softness, just *her*.

God, he wanted her. He did. She was worth all the discomfort, the questions and concerns from her friends and family, the constant desire to punch something. Or someone.

"I know they can be a bit much."

He laughed softly. "Yeah."

"They're just protective. They just—"

"Allie, I literally carried you out of your wedding in front of all of them. They have a right to think this is weird, to be unsure of me."

She pulled back to look up at him. "Is it weird for you?"

He looked her straight in the eye. "Yes."

She winced. "Sorry."

"I just need to ease into it, I think."

"They're not used to you being here. It will get better," she said.

"Devon and Jackson aren't usually here."

She lifted a shoulder. "They are, actually. I mean, we're used to having them around at different times. Jackson and Josh have always been friends, and through middle school and high school Devon was a pretty regular fixture here."

"Right." Gavin drew back, pushing a hand through his hair. He was the new guy, the one who didn't quite fit, the question mark.

"Gavin—"

"I'm gonna go for a drive."

Allie clutched his forearm. "No, just—"

"I need some breathing room."

"Let me come with you."

He shook his head. The last thing he should do was whisk her away from them again right now. She needed to be here with them, if for no other reason than so *they* could see *she* was okay. And frankly, he wanted to be alone.

If he wanted to be with Allie, he had to be with them too. At least for awhile. Until they all got to know him and understood how much he loved her. But he needed to take them in smaller doses. Which meant figuring out a plan to stay in Promise Harbor and not need psychiatric attention.

"No, you stay. I'll be back. Or I'll call you later," he said, stepping back.

"Gavin, I know this isn't your thing, but give them a chance. They mean well. And no one blames you for anything."

Oh, that so wasn't true. He gave her a little smile, kissed her forehead and then headed for the door. "I'll talk to you later."

Allie felt sick and numb as she watched Gavin pull the truck he'd borrowed from Hayley out of the driveway and disappear down the street. She hugged herself tighter and tried not to cry.

He said he'd be back. She had no reason not to believe him. That wasn't the problem.

What bothered her was that even though he'd come back, he wouldn't want to.

"Dammit," she breathed, her stomach cramping. She wanted him happy. She hated the idea that being here with her, and her family, was making him *un*happy.

She knew it was a lot for him to take in and deal with at

once. She'd been around all these people—often all at the same time like this—her whole life and they could still overwhelm her at times.

But she'd really hoped... She breathed out. Hell, she didn't know. What had she hoped? She had barely had time to think about Gavin's integration with her family. She'd been so focused on getting home and checking on everything that she hadn't thought much beyond the moment, to be honest.

And now, here they were. They had no experience here.

"Fuck."

She turned and bumped into Hayley.

Hayley's eyebrows went up. "I don't think I've ever heard you swear."

Allie gave her a weak smile. She didn't know Hayley well. They were friendly acquaintances for sure. Maybe more than that. But they hadn't spent a lot of time together, and certainly not one-on-one. "The swearing has been happening more and more often lately," Allie admitted.

Hayley glanced at the door Gavin had left through. "I can imagine."

"No, not because of him," Allie said quickly. Then she shrugged. "Yeah, okay, partly because of him."

"Gavin is one of the most stubborn people I've ever met," Hayley told her.

Allie nodded.

"But he's a great guy."

Allie nodded again. "You don't have to sell me on him, Hayley."

"Okay, good." Hayley smiled. "He's a little spooked. But give him time. He loves you, Allie. He's not going anywhere."

Her words poked at Allie's heart. They were what she wanted to hear. Or so she thought. They were meant to be reassuring, she knew. But something about it bothered her.

"He's not going anywhere *because* he loves me?" she asked.

"Right."

And, of course, she knew that. Gavin hadn't chosen to

come back to Promise Harbor for any reason other than because she was coming back. He never would have otherwise, she was sure.

Allie pinched the bridge of her nose. *He won't get on the plane without saying good-bye,* she told herself. *He's spooked, but he won't leave you.*

But that bothered her, too. He wouldn't leave no matter how miserable or uncomfortable or sad or frustrated he became, because of her. That urge to take care of him was strong, just like when she'd seen him after the polar bear died.

"I might have to break into your house later," Allie told Hayley. "He's sleeping on the couch, right?"

Hayley chuckled. "How about I leave the front door unlocked? Unless you've changed *a lot,* I don't see you being real great at breaking in and I don't want to have to replace a window or my door."

Allie smiled. "I think it's really in my best interest for you to believe that I would have no clue how to break in, no matter what the truth is."

"Agreed."

The girls headed back for the living room full of the people Allie loved most in the world. Well, all but one.

She glanced once more at the back door.

The *main* one was missing. But he'd be back.

She was pretty sure.

The clock said two a.m. Allie was just digging in her suitcase for her left shoe and mentally rehearsing how to tiptoe across her bedroom floor, skip over the creaky step that was eighth from the top, slip out the side door and borrow her brother's car to drive to Hayley's when she heard three quick taps, a pause and two more taps on her window. She spun, transported for a moment to third grade, fully expecting to see Devon's face in the window.

But it was Gavin.

"Oh, thank god," she breathed as she slid the screen out of the window and opened it for him. "Did Devon tell you how to get up here?"

"Yeah." He climbed through awkwardly, but before he was even solid on his feet, he was cupping her face in both hands. "God, I need you."

She felt the same way. The moment his mouth covered hers, she felt the tension and worry melt away. She drew in his heat, the firmness of his chest and shoulders, and completely immersed herself in the reality that he was *here*. He was here, with her, *because* of her...

She tried to pull away, to ask how he was, where he'd gone, but he wouldn't let her get far.

"I need you, Allie. I need to have you right now."

Hunger slid through her, attempting to block out the other emotions. She wanted him to have her right now too—to feel him big and hot and solid against her, surrounding her, moving in her. She craved the way he made her feel like she was the most important thing in the world.

If she was the most important thing to him, he wouldn't leave, right? He wouldn't break her heart.

But the intensity of his kisses, the way his hands gripped her hips and pressed her against the very obvious erection, the need in his voice all made her hot...and panicked.

God, just like always, the love and panic warred. But this time the panic wasn't for what he was making her feel, but for how *she* was making *him* feel. He'd do anything for her. Even something that was bad for him.

"Gav..." She wedged her hands between them somehow and pushed.

He relented enough to rest his forehead against hers, but his big hand cradled the back of her neck and the other stayed at her hip, not letting her pull away.

"Are you okay?" she asked, running her palm over the prickliness along his jaw.

He turned his head and kissed the middle of her hand, sending desire zinging through her. "I am," he said.

"Everything's fine."

"I was wor—"

"Allie, you love me, right?" he interrupted.

She frowned slightly. "Of course."

"Then everything's fine."

"You just seem..." She trailed off, not sure how to describe him. He seemed determined. Like he had when she'd first come to Alaska. Determined to make things right, to make her happy, to make it work.

Which was okay, wasn't it? Things took work. Relationships weren't easy. This was all new territory for them. She had to expect it to be a little rocky. Right?

"I just need you," he said, tipping his head to kiss her again. He kissed her softly at first, then opened slightly and licked along her bottom lip. "I need your body, your heat, your softness," he said huskily against her mouth. "Let me have you. Tonight. Now."

Sure, she was going to say no to *that*.

"Gavin." She whispered her surrender, her hands gripping the front of his T-shirt.

He lifted her to her tiptoes and she could feel the delicious, incredibly hard length of his desire behind his zipper.

When he let her up for air, all she could do was nod. If Gavin needed her, she couldn't deny him. For anything.

He started to back her toward the bed, but she dug her heels in. "Can't," she said shaking her head and grinning. "The headboard will bang against Danny's bedroom wall."

Gavin chuckled. "It's been a long time since I had to worry about a girl's little brother overhearing us."

She shook her head. "Don't want to hear your sordid stories. Just kiss me again."

He did. Hot and thoroughly. As he turned and walked her back to the wall beside the window. He pressed close, his hips to hers, making her moan.

She had been planning to go out to find him, but she certainly wasn't dressed in many layers. Gavin made short work of stripping off her light T-shirt and tossing it over his shoulder. Her bra followed and his hands cupped her, tugging on the tips that begged for his attention.

Her shorts and panties landed on top of the T-shirt and bra seconds later. Then his hands were everywhere. Insistent. Hot. Bringing her to the edge he knew so well. He stroked and sucked, pressed and plucked until she was writhing against the wall.

"Please, Gavin, please."

He didn't even undress. He unzipped—somehow keeping fingers thrusting deep, though not *quite* hard enough—and shoved his clothing out of the way so that when he bent his knees and surged upward, he slid home.

He filled her, stretched her, set every nerve on fire. She used his broad shoulders to lift herself and wrap her legs around his hips, pressing close and taking him fully.

"Yes, god yes, Al," he panted. "This. You. All I need."

His words, his strokes, the look of desire and love on his face were all she needed to thunder toward the crest and shoot over the top as her orgasm swept through her, shaking every cell.

Gavin continued to thrust, his gaze intent on hers. One hand cupped her butt, keeping her in place against the wall, while the other snuck between them and found her clit, circling, then pressing, then circling again.

Allie quickly felt additional tremors begin deep inside and sucked in a sharp breath. She tightened on his length, digging her heels into his butt so she could move with him. This time the orgasm came over her slowly, like lowering herself into a warm bath. But it was no less satisfying.

Gavin still thrust beyond her climax. She kissed him, curled her fingers into his hair and finally licked up the length of his neck, then whispered hoarsely in his ear, "I love you, Gavin."

He let go of his control then and pounded into her, coming hard in only minutes.

Gasping for air, he slumped forward, his forehead to the

wall over her shoulder. Allie just held on, her arms and legs still around him, her cheek against his shoulder.

"Damn, girl, that was good."

She laughed softly. "Feel better?"

"Much." He squeezed her ass before pulling back and letting her slide to the floor.

She felt pretty damned good herself. "Wish you could stay."

"Me too." He cupped her face and kissed her, then tucked himself back into his jeans.

Allie pushed her hair back from her face. She'd gotten used to sleeping in his arms. This was going to suck. "I won't be living here forever," she told him. "I'll um...have to...get a place." For some reason she felt like an idiot.

"I'll see you tomorrow." He leaned in for another kiss, then started for the window.

"Barbecue. At the Brewster's. Eleven o'clock, okay?"

He nodded as he swung a leg over the windowsill. "Hayley told me. I'm bringing chips."

She smiled, wishing it was all as easy and comfortable as it sounded. "See you then."

"Love you."

"Love you too."

Then he disappeared through the window and into the night.

In spite of the two a.m. booty call, Gavin awoke early.

He knew it was the tension that had been swirling in his gut since Allie had told him she was coming home to Promise Harbor, but hanging out with Allie's family, a long drive, an even longer run and half a bottle of Rolaids hadn't helped.

He heard Haley banging around in the kitchen and headed in for hot caffeine. Hayley made fantastic coffee.

"Morning, sunshine," Hayley greeted him with a grin. She was being annoyingly perky this morning and he knew it was just to drive him crazy.

"Hey." He poured coffee and drank without even letting it cool.

"So, two a.m., huh?" she asked, handing him a piece of toast.

It was an old house with plenty of creaking boards and squeaky hinges, but he'd been incredibly quiet sneaking out and back in. "How'd you know?"

"I'm a cop, Gav. You really think I'm not going to hear somebody going in and out of my house in the middle of the night?"

"Right." He grinned. "Thanks for not coming after me with your billy club."

She winked. "I won't do that unless you try to leave here without Allie, 'kay?"

He swallowed his coffee wrong and started to hack. He set his cup down, braced his hands on the counter and breathed until he could do it without coughing.

When he looked up, Hayley was leaning against the counter, watching him, munching on her toast. She was dressed in a simple T-shirt and shorts, her hair pulled back, but somehow she managed to look intimidating. "I'm serious, Gavin," she said when he stopped making so much noise.

"I'm not going to leave her," he said crossly. "Why'd you think that?" But he felt heat rise along his neck. Fuck. He wasn't *actually* going to leave her, but he couldn't deny that yesterday, for just a minute, he'd wondered if that would be best. Leave her here where she wanted to be, where she thought she needed to be.

"You looked pretty spooked yesterday." Hayley tipped her head, studying him. "And right now."

"I'm just not used to all of this." That had to be it. This would pass. Like a pair of new shoes: things felt tight and uncomfortable right now, but over time things would ease—or he'd build up some calluses.

Hayley gave him one of her cop looks. "Don't lie to me, Gavin. You don't want to be here."

"I'll get over it." He paced to the other side of the room,

feeling crowded by his best friend.

"Yeah, probably. Maybe. But the harbor doesn't have everything for everyone. And that doesn't make you a bad person."

He stared down at the pattern on Hayley's kitchen floor and let himself really feel all the things he'd been trying to keep tamped down since setting foot in his hometown. Finally he lifted his head and met Hayley's eyes. "You sure?"

She frowned. "What do you mean?"

"I don't want to live here in my hometown with my family and old friends. I want to take Allie away from her home, family and friends. Are you sure that doesn't make me a bad person?"

Hayley set her cup down on the counter beside her and crossed her arms. "I guess that depends on *why* you don't want to be here."

He could be honest with Hayley. She wouldn't judge him. She knew him. "I don't think it's good for her. There's a whole big world out there, Hayley. She loved Alaska. She relaxed. She saw new things, met new people. She could carve out the life she wanted somewhere else. Here there are expectations and history and...her mom's ghost. I don't think she'll ever be totally who she wants to be here."

Hayley swallowed and nodded. "See, that doesn't make you a bad person."

"Well, it's all convenient, considering *I* don't want to live here either."

"Why? Still your dad?"

"That and..." He took a deep breath. He was going to be honest and hope that he didn't hurt her feelings. "There's a lot more in the world than this little town, Hayley. Staying home is great for some people." He gave her a pointed look. "But it's not for everybody. Around here, though, you're a black sheep or selfish or just plain wrong if you don't want to live here with your family in your backyard, hanging out with the same people you've known your whole life."

Hayley cocked an eyebrow.

"I love you, you know that," he said quickly. "But our

relationship is great, it's strong, even across a distance."

She nodded and said softly, "I know."

"So, am I a bad person?"

"Not at all." She pushed away from the counter. "You could come visit more often though."

He smiled. "Yeah, well, in spite of my big speech, I'm not going anywhere."

Hayley sighed. "I knew you were going to say that."

"I can't." He stuffed his hands in his pockets. "She's not ready to go. If she ever is, I'll definitely be the guy to show her the world, but..." he sighed, "...until then, I'm here with her."

Hayley crossed the room quickly, wrapping her arms around him. "I have fantastic taste in best friends," she said against his shirt.

Surprised, he hugged her back. Hayley was definitely showing a softer side since meeting Jackson. "So, everything good with you?"

She pulled back and nodded, giving him a big smile. "Really good."

He was glad. This was certainly one bright side to staying in Promise Harbor. He'd love to spend more time with Hayley and Jackson. The guy seemed perfect for her. Which was a good thing. Gavin would have felt compelled to kick Jackson's ass and, frankly, he wasn't sure that would have gone his way. He didn't think it would be the smartest move to try to take on an ex-hockey player.

As she headed to retrieve her coffee cup again, Gavin finally accepted what he had to do today before he saw Allie. "Hey, do you happen to know where Dad and the guys are working today?"

Hayley looked over her shoulder in surprise. "Yeah."

She always knew stuff like that. She was a cop, and Montgomery Contracting was a big company with lots of employees and trucks out and around town.

"I need to talk to him. And not on the phone."

"Your dad?" She turned to face him.

Gavin nodded.

"Today?"

"Right now." He said it firmly and that was enough for Hayley.

"The church," she said.

"The church? There are like eight churches in town. Which one?"

"*The* church," she said, changing the emphasis.

"Wha..." Then what she was saying hit him. "*The* church?"

"They're adding on to the social hall," she said. "They were just waiting for the biggest wedding of the season to get over with so they could tear things up."

Gavin closed his eyes and ran his hand over his face. This had to be bad karma or something. If he believed in that kind of stuff.

"Okay," he finally said.

"You're going over there?"

"Have to."

Hayley looked worried and intrigued at the same time. "If things get bad, call my cell, not 9-1-1. I'm not on duty today and I want to be first on *that* scene."

"You're hilarious." But as Gavin headed for the shower, he had to admit that a big Montgomery family brawl in the middle of St. Mark's Methodist Church wasn't last on the list of possibilities.

Twenty minutes later he was on his way to the church, the knot in his gut tightening further with each block.

"Dammit," Gavin swore ten minutes later as he pulled up in front of St. Mark's for the second time in as many weeks.

Sure enough, his father's truck was here. He could tell by the Garth Brooks CD case, the empty Snickers bar wrapper, and the very faded orange Grand Canyon National Park cap on the dash. He couldn't believe his dad was still wearing that cap.

Gavin gripped the steering wheel and tried to calm down.

He needed to get this showdown with his father over with. The sooner he laid down the rules and said what he had to say, the sooner he could have some peace. And if he was going to live in Promise Harbor, he was going to have some peace. Even if it killed him.

But he *really* didn't want to do this.

He climbed the steps at about a fourth of the speed he'd used the last time. Two weeks ago he couldn't wait to get in there. Literally. If he'd waited, Allie would have belonged to Josh.

This time, he wanted to be anywhere else, doing anything else. Even having a picnic at Sophie's place with Josh and company.

He really didn't want to see his father.

He supposed he didn't *have* to. But...well, yeah, he did actually have to. He'd gotten a call on his cell yesterday while he was running. It was from Ken Martin, the long-time vet in Promise Harbor. He said he'd heard that Gavin was moving home and he wanted to talk about selling his practice.

Wasn't that convenient? It wasn't like Gavin didn't know his father and Ken had been friends and golf partners for years.

Convenient his ass. He had to nip this shit in the bud or his father was going to keep manipulating and interfering. There was no way Gavin was taking over the local practice. No way.

Gavin paused with his hand on the handle of the big, heavy oak door.

But maybe he should take it.

He didn't love his dad getting involved when Gavin had specifically told him not to, but he also couldn't deny that it was the perfect setup. This wasn't like his sophomore science class where his dad leaned on the right people to get Gavin the B he needed to stay on the football team. This wasn't like the party where the high school principal's car ended up in the river and his dad worked it so Gavin hadn't paid a penny or done even a minute of community service.

This time it made sense. It fit. It was something he'd earned—at least in part. He'd graduated top of his class in college and vet school. He was a great vet. Promise Harbor would be lucky to have him.

Even more, it would prove to Allie, and her friends and family, that he was serious. He was staying and that was that.

"Fuck." He arm outstretched, hand still on the handle, Gavin let his head drop forward and his eyes close.

He couldn't do it. He couldn't take something that had come to him through his dad's connections, whether he wanted it or would be good at it or not.

He'd made his life, his reputation, his relationships on his own, away from this place, for ten years. He could do it again. He'd work his way into the community and eventually establish his own practice.

And in the meantime, he'd make some money and work on his family relationships and see what happened.

"Dammit," he breathed. His stomach was churning, his heart and head pounded, but this was what he had to do. To be with Allie, he'd do anything.

He shoved the door open, the old hinges creaking, announcing his arrival.

But he'd stepped into the sanctuary. The social hall was the east wing of the church. He strode down the aisle with purpose, just as he'd done two weeks ago. He, of course, replayed every second of that day in his head and knew that he'd do it all over again. He didn't have a single regret.

Even as he crossed past the altar and then through the doorway that would lead to the hall where his dad and brothers were.

He wouldn't change anything.

His dad was up on a tall ladder, facing where Gavin emerged.

"Gavin!"

His face broke into a wide smile that brought Gavin up short. He'd seen photos of his family over the years. His mother made a point of emailing him pictures from family gatherings and an annual Christmas card with a photo of her and his father. But he wasn't prepared for the new lines on his father's face and the gray in his hair.

"Hey, Dad."

Greg Montgomery descended the ladder faster than he should have, but it only wobbled slightly as he jumped past the final three rungs and headed for Gavin.

He looked like he was going for a hug and Gavin instinctively stepped back. He definitely wasn't ready for that.

"It's good to see you," Greg said, stopping a few feet away instead of enfolding Gavin.

"Thanks."

"I'm glad you came by. Surprised, but glad."

Gavin pulled in a deep breath. "Dad, up front, stay out of my business."

"I...yeah." Greg cleared his throat. "You mentioned that on the phone."

"And I meant it."

"Okay."

He seemed sincere and Gavin felt his chest tighten. He wanted his dad to be sincere about a lot of things. He wanted this to be like any other son going to see his dad when he was home visiting.

But it wasn't. It just wasn't.

"Dad, this is going to be..." Fuck, he didn't even know what it *was*, not to mention what it was going to be. He tried again. "This is hard."

His dad looked uncomfortable, but he nodded. "I know."

"I just..." There were a lot of things he wanted to say. Things he probably *should* say. Things he definitely shouldn't say.

Then he looked into his dad's face. Damn, maybe there wasn't anything he shouldn't say. Maybe they just needed it all out on the table.

"Gav, I know there are things you can't forget."

"You're right," he said. "There are things I can't forget. And honestly, that's what kills me, Dad." He rubbed the middle of his chest, where everything seemed to be knotting up. "I look at you and I remember so many things. Like the time you got us behind the scenes at the aquarium. And how you had us make cards for Mom on Mother's Day. And that you introduced me to the reruns of *Night Court*."

His dad nodded, but Gavin noticed he wasn't smiling. He knew the other shoe had to drop. Gavin hesitated. Did he need to keep going? Did he really need to say the rest? They both knew what was coming.

But he really did feel like he needed to lay it all out there.

"As much as I hate it and wish it was different, I also see the guy who hurt my mother and never got anything honestly in his life."

Greg flinched, then cleared his throat again. "I know."

Well, of course he knew was Gavin's first bitter thought. But then he watched his dad's gaze skitter from his. Greg's neck got red and he shifted from foot to foot. And like touching a live wire, Gavin felt a shock rock through him all the way to his feet.

His dad was ashamed.

This was so far from the angry, cocky man Gavin remembered from high school that he had a moment of disorientation. But this was his father. He'd recognize the cowlick—the same one he struggled to control—and the calluses on his big hands and the scuffed brown work boots anywhere.

Gavin was used to his chest and gut hurting when he thought about his father. It was Greg's fault. He'd done it, he'd been the ass who'd messed everything up. But maybe ten years had given him some perspective or something.

Or maybe Gavin was just tired of being pissed off all the time.

Or both.

"Okay," Gavin slipped his hands into his front pockets, "we both know what happened in the past. But there are about ten years to catch up on. Maybe we'll just do that for now."

Greg nodded. "Sounds good."

Gavin looked around, not sure what to do next. "Where are Gabe and Garrett?"

"In a meeting with the church board," Greg said, waving

toward a doorway. "They're really running the show now. I just come to pound nails anymore."

At least he hadn't said "screw things", Gavin thought. Then grimaced and ran a hand over his face. None of it was funny. His father's past, his family's dysfunction, Gavin's inability to get past it all. Definitely not funny.

But it felt...old. And tired.

He'd been hanging on to his anger and self-righteousness for so long now that it suddenly felt as if it had dried up and shrunk a little. It was still there. Still ugly—maybe even more so now that it had rotted for ten years—but it wasn't as big and didn't feel like it pressed on his heart quite the same way it used to.

He took a deep breath. "I came by to talk to you about maybe working with you for a while. While I get to know the community again, maybe put out some feelers about vet services."

Greg was clearly shocked. "You want to work with *me*? With us?"

Not really, but it seemed like a good way to make some cash here while he kept paying bills in Alaska. He couldn't stay on Hayley's couch indefinitely. This would also show Allie he was trying at this family thing. "For a while."

"I thought Ken Martin—"

"Ken called," Gavin broke in. "I'm not doing that and you should know that."

"I didn't ask him to call you," Greg said quickly. "We were just golfing and you came up."

"Uh-huh." Gavin felt exhausted suddenly. "It doesn't matter. I'll do it on my own."

"Gavin," Greg said earnestly. "It was bad timing, I know. But Ken and I are friends. Of course it came up that my son was finally coming back. He told me about his decision to retire *after* he'd called you."

Gavin looked his father directly in the eye for the first time in ten years. There was sincerity there. And regret.

He tried not to be moved. He wasn't—not really. Anything

his father regretted was all his own doing. But the sincerity got to Gavin.

"Fine. Okay. I believe you," Gavin finally said. "I'm still not taking over the practice. Not right now. I just need to..."

Fuck. He just needed to take one thing at a time.

"You can definitely work with us," Greg said, when Gavin still failed to come up with more words.

That was all he wanted. He wanted work that would provide him a paycheck, a chance to reconnect with his brothers, maybe let go of some more of his anger toward his father, and concentrate on Allie. That was all more than enough right now.

"Okay," he said.

Greg handed him a hammer. "You take the ladder. I'm getting too old for that stuff."

Right. Gavin didn't believe that for a second. But he took the hammer and climbed the ladder.

It was a start, at least.

Chapter Thirteen

Allie sat with her dad on the big swing in Sophie's backyard. He had his arm over the back of the swing behind her, and she leaned into him. The scent of Tide and coffee surrounded her—the combination that would forever bring her father to mind.

The scene in front of them was very familiar too. The Brewsters, even Greta and her new boyfriend, Hank—it seemed everyone had been busy falling in love in the past two weeks— were gathered with Danny, Charlie and Lydia, Hayley and Jackson, and Devon and Josh.

Josh, as usual, manned the grill, while Sophie made sure everyone's glasses and plates stayed full.

Allie watched the woman she'd always thought of as her second mom. "Did Sophie go crazy with a church full of people and no wedding?" Allie asked her dad.

It was the first time she'd spoken of the wedding debacle with anyone here other than Josh and Devon.

Owen chuckled. "Of course. But everyone went to the party. They forgave."

"Well, they all got their gifts back, I assume," Allie said, pushing the swing lazily with her foot. "No one was really out anything but an hour of their time. And no one could say it wasn't entertaining."

Owen chuckled and squeezed her upper arm, but he said nothing more.

"Were you...disappointed?" she asked him. "Or angry?"

He didn't reply right away, and Allie looked up to find him seemingly thinking about her question.

"Dad?"

"Not angry," he said easily. "Not disappointed either."

Allie shifted so she was out from under his arm and could face him fully. "Then what? Worried? Shocked?"

"Surprised. You let it get too far. You didn't want it," he finally said in his choppy way of speaking. "But it was Gavin—not shocked."

"Really?" Allie was a little shocked at that. "Concerned then?"

Owen shook his head. "No. You wanted to leave. You're careful. You know what you want. You wanted Gavin, so I didn't worry. Just felt bad for Josh."

Of course he had. Everyone in the church had, she was sure. She knew that the town had quickly divided into Team Josh and Team Allie.

That had been apparent, even without Danny's explanation, when she'd gone to the grocery store that morning for fruit salad ingredients and more hamburger buns. She'd been greeted and glared at equally, but she definitely hadn't gone unnoticed.

Some thought she was the biggest bitch to ever set foot in the harbor for leaving Josh. Most thought she was crazy. Apparently there was a rumor going around that she'd been kidnapped by Gavin. Another rumor was that Gavin was blackmailing her and another that she was pregnant with Gavin's baby. But there were also some people who thought Gavin's actions were romantic and that if Allie didn't want to marry Josh, then it was good she hadn't gone through with it.

Several thought that Josh was, and always had been, too good for her anyway.

"Sorry about the gossip. And the money," she said.

"I've survived worse," Owen said with a smile.

She leaned over and hugged him. "Thanks, Dad."

"You and Gavin might have to do smaller," Owen added when she released him. "Can't swing another open bar too soon."

The comment was casual, even a little teasing, but Allie felt the sharp clench of *I want that* in her chest. She wanted a wedding with Gavin.

She swallowed hard before she could respond. "We don't need anything fancy."

Did that mean she was considering marrying him? But the answer came immediately. Of course she was going to marry him.

"How long are you staying?" Owen asked, his eyes on the party rather than his daughter.

"Staying?" Allie looked around. Everyone was very settled in their chairs, their stomachs full and their loved ones gathered around. This party wouldn't be breaking up anytime soon. "A while. Gavin's not even here yet."

Which, if she thought about it, flipped her stomach. He wasn't just late—he'd missed lunch entirely. The barbecue had started two hours ago.

Where was he?

She was better just not thinking about it. They didn't need to be together twenty-four/seven. And he had old friends here. Maybe he'd run into someone. Maybe he was just sleeping late. Lord knew that she was all about shutting down when things got crazy. Besides, he'd still been very awake as of two a.m.

She knew he hadn't actually *left*. Not back to Alaska anyway. But he also wasn't *here*. He hadn't called or sent a message with Hayley.

Allie was trying to be cool about it. This was a lot for him and it would make sense that he'd dawdle on his way over.

But two hours was beyond showing up fashionably late or making a grand entrance.

"No, when back to Alaska?"

Owen's question yanked her back to the moment.

"What?"

"That's where Gavin lives?" Owen frowned like he was trying to remember something.

"Yes. That's where I've been."

"You'll be going back."

She sat back. "I will?"

"Why not?"

She stared at him. "Dad? Do you mean on a vacation, to visit?"

Owen focused on her. "You want Gavin?"

"Of course." That question, at least, had an easy answer.

"Then you'll move to Alaska."

Unbelievable. Allie couldn't quite wrap her head around her dad's assumption she was moving to the opposite side of the country.

"We might stay here." But even as she said it, it didn't feel good. Staying here didn't feel like it fit.

"Why?" Owen asked.

"For *you*," she said. "I'd stay for you."

Owen looked genuinely surprised by that. "Why?"

"Dad," she said, finally exasperated. "I do *everything* for you."

"I'm gonna have to work harder."

"Work harder? You make it sound like all this time you could have been doing all these things if you wanted to."

"I'm spoiled and lazy. Your mom did everything. Then you," he said. "But I can do things. Sophie will help me. Or I'll hire help. Really don't want to scrub toilets."

She blinked at him. "Seriously. You think you'll be fine if I pack up and move four thousand miles away."

"Gavin has a plane. You can come visit a lot. And I'll come visit you."

He made it sound so simple.

Which was ridiculous. Something like this couldn't be simple. Could it?

"What if you need something?" she asked.

Owen looked around the yard and grinned. "No problem, honey."

She looked around as well. He had a point. Then her gaze landed on Lydia and something in her heart clicked into place. She felt herself smile. With Lydia here, everything would be just fine.

The girl was a natural-born caregiver. She'd loved taking care of Gavin. Now she'd have Charlie, Danny, Owen, Sophie and who knew who else to boss around, organize and take care of. If anyone could herd this group, it was Lydia.

Wow. Maybe...

"I need a refill," Allie said. "How about you?"

"I'm good." Owen stretched to his feet with her and pulled her into a hug. "Be happy. Okay?"

She gripped the back of his shirt in her fists, breathing the Tide-coffee scent in deeply. Then she blinked against the moisture in her eyes and let him go. "I will, Dad. You too."

"Always have," Owen said. "Might not have done everything right, but always done that."

Allie looked up at him and felt the tears threaten again. She'd spent so much time paying attention to the things he needed that she hadn't really paid attention to *him*. Owen was happy. He really had always been happy. Her mom's illness and death had, of course, been a blow, but looking at him now, Allie had no doubt that he was happy and content and thankful. He was looking upon the gathering of family and friends with a pride and affection that was deep and genuine.

Okay, she could do that too. She *would* do that. And she was going to start by finding the man who had a lot to do with her happiness.

Hayley and Jackson were by the buffet table on the patio and Allie headed in that direction. Surely Hayley had an *idea* where Gavin might be.

"Hayley, did you talk to Gavin this morning?"

"Um..." Hayley looked at Jackson worriedly. "Yeah."

That was weird. "You okay?" Allie asked as she picked up the pitcher of homemade-with-freshly-squeezed-lemons-just-that-morning lemonade that Danny and Lydia had made. How had she not immediately seen how great Lydia would be for her brothers and dad? Shaking her head, Allie poured a glass, then turned to face Hayley and Jackson.

"I wasn't going to tell you," Hayley started out.

Allie straightened. She already didn't like whatever Hayley

was going to say. "What?"

"Because you'd worry," Hayley said.

"*What*, Hayley?"

"I don't know why Gavin's so late."

"But you know where he is," Allie guessed.

Hayley glanced at Jackson, then back to Allie. "Yeah. He went to talk to his dad."

Her words made Allie's breath catch. For some reason, she looked over to where Lydia was sitting with Charlie. The girl had obviously overheard. In fact, everyone had overheard, and all were watching her with varying degrees of curiosity and concern. Lydia definitely looked concerned.

"I thought Gavin didn't have contact with his parents," Charlie commented.

"Yeah," Allie said quietly. "I did too."

"He doesn't," Hayley added confidently. "It's been years. But he asked if I knew where his dad and brothers were working today so he could go see them."

"For what?" Allie's gut told her this wasn't good.

"He just said to talk," Hayley said. "But I know that Ken Martin called him yesterday. He's offering to sell his practice to Gavin."

Allie went cold. She knew Ken Martin. She also didn't think Gavin would have initiated that contact. "Does Ken know Gavin's dad?"

Hayley frowned. "Yes."

So Greg was up to his old tricks. He was getting Gavin a job. Dammit. That would piss Gavin off. It pissed *her* off. Gavin was perfectly capable of getting his own job, starting his own practice, whatever he wanted. And it didn't matter. He had a job, a thriving practice that he loved. He didn't need work in Promise Harbor. And he definitely didn't need his dad pulling strings and cashing in favors.

"Dammit."

"Yeah," Hayley agreed grimly. "And Gavin went to talk to his dad almost four hours ago."

"Okay. Where are they working?" Allie was going over there. Whatever was going on, Gavin needed her with him.

Being in love with him obviously made her feel protective— but *dammit*, Gavin was amazing; he'd done everything he set out to do with his life. His dad just needed to leave him the hell alone.

"Come on, Hayley," she said as she started for the sliding glass door leading into the house.

"I'm coming?" But Hayley was already following.

"Well, you can take me over there in your truck or ticket me for speeding in my own car."

"You're right. This is more efficient."

"I'm coming too," Jackson said, shoving back his chair and grabbing a handful of pretzels on his way to the door.

"Well, *I'm* not missing this," Devon said, getting up as well.

"Are you going to tell her where they're working today?" Josh asked, also getting to his feet and pulling his car keys from his pocket.

Allie stopped in the middle of the kitchen and looked at Hayley. "Where are they working?" Why did that possibly matter? It was a construction site. Gavin's dad and brothers owned Montgomery Contracting.

"Um." Hayley looked at Josh. He shrugged. "The church."

Allie frowned. "What church? There are eight in town."

"*The* church," Hayley said. "Your church."

"My...oh." The setting for the Wedding That Wasn't. "Got it."

"I'm so coming," Charlie said, tugging Lydia along with him. "Gavin came storming into that church to rescue you and now you're doing the same thing for him. Awesome."

Yeah, awesome.

Allie took a deep breath. Well, she was doing this anyway. Gavin was there so she was going to be there. It really was that simple.

Hayley made record time to St. Mark's. Allie, Hayley and Jackson piled out of her car while Charlie, Lydia and Danny pulled up at the curb with Josh, Devon, Sophie and Owen, and

Greta and Hank right behind them. Everyone headed for the front of the church together.

Allie threw open the doors and rushed inside. And came up short.

It was pretty anticlimactic really.

The sanctuary was empty.

She turned in a full circle. "Where are they?"

"Social hall." Hayley pointed to the east.

They burst into the great room a moment later. Allie actually slid a little on the slick tile floor with her flip-flops as she tried to slow her momentum.

Again, though, the room was empty.

Well, dammit.

She swung to face Hayley. "Well, where are they?"

Hayley looked around. "I don't know."

The rest of their gang crowded through the doorway, then stood looking around.

"They're not here?"

"What's going on?"

"Should we call him?"

Hayley held up a hand. "Shh! Listen."

They were all quiet immediately—that alone was amazing—and tipped their heads.

There were voices coming from the kitchen.

Angry male voices.

Allie started across the huge room for the swinging doors that led into the kitchen.

"Allie." Hayley followed.

"No, dammit!" someone inside the kitchen yelled.

It sounded like Gavin, and Allie picked up her pace.

"It's not a big deal," another voice said.

"It's a *huge* deal. This is bullshit. I told you not to do this."

"It's the best way."

"You never fucking listen!"

"Gavin!" Allie burst through the doors. "I'm here! Stop!"

Two men were squared off near a huge hole in the wall near the ovens. But neither of them were Gavin.

Gabe and Garrett Montgomery stared at her.

She stopped so quickly that Hayley plowed into her and Gabe lunged to catch her from going face-first into the kitchen floor.

He set her back on her feet, hands gripping her upper arms. "You okay?"

Allie pushed her hair back from her face. "Yeah. Where's Gavin?"

Gabe's mouth curled into a smile very much like his brother's. It didn't make her tummy tingle, but it was plenty charming. "He and Dad ran over to the office. Should be back soon."

"Al! They just pulled up!" Danny yelled from the social hall.

She stomped back into the big room. "Where?" This was getting ridiculous.

Danny was near the windows. "They're heading for the front doors."

Okay, this was it. She beelined for the sanctuary and was in front of the altar when Gavin and his father came through the main church doors.

"I think you and Gabe can get most of the kitchen sorted out," Greg was saying.

Neither man noticed her at first. She was aware of the crowd of people in the doorway from the social hall, but they all seemed to be hanging back, giving her space.

She put her hands on her hips.

"If he can handle the electric, I'm fine with the drywall and flooring," Gavin told his dad.

"Oh, hell no."

Both men looked up quickly and froze.

"Allie?" Gavin was clearly surprised to see her.

"We need to talk." She strode forward and grabbed his hand.

"We're just..." He let her lead him a few steps back down

the aisle before stopping her. "It's good, Al. Things are okay."

"Yeah, well, that's not good enough," she said firmly. She started tugging him toward the church doors again. Over his shoulder she noticed that their gang had moved partway into the sanctuary to get a better view.

Gavin stopped her movement. "What's not good enough?"

"Things being okay. I want things to be great. Wonderful. The best they can be."

"Nothing's perfect," Gavin said, pulling her close.

"I know. I don't want perfect. I just want things to be right."

"They will be."

She shook her head, knowing that coming back to the harbor had been good. But it wasn't *for good.*

"You said you weren't letting me go again, right?"

"Yes," he said resolutely. "I'm going to be wherever you are from now on."

"Good. I'm going to be in Alaska."

He stared at her, then narrowed his eyes suspiciously. "Why?"

"I love it there," she said simply. "It's good for me to be there. And for you."

Gavin looked like he was pondering something very serious. Finally he asked, "Who's going to take care of everyone here?"

She looked over her shoulder at their families and friends. "They'll take care of each other."

He moved a little closer. "And what if something comes up they don't know how to handle?"

She lifted a shoulder. "They'll figure it out. Or—" She glanced at Lydia. "They'll ask someone." She looked back at Gavin with a big smile. "Maybe even me sometimes."

He nodded solemnly. "So you're telling me that you're ready for me to be your broccoli *and* your chocolate frosting."

She smiled and stepped even closer. "No. I'm telling you that I've realized that you already are my broccoli, my chocolate frosting, my meatloaf, my potatoes, my bread—"

He interrupted her with a quick, but possessive, kiss. "I

accept," he told her when he'd lifted his head.

"You accept me going back to Alaska?"

"I accept your marriage proposal."

She felt her heart flip, but she raised an eyebrow. "That was a marriage proposal?"

"Babe, you know you're never going to find chocolate-covered broccoli like me again. You better tie me down while you have the chance."

She pretended to shudder. "Chocolate-covered broccoli?"

"I went too far with the analogy?"

"Maybe a little."

"Still," he said with a huge, cocky grin, his hands on her hips. "You've finally realized that I've got everything you need."

She laughed and wrapped her arms around his neck. "Yes. You definitely do."

"Damn right I do," he muttered before kissing her again for several long, sweet seconds.

When they finally took a breath, she said, "And when they all come visit, we're *definitely* going up for a flight-seeing tour."

He smiled. "Definitely."

"So, let's go." She pulled back and started for the doors again, his hand in hers.

"Hold on. Now? Today?"

She turned back. Gavin stood in front of the altar where he'd saved her from her wedding. His dad was just behind him, and his brothers, hers, her father and everyone she loved most were gathered to the side, looking on, their arms around one another.

Most importantly, everyone was smiling.

"We'll have to pack and say good-bye to everyone. But, yes. Today. I have to get back."

Gavin's eyebrows went up. "You do?"

"The sooner I get back, the sooner I can start mountain-climbing classes," she said with a smile.

He chuckled. "Is that right?"

"And speaking of fun," she said with a grin. "I have some

ideas for the kitchen now that Lydia won't be there."

Gavin glanced toward the girl, then back to Allie. "I do still like your lasagna best."

She laughed. "Well, if lasagna is a euphemism for sex, then we're totally on the same page."

"Yep, definitely time to go home," Gavin said. "Right after we get hitched."

Allie felt her heart expand in her chest. "My dress is still in Alaska," she said, as her eyes filled with happy tears.

"You are *not* wearing that dress. Ever again."

"There's still leftover food in the freezer!" Sophie called.

Allie giggled and gave Gavin a huge smile. "What do you think? Do you mind using leftover wedding cake at our wedding?"

Gavin pulled her close. "As long as *I'm* the one you're saying I do to...and as long as it will be thawed out by tomorrow morning."

"Tomorrow morning?" she asked, wrapping her arms around him, "I have to wait that long?"

Epilogue

"Dearly beloved, we are gathered here today to unite this man and this woman in holy matrimony."

Reverend Morgan paused at the spot the last wedding he'd officiated at had been interrupted. He hadn't really meant to, but now that he'd stopped it was obvious to everyone what he was waiting for.

He'd valiantly resisted all attempts to pull him into conversation and speculation about the first wedding debacle. But when they'd found out about today's wedding—and who the bride was—the other pastors in his Friday breakfast group had insisted that, if it happened a second time, he had to work it into a sermon somehow.

It seemed that the whole congregation was holding its breath this time.

But no one said anything like *No* or *Stop*. And no one came storming down the middle aisle.

Which was great. Really. He was going to have to come up with something else for Sunday, but he was fine with that.

He took a deep breath, grinned at the congregation and went on. "Marriage should not be entered into unadvisedly or lightly, but reverently, discreetly, advisedly and solemnly. Into this holy estate these two persons present now come to be joined. If any person can show just cause why they may not be joined together, let them speak now or forever hold their peace."

Reverend Morgan paused again—but he always paused at this part—and looked at the happy couple before him.

The groom was wearing one of the biggest smiles he'd ever seen and the bride was...frowning.

"Wait," she said.

He stared at her. *No way.* He clapped the Bible he held

shut. Now he owed Pastor Richards a jumbo muffin and a decaf latte on Friday.

The groom turned wide eyes on the bride. "Seriously?" he asked.

"There's something I need to know," she told him.

He turned to face her fully. "Now? You're kidding, right?"

She shook her head. "Now is the perfect time actually."

The groom glanced around at the friends they had standing up with them, then out at the church full of people. Then he took a deep breath and focused on the woman in white beside him. "Okay, what?"

"What did you come four thousand miles to say to me?"

He stared at her for three heartbeats. "Really?"

"You said I'd always wonder what you came four thousand miles to say, but you never actually said it."

Reverend Morgan saw Gavin's eyes dart to Devon Grant, the maid of honor, then out to the congregation, where his family sat in the second pew. Then he glanced over his shoulder at his best man—or rather, his best woman.

Hayley Stone gave him a big grin. "Yeah, let's hear it, Gav."

Gavin gave her a frown, then turned back to his bride. "Hasn't everything that's happened since I broke up your first wedding proven what I wanted to say without needing the words?" Gavin asked. "In fact, didn't *breaking up your wedding* more or less prove what I wanted you to know?"

Allison smiled but shook her head. "Oh, no. I want to hear the exact words. I think everyone would like to."

Reverend Morgan looked up to see the church full of smiles and nodding heads. If *most* of the town had shown up for the Brewster-Ralston wedding, the entire population was here for this one.

He had to admit, he wouldn't mind hearing the words that had fueled the previous wedding drama.

He just wished he had a pen and paper.

The other pastors would insist on having it quoted word for word on Facebook, he was sure. "You did have an actual speech prepared, didn't you?" Allie asked him, her tone teasing. "You wouldn't just charge into a wedding fueled purely by emotion without a specific plan, would you?"

Gavin took a deep breath and leaned closer to Allie, lowering his voice. "I was kind of...winging it that day."

Allie smiled knowingly. "No kidding."

"Speak up! We can't hear in back!" someone called from the pews.

Everyone laughed and the groom's shoulders seemed to relax. He took Allie's hands in his.

"But I think I can do this. You ready?"

She smiled up at him, the love clear in her eyes. "You don't have to. I was just joking—"

"Oh, no. You started this," Gavin broke in. "I think you do need to hear this."

Allie's eyes were wide as she nodded. "Okay."

Gavin lifted one of her hands to his mouth and kissed her knuckles. Then he said, loudly enough for everyone to hear, "Allison Ralston, I love you. More than anyone else ever will. Let me be the one to love you for better or worse. Let me be the one to take care of you in sickness and in health. Let me be the one to buy you Froot Loops and the one to dance with you in the rain and the one to kiss you good night every night." He paused and took a deep breath. "Let me be the one to love you for the rest of your life."

Allie blinked at him, then opened her mouth, then shut it again without making a sound.

Gavin gave her a smug grin. "See, told you I could do this."

"Way to go, Gav," Hayley said from behind him.

Devon wiped away a tear.

Reverend Morgan chuckled. Looked like he was going to get to finish this wedding ceremony after all.

Pastor Richards was buying the coffee and muffins on Friday.

"Well, I think that sums everything up nicely," he said. "Allison, do you take Gavin as your lawfully wedded husband?"

Allie cleared her throat and swiped at the tear that balanced on her lower lashes. "I most definitely do."

And this time when Gavin scooped Allie up into his arms in front of all their friends and family, it was Josh Brewster who held the church door open for them.

About the Author

Erin Nicholas is the author of sexy contemporary romances. Her stories have been described as toe-curling, enchanting, steamy and fun. She loves to write about reluctant heroes, imperfect heroines and happily ever afters. She lives in the Midwest with her husband, who only wants to read the sex scenes in her books; her kids, who will never read the sex scenes in her books; and family and friends who say they're shocked by the sex scenes in her books (yeah, right!).

You can find Erin on the web at www.ErinNicholas.com, ninenaughtynovelists.blogspot.com, on Twitter (@ErinNicholas) and even on Facebook (www.facebook.com/erin.nicholas.90).

You're invited to the wedding of the year

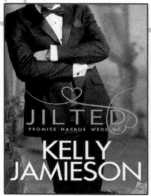

JILTED
PROMISE HARBOR WEDDING
KELLY JAMIESON

Book 1

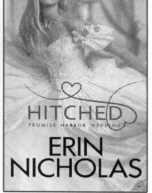

BOLTED
PROMISE HARBOR WEDDING
MEG BENJAMIN

Book 2

BUSTED
PROMISE HARBOR WEDDING
SYDNEY SOMERS

Book 3

HITCHED
PROMISE HARBOR WEDDING
ERIN NICHOLAS

Book 4

Don't miss any of the books in the
Promise Harbor Wedding series

WWW.SAMHAINPUBLISHING.COM

SAMHAIN

PUBLISHING

It's all about the story...

Romance

HORROR

www.samhainpublishing.com

Made in the USA
Lexington, KY
08 April 2016